maurice
in
london

Xavier-Marcel Boulestin

maurice in london

Translated from the French by Nancy Erber

— or — "The Company He Keeps"

MAURICE IN LONDON
Xavier-Marcel Boulestin
Translated by Nancy Erber

ISBN 978-1-59021-784-9

First published as *Les Fréquentations de Maurice: Moeurs de Londres*
in 1911 by Sydney Place (pseudonym of Xavier-Marcel Boulestin)
Paris: Dorbon-Aîné, 1911

Les Fréquentations de Maurice was first published as a serial novel in *Akademos*
in 1909. Cahiers Questiondegenre-Éditions GKC reissued an annotated version
in 2022.

introduction

Maurice in London was published as a serial novel in a French gay arts journal, *Akademos*, in 1909. Xavier-Marcel Boulestin, the author, had just moved from Paris to London where he used his French connections to eke out a living as a freelance journalist, publishing sketches of life in London in newspapers and magazines back home. He saved the campy insider's tour of queer London for his novel though, where the main character Maurice Verdal mingles with artists, critics, chorus boys and the generous male and female patrons who support them.

Readers see pre-war London and its queer subcultures through Maurice Verdal's eyes. This main character, an independently wealthy, well-connected, homo-curious French man, might seem like an odd choice for a gay writer, but think of Marcel Proust, whose narrator Marcel pines for Albertine, Gilberte and other girls throughout *In Search of Lost Time*. Maurice's charm, impeccable wardrobe and unlimited income are his passport to turn of the century London. He befriends young men trying to make their way in the theater and as escorts, drops in on a gay house party, visits popular cruising spots in parks and theaters, goes boating on the Thames with bright young things, and discusses tailors, beauty consultants and the attractions of the Horse Guards with his London friends. Fashionable young men living on a shoestring explain to this curious outsider the etiquette of avoiding bills and nabbing invitations to trendy grill rooms, fashionable resorts and prime addresses in Mayfair and Piccadilly. This is a world the author, Boulestin, came to know well: its elite society seasons and rituals, the hansom carriages, music halls, poisonous fogs, glittering high life and working-class slums. This is London after Oscar Wilde was condemned to hard labor and in the calm before the storm of World War I.

As early twentieth century moderns, Maurice and his crowd gently mock the now-passé lifestyle of London's "fossils," the aesthetes and dandies who are holdovers from Oscar Wilde's London. Though he and his friends rarely detour from the London circuit, they chat knowingly about Paris nightclubs, music hall stars and lesbian salons. Boulestin was a close friend of the great French novelist and queer icon Colette, and his gossipy letters to her include some of the same insights into London's LGBTQ communities and its scandals that he fictionalized in this book.

Boulestin settled permanently in London and after his stint in journalism, he opened a short-lived interior design business and then a very successful French restaurant called Boulestin's, frequented by Virginia Woolf and the Bloomsbury crowd. In the 1950s he became the BBC's first television chef. Although his novel was published as a book in Paris a few years after it was serialized in *Akademos*, Boulestin regretted never seeing his novel translated into English. This is for you, Monsieur Boulestin!

— Nancy Eber

Maurice in London

or

The Company

He Keeps

C H A P T E R   I

*paris-london
via boulogne*

"Yes, moods are delightful..."
R. Hitchens

MAURICE VERDAL WAS BUSY EVERY day, quite simply living his life, when he realized, as Laforgue wrote: "Oh, how routine my everyday life is!"[1] But especially fond memories of London kept intruding, putting a damper on the joys of life in Paris. He had moved to the eighth arrondissement recently. At first, decorating his new apartment on rue Montaigne occupied every minute of his time with thrilling decisions and fascinating challenges. Now that the last nail had been hammered in and the last book was gorgeously bound, lovingly and definitively given its rightful place on a shelf (though he would never pick up that book again), Maurice was truly, definitively, at a loss.

One day, he decided to have tea on rue Cambon[2] in English territory and came home feeling more disoriented than ever. At the next table, two old ladies and one young subject of King Edward VII went on and on about the latest Oxford-Cambridge match. Back at his apartment, he lit a cigarette and lost himself in daydreams, summoning up happy memories. As the sun set and the sky darkened, his thoughts took a gloomy turn. He quickly shook off his melancholy mood,

---

[1] Laforgue, *Les Complaintes*, "Sur certains ennuis" (1885).
[2] The "British Dairy" at 11 rue Cambon.

though, and decided to have dinner at Fouquet's bar on the Champs-Élysées. At the bar, he spotted an old etching of "Ye Old White Horse Cellar" hanging above the mirror. It had caught his eye at least twenty times before. Piccadilly! All of a sudden, the jumble of thoughts and feelings came together in a few short and bittersweet words from Laforgue: "Oh ungrateful and monotonous homeland!"[3]

So, why stay in Paris? "That's it!" Maurice decided. He would leave. There was nothing keeping him here, no casual flirtations, no serious affairs, not even the hint of a new encounter. His apartment no longer interested him now that it was entirely arranged to his satisfaction. "I'm leaving. I'm leaving," he repeated to himself gaily as he walked along the avenue. "It's a mistake to mull things over and make a decision after careful consideration. You only waste precious time and get caught up worrying about duty. I've always thought that you should either take action or not, but do whatever it is quickly. Your first choice isn't always the worst. You should never indulge in regrets or scold yourself for stepping back. Don't say, 'Oh, if only I hadn't thought it over.'"

Thus, it happened that one fine day in May, Maurice left for London, where he had charming friends, faithful comrades, and social connections just waiting to be revived. But for no reason at all, instead of traveling straight to London, he stopped at Boulogne. He told himself that at least he could enjoy the sea view there for more than an hour and fifteen minutes. Resorts like Boulogne had always fascinated him. Even the sight of a casino was thrilling. If his memories were accurate, its casino was the epitome of tacky elegance and mixed company. Footmen in their Sunday best rubbed shoulders with tourists from Paris decked out in shabby white pique there, and the black satin gowns of the local ladies brushed against the brightly printed muslins of English day-trippers. French excursion trains and London "Bank Holiday" specials seemed to disgorge their hordes of passengers directly into the gambling halls. The noisy and demanding "trippers" in all their horrifying splendor there could put off even the most dispassionate croupiers.

"One ought to see Boulogne out of season," Maurice mused as he lounged near the lighthouse. "The end of May is especially lovely, with a calm sea under a deep blue sky, the beaches deserted except for the lapping waves.... I have the hotel and the shore to myself. In the evening, I'll look for two distant blinking lights, which are probably all I can see of England. I'm even afraid sometimes that the wind will blow them out!" He watched the steamers coming and going in the harbor every day,

---

[3] Laforgue, *Les Complaintes*, "Sur certains ennuis" (1885).

thinking that soon one would take him to "dear old London!" But he forced himself to wait in Boulogne until he couldn't put off the crossing any longer.

He boarded, settled into a deck chair and took in the view. The greyish outline of the town stood out against the muted colors of the harbor. The cathedral spire rose up from a thicket of trees. Fishing boats bobbed on the water, straining at their anchors. Some carpenters on the dock were busy repairing a ship's mast while nearby a customs officer was smoking a cigarette, his pistol in a holster stretched across his chest. Little by little, the steamer was readied for departure. Giant cranes hoisted the baggage and gently deposited it in the hold while the passengers themselves hurried on board to take the best seats. A few scanned the horizon with a falsely nonchalant but clearly anxious air.

Outside the harbor, the glassy seas erupted into jagged whitecapped waves, an ominous sign of an unpleasant crossing. "Oof, as long as I don't get seasick," Maurice muttered to himself. "That would be idiotic." And he reviewed the advice seasoned travelers gave in these circumstances: "Eat nothing; eat a hearty meal; lie down in your cabin; stroll about in the fresh air; smoke; don't smoke; flirt with someone…." He smiled, remembering the English-speaking guide on the dock who accosted him, asking "Would you like a guide, sir?" He always enjoyed being mistaken for a foreigner.

The boat had left its berth smoothly and swiftly picked up speed, like a prisoner escaping from jail, but it entered rough water after passing the second lighthouse. Maurice distracted himself by focusing on how he felt. *Thank God. I'm not seasick. I'm not at all upset. But the other passengers!* Every now and then a fine lady or gentleman would stand up, abruptly throwing off a shawl or an overcoat. Looking quite discombobulated, they would weave this way and that heading for a railing over the heaving waters. They often reached the railing just in time. But other passengers were not taken off guard. They had enough time to return to their cabins at a stately pace and, once inside, discreetly dealt with their malaise. Still, other passengers couldn't even muster the strength to stand up. They unashamedly availed themselves of the zinc basins the crew handed out.

The sea was boiling and howling furiously. The steep rises and falls, the boat's pitching side to side jostled people's innards as roughly as the waves pummeling the steamer. A teenage boy, about fourteen years old, confided to Maurice with a certain smugness that he truly enjoyed the stormy weather that put everyone else off. He boldly surveyed the passengers turning green around the gills and gave

Maurice a running commentary. "Only three ladies left," the boy shouted, on the lookout for new signs of distress, "and another who's looking awfully pale! Okay, that's it. All done," he announced triumphantly two minutes later.

"Are you traveling alone?" Maurice asked.

"Oh, no. I'm with my father and my sister. They're resting… below decks," he smiled mockingly. Like someone in the know, he explained, "This is a fine boat. It's handling everything well. I prefer a turbine-driven steamer, don't you?"

"Me, oh naturally, of course I do," Maurice replied though he wasn't exactly sure what a turbine was. He only knew that their steamer, the *Onward*, made the crossing in an hour and ten minutes.

"Yes, what a magnificent vessel! Have you seen the dining room? It's just like an ocean liner…. Ah, here's the coast. Too bad!"

In fact, the gray cliffs of Folkestone were visible on the horizon. The sight of land brought a measure of calm to some agitated faces.

"Well, this felt like a very short trip," Maurice told the young man.

"A calm stomach, there's nothing like it to make you appreciate life…. Oh, you're stopping at Folkestone? I'm not. Well, take care. Be good. Good-bye!"

Such a charming boy; nothing fazes him, Maurice thought. *A fine young example of British pluck, I guess. And I do like that, though…. Now, I need to find a cozy spot on the train, a seat in the dining car facing away from the port, a tea basket, some English newspapers, and what else? Ugh, as usual, I don't have any change. Why does one always forget to bring change when one travels?*

There's no point asking the porter carrying my bags to give me change. My God, I hate traveling with luggage. I'm worried about my suitcase and my personal items. That always ruins my getaways in the countryside. The next time, I won't bring any. But it's such a lovely suitcase. It's made for keeping at home, in its wrappings, and not for traveling. Reggie will agree, I'm sure, that good quality luggage is indispensable for inspiring confidence in hotel keepers, but if one is sure to pay the bill, fine luggage is unnecessary. But my toilet bag? I'm going to give the porter two shillings. He only bumped and scraped the luggage three times. All right. It's all fine!

Maurice settled in with his French novels, English novels, a box of cigarettes, the *Vie Parisienne* and *The Referee*, the *Mercure de France* and *The Academy*, and even *The New York Herald* for its society news, but he didn't read at all. He gazed through the train car windows at the countryside rushing by, green and hilly. The sight was not particularly scenic or memorable, but even so, he exclaimed, "Oh, it's so English, isn't it?" He felt especially sensitive and authentic. In his compartment, two British tourists were mulling over the joys of Paris they left behind. A woman mentioned the "naughty Folies Bergères" with a smile.

The train passed through the stations on the line, roared through intersections, and finally reached the outskirts of London where row after row of gloomy look-alike houses, low and gray, seemed to stretch out endlessly. The very thought of them was alarming; all the people in those houses lived out their lives, merely waiting to die. The train kept going, and more tracks came into view, crossing, extending, and making infinite connections. The whole of London seemed to sum itself up in two postcard views: on the left, Parliament, and on the right, London Bridge. And then, at long last, the train reached Charing Cross station, discharging passengers into a vortex of sights, sounds, and smells.

Maurice's friend Roy Horner, a clubman and novelist, was there to meet him with a friendly "Hullo" and a quotation from Browning. Roy was the type of Englishman you saw at Biarritz, Paris, Monte Carlo, and Florence, spending a month here and there but he was always back in London for the season. "I've got a car," he announced. "Grab your bags and go get changed. We'll meet at the club. Be sure to dress for a night out. After we meet at the club, I'll take you along, somewhere. Where exactly? We'll see. So, shall we dine at the Reform or the Isthmian tomorrow? It's absolutely your choice. The Isthmian might be better because of the trees shading the park. I say, Maurice, did you have a good crossing? And how is *dear old Paris?*"

"Paris is doing fine, Roy, and so am I. The crossing was atrocious," Maurice exaggerated a little without even being aware of it. He added dramatically, "Everyone on board was seasick."

"Except you," Roy countered.

"I and a few others. A fine vessel, my dear, the *Onward* has turbine propellers. It's a real ocean liner and so even-keeled… so even-keeled, as a fine boy whom I met on board assured me. Can you believe that boy spent his time mocking the passengers who got seasick?"

The customs agent was getting restless waiting. "Oh, there's nothing here. Just my linen, clothes and personal items….

"Yes indeed, Roy, the boy spent the whole trip watching the other passengers turn green around the gills…. Well, if I've got all my things, I'll tell you the rest of it in the car. Where's the car?"

A police officer offered to get it. *What a wonderful country*, Maurice mused, where the police offer services and don't turn down a tip.

"Where am I going to live? But naturally at 7 St James Place, as I always do. I keep to my little routines and my own bachelor rooms. All right, then, it's agreed: the Isthmian Club!"

"At eight on the dot. Don't be late. You know how much I hate waiting."

"Me too!"

WHEN MAURICE ARRIVED AT THE club at 8:25 pm, he found Roy deep in conversation with Harold Barnes. "Harold is free. He'll dine with us," Roy said. "But of course. Such a pleasure," the young man answered, gratefully. "It's been ages, Maurice, since I last saw you. How are you?" "Well, why don't you ever come to Paris? You'd see me there. It's worth the trip...." "My dear chap, I leave for Paris once a year, on August 1st." "Oh, that's too late." "And I always stop in Dieppe before I go back to London. You can't be a theater critic without getting absolutely worn out in that godforsaken city!"

Harold Barnes, or Harold for short, was a real London type; you'd see him everywhere, and everybody knew who he was. Some of his most fervent admirers hadn't read a single word he'd written, and others criticized him for no reason at all. It ought to be impossible to have published so little and be such a well-known writer, but that was the case. His collected works amounted to three short monographs and two one-act plays. He was talkative and not at all shy about his witty, often contrarian ideas, A confident and astute flaneur who enjoyed life, Harold's exaggerated courtesy was spiked with mockery, and people often thought he was a bit too full of himself. He did feel secretly superior, but he rarely let it show. Roy admired his friend Harold greatly and liked Maurice's fine *sense of humor*, too, so like Harold's. He enjoyed Maurice's company, sure that his French friend would never judge him and always give the benefit of the doubt.

Actually, Maurice's strong sense of self, his egoism in fact, was a substitute for empathy and served him quite well. He was always open-hearted and friendly when he thought it was worth the effort and felt satisfied if he got as much as he gave in a relationship. Now that he was in London, he was determined to stick to his new philosophy of life and not try to control other people or change the course of fate. He explained to his friends, "You have no idea how much I've simplified my life. I've locked up my sense of morality, for one thing," he explained to his two friends.

"So very practical!" Harold exclaimed. "In any case, that took up too much room, and now I've misplaced the key...." "A wasted effort!" "So, now, after so many short affairs, great loves, and passing flirtations, I believe I've made an important discovery. We've got to savor our unhappiness as much as our joy. Everything is worth something; we just have to know how to understand life. Every petty thing is as valuable as every overwhelming passion. It's all interesting, and it's all useful." Roy interjected in a friendly tone, "You know, that's not particularly new." "But it's new to me because I've just discovered it. And that's all right. Remember, my dear Roy, how sincere I was when I told you I loved Maggie, and that 'no matter what happens, this will be a lovely memory!' And now I can say equally sincerely, and with a wry smile on my face: 'What a bitch, that Maggie!'" "And isn't that also a 'lovely memory?'" "Exactly! From now on, I'm going to savor every minute and enjoy what happens. Nothing more, neither sweet memories nor grand ambitions. They're equally pointless. I still want to be somebody's fool and experience a broken heart, but I do so consciously so I'll come out ahead. And then I won't regret anything because I will never blame myself. I'm convinced this is the first step on the road to wisdom."

Harold sighed, "But there are so many things that one believes are the first step to wisdom. There's no end to it!" Maurice smiled and said, "Harold, please stop joking. I'm awfully serious." Roy chimed in, "Harold is serious too, don't you see? First of all, he never jokes. But, tell me, Maurice, all the things you told me last year at Dieppe, mostly at midnight as we were leaving a bar...." "Oh yes, those moist lips... revisiting splendid moments...the time we spend waiting eagerly to start a new affair. No, I don't talk like that any longer. I'm living a quiet life. Look at how lovely and green the trees are in the park and that lovely golden haze like a Dutch painting. Isn't this an exquisite moment?" "Of course, of course," Harold assured him. "And you are even more exquisite. I can't think of anything more pathetic than your sincerity. It's wonderful, touching, superhuman. But that in no way rules out that tomorrow perhaps...." "Tomorrow! That's what I've been telling you. How wonderful not to know what one will do tomorrow." "Yes, I understand." Roy added abruptly, "But let's move on to something serious. Look here..." He covered both ends of his mustache with his hands, shrinking it to half the size. "Well, what do you think? Should I trim it? Or leave it the way it is? Or shave it off completely? I can't stop thinking about it…. Shall we take our coffee in the smoking room? Remind me to tell you all about my latest masterpiece, won't you? It's shockingly new."

The men settled into enormous leather armchairs and decided not to go on to the theater after all. They'd rather spend the time talking about this and that. Since Maurice hadn't been in London for several months, he absolutely had to be brought up to date. Harold cleared his throat and said, "Yesterday I read in a reputable newspaper that the King of Spain…." Roy, at the same time, started to gossip, "People are saying that Mrs. Henderson–" Maurice smirked, "Oh, I'd rather hear about that. But why, for God's sake, do you take such an interest in talking about unsavory characters, Roy? I'm a foreigner, just passing through, I go anywhere and everywhere, and no one has a single word to say about it. But you…." "I? First of all, I don't go anywhere and everywhere. I don't spend my time with what you might call 'loose women.' I know a few by sight, naturally. And, if I pass on any gossip about them, it's strictly because I enjoy it, and so do you. Do you think we don't have loose women in London or any sketchy neighborhoods of the "Cythera"[4] variety, as the special guidebooks call it? Big thinkers like me need petty distractions and the scandals of the 'smart set' and 'fast people,' whether true or not, fill the bill. The actual stories of adulterers just bore me nowadays. Besides, we can't spend all our time discussing George Bernard Shaw!

"The last time I saw Shaw," Harold continued, "was at Covent Garden. It was some sort of performance, I can't quite remember what, and I caught a glimpse of him sitting between a fat lady wearing a gorgeous feather boa and a bald-headed diplomat. Shaw was wearing a top hat and evening dress like everyone else, not the cap and ordinary suit I expected.[5] He was virtually unrecognizable and madly paradoxical. I was dumbfounded. It would be like seeing Willy without his top hat[6]…." he added in a very Parisian aside.[7] Whiskeys and sodas were served all around.

---

[4] A reference to the mythical island of love, popularized in Watteau's painting "Pilgrimage to Cythère", in Offenbach's comic opera *Les Braconniers*, in compositions by Poulence, Satie, and others.

[5] Shaw was famous for wearing a Jaeger wool suit and woolen underwear.

[6] Willy is Henry Gauthier-Villars, the French writer and man-about-town with his signature top hat. He was the first husband of the famous author Colette. Boulestin briefly served as Willy's "secretary" and ghost writer.

[7] "Very Parisian" was regularly used in gossip columns and caricatures to describe Colette and Willy's free-wheeling marriage. Here it's an inside joke by Boulestin, who became Colette's close friend and ally when he lived in Paris.

C H A P T E R   I I

*mr. reginald de vere
and his friends*

S HRUGGING OFF HIS JACKET AND without waiting for a reply, Reggie de Vere asked Fred Fisher, "Is it all right if I get undressed?" He took off the rest of his evening wear, put on a pink pajama suit with mauve stripes, and dusted his face with Rachel powder.[1] He called out from the bedroom, "Go ahead, have a cigarette. There's whiskey and soda on the table. Make yourself at home," He came into the sitting room with an easy smile, "The fact is I hate wearing evening clothes after closing time.[2] In any case, I'm at home and I've every right to be comfortable. Naturally, I wouldn't do this in anyone else's place." He laughed as he always did, a sort of open-mouthed shriek that bared all his teeth. "Unless they asked me to!" "Of course," Fred nodded agreeably.

Mr. Reginald de Vere was born in Jersey and grew up in London. His accent was untraceable, embellished with nuances of several hard-to-identify foreign languages and sprinkled with slang from various countries, along with some of his own invention. His conversation was quite unique, an extraordinary combination of stupidity and brashness that was hard to imagine, where superficiality reigned

---

[1] This popular face powder, named after the celebrated actor Rachel, was advertised as 'fine... light pink, ideal for pale skin."

[2] At this time, pubs closed at 11 pm.

supreme, but was overruled by a certain type of slyness on special occasions. He lived on a tiny allowance from his mother, a very elegant lady whose friends were eager to keep her at home in Jersey. Reggie, haphazardly brought up by this young and frivolous mother, had decided at the age of seventeen to live a completely idle life since the very idea of work absolutely horrified him. Being young, presentable and a new face in London, a few people took an interest in him and generously helped him out from time to time. This is how he managed to live quite comfortably on his meager allowance.

He also ran up debts. For the last year and a half, two people in particular bailed him out when he needed it. One was a very wealthy married man, Mr. Alec Kemball, who lived in Liverpool, and the other was Mrs. Henderson. Everyone who was anyone in London knew Mrs. Henderson. She was at least forty but dressed like a twenty-year-old, owned a stylish electric coupe, and supported a coterie of young men. Her connection to high society was rather ambiguous; she was part of that world though she rarely spent any time there. Once in a while, a former lady friend would catch a glimpse of her at the Savoy Hotel or on Bond Street, but would pretend not to have seen her, as a sign of discretion. A few gossips even claimed she had a husband somewhere in the colonies, though she herself never mentioned him. She went out frequently, hobnobbing with a few actresses and cosmopolitan types she had met on the Riviera, but nowadays she was escorted around town by Reggie, which flattered him immensely. He was quite proud of his standing.

Of course, Mr. Kemball couldn't help but hear about Mrs. Henderson even though she, on the other hand, knew nothing about him. He occasionally mentioned that his uncle Alec from Liverpool was spending a few days in London, and naturally he would have to go out with him occasionally. These visits usually occurred once every three months, and cost Mr. Kemball dearly. Reggie, with the mind of a cheap floozy and the stomach of an ostrich, insisted on expensive dinners and when the good uncle came back to his rooms for a nightcap, he would invariably find a few large and urgent bills waiting there. But Reggie had to be well-dressed, didn't he? And have fine linen, exotic cigarettes and bouquets of flowers brightening up his rooms. It all added up! And the man from Liverpool began noticing that these trips to London were getting awfully expensive. It was true that the young man was charming, well-built, and had a sweet disposition. When all was said and done, he got some satisfaction from the deal, but still!

Reggie realized this, and it troubled him. He also knew that Mrs. Henderson's indulgence would not last forever. Besides that, the mountain of debt he was accumulating worried him. "I'll have a few drinks tonight to cheer myself up," he told Fred. "To be honest, I'm so depressed, I don't know what to do…. Oh, speaking of which, how do you like my new apartment? I absolutely had to have the ground floor. It's more convenient." Fred looked around as Reggie babbled on. "It's cozy, isn't it? Not badly furnished and it has electricity. My bedroom's over there, and my bathroom. To top it off, this is a fashionable street. My word, Clarges Street.[3] I can put Mayfair on my stationery and my cards. That's excellent. Are you still living on—what was it now? Katherine Street?[4] " "Yes, indeed," Fred replied with a quick smile. "I don't move house as easily as you do! And Mayfair or St. James are a bit too pricey for me … since I have to pay my own bills." Reggie wasn't at all insulted by the subtle dig. He laughed instead. "Oh my, that's the least of my worries. Everybody knows that! But tell me about yourself, Freddy dear." He put an outsized emphasis on the "dear."

"Freddy dear" was tall, blond, and broke. He didn't have Reggie's stylish wardrobe or bubbly personality. He was quiet and a little subdued. His rather haughty smile and affected mannerisms made him seem conceited sometimes and quite decadent at others. He was 'arty' in the sense that he was an esthete from the early 1890s; he first came on the social scene when stylized flowers, paradoxical epigrams and jewelry studded with rare and unusual gemstones were in fashion. He was a victim of his own style choices. He didn't evolve with the times, and nowadays he seemed awfully out of touch. He worked in theater, naturally.

"I hear you're going to be doing Shakespeare," Reggie said in a friendly tone. "Yes, Osric in *Hamlet*[5], on tour." "Really? Really? That's fabulous. You'll have to get some postcards printed up. I still have mine, you know, from *The Magic Slipper*[6] at the Prince of Wales theater. I was one of the 'chorus boys' with a Panama hat." With this, he flourished a photo. "You see, always with a big smile! I had a three-week engagement and I always arrived at the theater in a hansom cab, decked out in a new suit. The director couldn't believe I managed it all on thirty shillings a week! So that was that! Everyone in town was talking about me, though, and I can still say, 'When I was in *The Magic Slipper*….' That's enough for me." "You're a lucky man, Reggie." "Me? Not at all. Listen, I've never been as broke as I am right now.

---

[3] Clarges Street in London is not far from the Green Park underground station, Curzon Street and Piccadilly.

[4] Probably a reference to Catherine Street, a less fashionable address near the docks.

[5] Osric is a minor character who first appears in *Hamlet* in Act V scene 2.

[6] This was a musical based on the Cinderella story, performed in London in 1904.

And my tailor just sent me a bill——" He was about to launch into a tirade about his creditors and their annoying habits when they heard voices outside. Reggie rushed to the front window and opened it. "I have some friends with me, Reggie," a man called out. The shadowy figures on the sidewalk waited. "May we come in?"

"Come in, come in. I've got cigarettes and whiskey. It's fine, of course. Let me open the door. Don't make too much noise," he screeched. "And don't mind me. I'm in my pajamas." He shut the window abruptly and hurried to the door. "Fred, be a darling and get out some more glasses." Reggie's voice and his laugh echoed from the hallway. "How are you? Oh! Paul, I had no idea you were in town. How are you? Fred Fisher is here. Do you know him?" Four young men came into the living room. "Do you all know each other? No? Well, Mr. Fisher, Mr. Hmm, I don't recall your name. George, why don't you introduce your friends? I've never been able to make proper introductions. Have a drink." They settled into armchairs and Reggie kept on chatting. Sometimes, in the midst of the hubbub of voices, his shrill voice rose above all the others. He laughed and laughed; he had perfected the knack of chortling after every sentence, so that he sounded witty. He had a weird sense of humor that was strangely flat-footed, and he sometimes blurted out painfully indiscreet truths, always with a laugh and a self-mocking attitude. He spread rumors so diligently about everyone and everything that hardly anyone took him seriously, but people were afraid of him, nevertheless.

"Oh, this is so like me," he groaned. "I invite people to dinner and it's Hutchinson who pays! I hope I'm not shocking you, Mr. Bulter. I love to play the flirt... I won't say I am one, not really! But I adore acting like a tart; I have tendencies in that direction. I must have inherited them from Mummy! So, are you going back to Oxford? Do you know Harry Peile? He's a dear friend, a good-looking chap, wouldn't you say? So, you all dined at Trocadero?[7] I almost went there myself. That's too bad. We could have dined together.... When are you going on tour, George? You're also doing *Hamlet*? Osric, perhaps? Playing Osric in *Hamlet*? That's hilarious. All the boys are playing Osric in *Hamlet*. What in the world does that mean?" "It means not everyone can be a 'Panama boy' at the Prince of Wales, Reggie!" "True that!" Paul Haret interrupted, steering the conversation in another direction. "Let's talk about the Maidenhead[8] scandal." He was a young Frenchman studying English in London, blond, easy-going, and

---

[7] This was a restaurant operated by Lyons, the famous tea shop and Corner House company. Opened in 1896, the Trocadero was known as a cruising spot for gay men.

[8] The resort town of Maidenhead, with many hotels and restaurants, was popular with Londoners. An easy train ride away, it was nicknamed the "cheating capital."

generally mild-mannered although at times he showed himself capable of violent affections and vicious hatreds. He mingled in the sort of louche Piccadilly crowd that would upset his bourgeois provincial family if they ever found out. Reggie thought he was charming. "Such a dear!"

"Maidenhead!" Reggie cried, pretending to be angry. "That's my bad luck. You know I met Hutchinson at the beginning of last season when he was living in a very chic villa on the river." "Last year, he had a flat on Park Lane."[9] "And I met him in Monte Carlo when he was leaving the Riviera-Palace!"[10] "And in Paris he lived on the avenue du Bois."[11] "I know, I know. Will you let me talk? You're not telling me anything I don't already know. He's a lunatic. In fact, it's unbelievable that with his pots of money, he hardly knows anyone…. Anyway, once…. And his mania for dressing in women's clothes! Anyway, once he told me he wanted to give an elegant dinner party, and that I could invite whoever I wanted, etc. etc. We had the catering done by Benoist,[12] hired a gypsy orchestra, decorated the garden with Japanese lanterns and masses of orchids everywhere. He must have spent 300 pounds. It was madness, all this for the forty guests I had invited. But it turned out quite badly. First of all, he insisted on dressing as usual and greeted everyone wearing a lovely blue chiffon gown trimmed with antique lace. Stunning, and with a four-meter-long train. Since I knew the dinner party would be very, very *smart,* I invited only the chicest people…. My word, how I had to finesse the introductions, you know what I mean, saying over and over, 'Yes indeed, he's very eccentric,' and a whole lot of other nonsense to Mrs. Morell and Mrs. Henderson. It was excruciating. Then, when we finished dinner, he went out on the balcony and started throwing fruit, flowers, and shillings to the crowd below since all of Maidenhead turned up there to watch the show…. It was awful and at the end, people started throwing stones and smashing windows. We had to call the police…. Actually, at that point I jumped into a canoe with Mrs. Henderson, and we paddled all the way to the bridge at the railway station. We left the canoe and the entire circus behind!"

Reggie's guests were mesmerized by the story. His wild gestures and facial expressions completed the thoughts he left dangling. He was a good mimic. He told the tale with incredible gusto and his usual over-the-top energy. Perched on the arm of his chair, he smoked, drank and acted out the drama at the same

---

[9] Park Lane was conveniently located in Mayfair near Hyde Park, thus not far from a celebrated cruising spot.

[10] The Riviera-Palace had rental apartments.

[11] The Bois de Boulogne was another cruising spot.

[12] Benoist was a stylish French caterer located in Piccadilly.

time. "Well, now, that was my bad luck!" He banged his fist on the armchair for emphasis. "Naturally, I thought that was the end of it, that business! But no, not at all. Three days later two newspapers covered it in depth and printed all the guests' names, don't you know? Everybody who's anybody in London heard about it and Mrs. Henderson was furious! I didn't want to have anything more to do with that madman Hutchinson. First of all, he's utterly useless. I know the type…. He'll throw away 300 pounds on fancy dinners or gowns but won't even lend you a *fiver!*"

"So, Reggie," Paul said provocatively. "You know that when other people tell this story, they say you were dressed in a gown too, and that…""Oof! Really! Anyway, I couldn't care less…. What? Are you going so soon? Are you sure? Well, I have to get up early tomorrow too. I'm *lunching* at one o'clock though why anyone would care to *lunch* that early! Listen, come back whenever you please and let's go out for tea somewhere or meet for drinks after 12:30 at night. I'm always at home and I adore it when someone stops me from going to bed too early! Bye-bye…. No doubt I'll meet you at Trocadero or the Arcades.[13] Good night! Paul, it really isn't very late. Stay a little longer. I have lots of things to tell you…. Good night, George!"

Reggie heard footsteps echoing on the deserted sidewalk, and then fading away into the distance, replaced by the rumble of a hansom cab and its jingling bells. Paul stayed behind. Reggie sprawled in an armchair. "*Dearest* Paul! It's been ages since I last saw you." "Actually, it was two weeks ago, Reggie, when we were in Paris." "Really? It feels longer than that…. I'm feeling blue tonight, Paul. I need to cheer myself up." "I wouldn't have thought so, seeing how you were chatting and laughing." "Yes, I know. When I have an audience, I get excited and can chase the blues away. But now… I just don't know what to do…." "Money trouble?" "Of course! What other sort of trouble matters? The truth is, my dear chap, that I'm afraid Kemball is fed up with me. He's very kind, naturally, and has never refused me anything, but every day I look for a letter telling me that it's over. If I see an envelope addressed to me in his handwriting, I start shaking! It's absurd… I can't ignore this feeling, even if he still feels the same about me." "People say, 'it comes with the territory,' Reggie." "I can't argue with that. This stupid Maidenhead business is going to turn into a disaster. Mrs. Henderson is still angry, and Alec is going to hold it against me, just when I really need money! I don't know what to do, Paul, but I have more and more troubles and more and more debts. It can't go on this way. Do you think I even have thirty shillings in

---

[13] The Burlington Arcades in Piccadilly were lined with shops and were also a notorious cruising spot..

my pocket tonight? My cigarette case is empty, and I owe three weeks rent here. That's not counting all my other bills. What a mess! To get out of this, I'd need 200 pounds; that would put me right. My word, it wasn't too long ago that I had almost 100 pounds to my name. That didn't last, though, and I'm embarrassed to ask for more so soon." "The fact is—"

"You know, I've often thought I've had enough of this… I'd rather go to Paris or marry a rich woman…. There's a thought. I've actually got someone in mind…." Paul was speechless. The image of Reggie de Vere as a married man dumbfounded him. "Well, in the meantime, my dear Reggie, one of these days I'll bring you to Hurlston's flat to distract you." "Oh really? He has a lovely flat in Artillery Row.[14] A clever idea to live there, wouldn't you say, when one has money to spend? He's very hospitable, isn't he? I'm going to try to win him over… that will bring lots of new friends!" "Do you realize, Reggie, how hard I had to fight to get you an invitation? He's afraid of you, of your malicious gossip and your bad reputation, apparently." He was thrilled, and not at all shocked. "That's my luck, Paul. Absolutely!" "Well, in the end I convinced him that you were charming and not at all dangerous." "And you, *dearest,* are more charming than ever. Have another whiskey?" Paul protested that it was getting awfully late, impossible to stop any longer, but perhaps he'll have one more cigarette…. "Then, come smoke it in my bedroom. If you don't mind, I'm going to stretch out while we chat for another five minutes…. I'm so glad you stayed when the others left; it's better, more cosey, just the two of us…." Reggie lounged on the bed. "There. Sit on the foot of the bed. Ouch! Not on my foot…. Can you guess who I saw at the Savoy Hotel? Maurice Verdal, looking very chic, with—"Paul interrupted brusquely, "I don't like him." "What? Why not?" "Oh, nothing. An old story…." Reggie's interest was piqued. "He invited me to dine one of these days. Of course, I said yes. Besides, I think he's charming. He's a broad-minded chap, isn't he?" "Verdal? Hmm. I suppose so." "Ah, so much the better, " Reggie murmured, though he was sure of it already. "As broad-minded as you are, *dearest?* Or perhaps a little less? Because, let's be frank, you're as bad as I am. You don't have a Mrs. Henderson or a Mr. Kemball, but besides that…. Anyhow, you'd be wrong to act any differently. You have to do what you like…. Do you know, Paul, you are utterly charming? Oof, I'm making a fool of myself tonight. It true and it's too, too bad. I'm just so glad to see you. Give me a light, won't you?"

---

[14] Artillery Row is located near Victoria Station in Westminster, and as the name suggests, near an armory. Reggie implies that there would be easy encounters with soldiers.

The young man came closer, stretching out next to Reggie, propping his elbow on the pillow and grazing his bare arm. "Oh no, don't tickle me," Reggie cried. "I'll never get to sleep then." He wriggled nervously. "See here. *Don't be silly.*" Outside in the street, inspecting every locked door with his lantern, a policemen plodded by on his rounds.

C H A P T E R   I I I

a cottage in mayfair

MAURICE VERDAL TOOK A STROLL through the Burlington Arcade every morning. Walking down Bond Street before lunch, he always stopped in front of the same shop windows, looking at the same neckties, jewelry, and cigarettes on display, sure that he'd run into someone he knew and that they would window-shop for a while together. That morning a tall young man wearing a jacket that was really too long for him and with cheeks that were honestly too rosy stopped him at the corner of Conduit Street. "How are you?" he exclaimed. "I haven't seen you for ages!" Maurice, a bit taken aback, replied "I just got in from Paris." He had no idea who the other man was and as he got closer, the tall man's pink cheeks looked positively mauve.

"I see you've forgotten me! Fred Fisher.... We met at de Vere's place." "Ah yes, of course. And what are you up to? Are you in a play at the moment?" Maurice tried very hard to seem interested. "No, actually, I turned down a part in *Hamlet* in a touring company, absolutely impossible people. I really don't want to leave London at the moment. I've just moved." "Oh, what fun," Maurice murmured, thinking of his newly decorated apartment in Paris. "Quite so. What's the point of living if you don't move house from time to time. Modern life is so boring.

As dear Oscar always said...."[1] Maurice realized he was chatting with an esthete. "Yes indeed," the young actor droned on. "I found the perfect spot, a real country cottage in the middle of Mayfair, a stone's throw from Park Lane and the duchess of Harland.[2] You must come and see me. I'm at home every Sunday now, and lots of people come, Lady Ward, Mrs. Nordon, Reggie de Vere, Miss Houston, you know the lady who sings so delightfully in French. Ah! Lady Ward said something so witty the other day...." Maurice realized that Fred was not only an esthete, but also a dyed-in-the-wool snob. They chatted a little more about the theater, about books. "Have you read Maeterlinck's latest?[3]" Fred asked eagerly. "I couldn't put it down. It was as enthralling as Saint Augustine's *Confessions*." And so, he learned that his acquaintance was also a man of letters. He would certainly visit him for tea next Sunday, he thought. He was curious about his cottage and his guests.

THE NEXT SUNDAY, AFTER WANDERING around for a quarter of an hour, Maurice finally found the celebrated cottage inside a courtyard. He walked through a carriage entrance, gaping wide open, then went past two or three stables, a water pump and a pile of odds and ends. A servant in livery decorated generously with buttons came to the cottage door, and Maurice stepped into the drawing room, a cramped space with low ceilings. It was overflowing with vases of flowers, imitation antique prints, copies of Beardsley[4] drawings, pleated cotton curtains, pink lampshades and three ladies sitting in three armchairs. "How nice of you to come!" the host cried. "Let me introduce you to Lady Ward... Mr. Verdal... Mrs. Nordon... Mrs. Hallett... Cyril Flint, one of my friends from Cambridge... Mr. Verdal. Would you like a cup of tea?"

"Mr. Fisher has such a charming house," Lady Ward ventured. "It's so deliciously bohemian!" She smiled, looking condescending and awestruck at the same time. "And that's not all, Lady Ward," Fred exclaimed. "I have my cellar down below, my bedroom and my chapel." "Your chapel?" "Of course, Lady Ward. I'm a very devout Catholic." "Oh really?" the lady said brightly, taking another cup of tea. Maurice was enjoying himself enormously, surreptitiously taking stock of the

---

[1] A casual reference to the author Oscar Wilde.

[2] This fictive duchess may have been given the name of the literary editor of the notorious "Yellow Book" illustrated quarterly (1894), Henry Harland.

[3] Maurice Maeterlinck was a prolific and successful author. Debussy's opera *Pelleas et Melisande,* based on Maeterlinck's play, was performed in London in 1909.

[4] The artist Aubrey Beardsley was associated with the Yellow Book and Oscar Wilde's writing. Collecting his work was another indicator of Fred's Decadent esthetic tastes.

other guests. Lady Ward, a slightly worn-looking blond, ruled the roost from her seat on the nicest armchair. She had a strange habit of throwing off her furs and then clutching them around her neck as if she was suffering from alternating sensations of hot and cold. She held her right hand up to her forehead to shade her blinking eyes from the nearest lamp, which wasn't actually very bright. As for her dress sense, Maurice noted that her hat was rather ordinary, and her earrings were out of date. Her neighbor, Mrs. Hallett, whose first name was Caroline, proudly sported a triple strand of false pearls, a black satin dress and eyebrows penciled in with vigorous black strokes. Her hair was sparse and graying around the neckline but waved over her forehead in magnificent black bangs. The hairpiece, the eyebrows, all the youthful touches didn't fool other people, but Caroline liked them and kept to the same look for thirty years. She seemed to be a close friend of Lady Ward's and awfully smug.

A few somewhat ordinary-looking young men arrived as the flowers began to wilt in their metal vases and the cheap cigarettes bought by the pound pretended to be better than they were, displayed in a Philip Morris box.[5] Maurice stood next to Cyril. "It's nice here" he said. "Yes," he replied, "the postcards, the souvenirs, the family photos." They both smirked and sensed an immediate connection. "Are you still at Cambridge?" he asked. "No, I've finished. I live in London now." "So, was Fisher with you at Cambridge?" "No, not exactly. I mean, he was there for three days with a touring company last year. I don't remember how I met him but that's how he claims me as 'one of his friends from Cambridge.' Maurice chuckled. "That's clever… and a bit naive." Cyril nodded, saying "Well, he makes me laugh." "Yes, he is charming" Maurice added, "when he's serious… but he doesn't care much about that. What a strange collection of people! Who is that lady with the complicated hairdo?"

"Mrs. Nordon? She's one of your compatriots, my dear Monsieur. She's married to Mr. Nordon, who's nobody in society, but is musical. I think she might be a singer herself, but it wouldn't be much fun if she launched into an aria here. I'd rather have a good conversation." "Why does everybody laugh whenever she says something?" "Oh, people say she has quite a funny accent when she speaks English, and she enjoys it when people laugh. She's actually expecting it, like a kind of tribute, and then she thinks she's said something witty." "That's too bad. I couldn't possibly…." "Well then, you won't be in her good graces. Sorry, I must

---

[5] At the time the Philip Morris company was King Edward's supplier and based in London. The tobacconist's metal boxes were much sought after.

go," Cyril said. "I've other Sunday visits to make, but I'm glad to have met you. Come see me any day of the week, around five o'clock at the Bath Club. Good-bye for now, Verdal."

A minute later, Maurice told Fred, "Your friend is charming." "Yes, charming and remarkably intelligent," Fred replied solemnly. Then he busied himself with the other guests. He turned to Mrs. Hallet, "Have you seen the latest show at the Gaiety?"[6] She shook her black bangs to say "no." "All right, don't go. Anyways, all these musical comedies.... English theater is in a bad state." A thin young man with a clumsily shaved face spoke up. He had once acted in an Ibsen play. "I beg your pardon! How about the Court Theater?" [7] "But that is so different!" "I never go there," Lady Ward exclaimed. "It's too far from my house. Caroline wanted to take me one evening, but there was an awful fog, and we couldn't find our way.... I still get the shivers just thinking about it." Mrs. Hallet added, "It's very intellectual."

"Indeed," Fred replied. "But the other theaters!" And he launched into a diatribe. He kept on, taking aim at one critical disaster after another, leaning against the mantelpiece, lost in his train of thought. He denounced long-running plays with famous actors in a few well-chosen, vitriolic phrases. 'The latest comedy at the Haymarket Theater[8] only survived for a month; the play at the Apollo[9] was mind-numbingly stupid. Mr. George Alexander[10] had never looked worse; Mrs. Patrick Campbell[11] doesn't have the faintest idea of what acting is. As for Mr. Beerbohm Tree,[12] he shouldn't be allowed on stage."

Only Ellen Terry[13] was spared Fred's wrath. She was, after all, a national treasure and everyone agreed that her performances were delightful, smiling warmly at the very thought. After that, Fred, the young Ibsen disciple, and another young actor told a series of anecdotes while the ladies listened raptly. Their stories featured well-known society people that they didn't actually know personally. Harold was mentioned condescendingly. Maurice, impassive, didn't move a

---

[6] A theater for variety shows, burlesque and chorus girls. It was located on Aldwych near the Strand.

[7] The Royal Court Theater had a reputation for more high-brow performances.

[8] The Haymarket Theater often showcased Oscar Wilde's plays.

[9] The Apollo Theater specialized in comedies.

[10] George Alexander (1858-1919) was an actor and theater manager, most notably of the chic West End theater, the Saint James.

[11] Beatrice Rose Stella Tanner, aka Mrs Patrick Campbell (1865-1940) was a stage actor, known for serious roles in Shakespeare, Ibsen, and Maeterlinck among others.

[12] Beerbohm Tree (1852-1917) was a well-known actor, and the half-brother of the celebrated caricaturist Max Beerbohm.

[13] Ellen Terry (1847-1928) was among the most celebrated actors of the time.

muscle. Then, the men downed glasses of whiskey and moved on from criticism to comedy, trotting out hoary old witticisms, stale jokes and well-worn cliches one after another, convinced that they were being so very original. Fred was so wound-up that even Maurice was taken by surprise. The others thought he was "so funny," "so delectably naughty" and looked uncomfortable when he veered into feeling "awfully morbid" or "exquisitely Byzantine." Without missing a beat, he announced that he "only liked strawberries in March" and "personally found Shakespeare utterly boring." When his diatribe wound down, he recited verses by Swinburne[14] in lyrically decadent fashion and sang a few stanzas of a sentimental ballad he had written that set Henry VIII's poetry to music.

The funny French woman obliged by singing off-key, and then everyone, clearly feeling exalted by the experience, began taking their leave. Lady Ward invited Maurice to her 'at-homes' and Mrs. Nordon gave him a rather tepid good-bye. Fred said, "Come again, soon." "Certainly, I'll be glad to. I enjoyed myself immensely." "Oh, we're quite simple and cozy here, no posturing or grandstanding...." "Quite so. Come by my rooms some morning, before noon, won't you?" "But I'm never up then," protested his host. "So, you're as slug-a-bed as Reggie de Vere! And, by the way, he didn't come today?" "Gosh, no. I completely forgot about him!" And with that, Fred with a grand proprietorial smile, shut the cottage door. At the other end of the courtyard, a groom straddled a chair outside a stable, smoking a stubby pipe, at ease and a bit disdainful of the Sunday visitors filing out.

---

[14] Algernon Charles Swinburne (1837-1909), poet, critic and novelist was emblematic of the Decadent movement in English literature. Fred's taste reveals him to be stuck in the past, an 1890s esthete.

at the savoy hotel:
dinner and gossip

BATHED IN THE SOFT ELECTRIC light of a chandelier and under the indifferent gaze of footmen in sparkling yellow and white livery, diners made their way through the stately lobby of the Savoy to the hotel restaurant. Men were elegantly dressed in white close-fitting three-button waistcoats. Women rustled past in a blaze of colored gowns, their shoulders and arms bare, their hair either elaborately coiffed or ostentatiously tousled. Gossamer scarves, so beloved by English ladies, were draped around their necks. Anyone could see that these society folk were doing their duty, taking part faithfully, rigorously, in a ritual. They descended the staircase at a dignified pace, and approached the dining room in a solemnly, looking pensive. Only a few foreigners dressed in Paris fashions acted as if they were there to have a good time.

A mournful-looking host greeted the *parties* at the entrance and showed them to their tables. Roy, Maurice and Mrs. Atwell, terribly late, rushed to theirs. "We'll never have enough time for a proper dinner before closing time," Mrs. Atwell groaned. "To hell with *closing time* and English laws!" She was now regretting that she had stayed to hear the finale of *Madame Butterfly*. She was a close friend of Roy and Harold, and was very intelligent, very lazy, and a bit clairvoyant. Since she moved in literary circles, she had tried her hand at writing a novel once, but soon put it aside, quitting after the third chapter. Although she wasn't conventionally pretty, she exuded a sort of mysterious attraction though she seemed to have nothing to hide. A well-known author had dubbed her "the Sphinx without a secret."[1] Mrs. Atwell knew everyone in society by name and by reputation and was said to be, perhaps accurately, the most well-informed woman in London.

"At least in Paris," Roy observed, "if you're hungry after midnight..." Maurice interrupted him impatiently, "Yes, yes, Roy. We all know it. But that doesn't mean Paris nightlife isn't overrated! It's like the younger generation in America. Everyone's been going on about it for 300 years!" "And Montmartre?" "Oh, Montmartre." Mrs. Atwell smiled to herself, remembering. "The last time I was there... I saw nothing but rich American women in couturier frocks and chic whores dripping in diamonds. At least here..." Maurice burst out, "Don't say anything bad about the Savoy, Mrs. Atwell. It's the most English place in London." Roy steered the conversation in a different direction, asking, "Well, Maurice, what have you been doing these past few days?" "I? Nothing much.... Oh, yes! I've been out and about." "In society!" "Of course. Actually, Mrs. Atwell, do you know Lady Ward?" "Lady Ward? Give me a moment, let me think.... Oh, yes. A wonderful woman. I know her a little. She married Mr. Ward, who does something in the City and became a peer? That's how she became Lady Ward. You know the type. A nice, inconspicuous sort of person, the kind you don't notice in the chic salons. In some other drawing rooms, though, she's the one they point out, saying proudly 'We've got Lady Ward here' or 'Lady Ward has just said something so witty'.... Poor old Fred Fisher!" Maurice stifled a laugh, and Roy looked stunned. "What have you been up to with these impossible people?"

"Did you meet her at Fisher's?" Mrs. Atwell exclaimed. "I didn't realize you knew that young man. Incredible! That's exactly the sort of place where she can play the queen bee, and relish the part, though she'd never admit it. And with good old Mrs. Hallet at her side, I assume? All draped in black satin and gold chains.... You know her, Roy. It's the lady whose back is as curved as her chest, who has a thicker crop of eyebrows on her forehead than hair on her head, or is it the other way round? Still, an absolutely respectable woman." "She honestly has no good points. With a nose like hers, she's not likely to embark on any love affairs!" "And nor will Lady Ward, except that she's been mad about Sidney Martin ever since her

---

[1] "The Sphynx Without a Secret" is the title of a short story by Oscar Wilde, first published in 1887.

husband passed away. She saw him in *Monsieur Beaucaire*.[2] They say she still writes him from time to time. Anyway, she has a weakness for young actors. She takes them under her wing, invites them to tea, sends them boxes of sweets and handy little presents. But that's as far as it goes. She's not at all like Mrs. Henderson." "Everyone finds pleasure where they will, as the old saying goes," Maurice said. Roy groaned, "The tattletale Sphynx is off and running. She won't let up. You do realize we only have twenty more minutes here?"

"Roy," Maurice protested, "these stories are fascinating. Hearing local gossip is much more interesting than learning about statues or monuments or reading history books or even penny-dreadful tabloids! Gossip that's passed from person to person, picking up new details and nuances along the way, is what gives spice to life, as our ancestors in the eighteenth century knew well. Alas, socialism and our modern-day press have destroyed it. Tell me, what does the good lady Hallet think of Lady Ward's Platonisms?" "Oh, I think she ignores them. She passes over them in silence. She simply folds her arms across her chest and shakes her false fringe. Mrs. Hallet always uses her hair to express her opinions," Maurice said. "She must be muttering to herself, 'Poor Lady Ward is so reckless!' but she would never venture to say this to her friend. Lady Ward would certainly chide her, "Caroline *dear*, mind your own business!'

"Now then, what do you know about Fred Fisher?" he continued, making the most of this opportunity. "My goodness!" Mrs Atwell protested. "I feel like I'm taking an exam or testifying in a divorce case. Freddy! My dear Mr. Verdal, I've known him since he was seventeen years old... so that makes a good twelve years. A brainless boy who thinks he's very smart. He's awfully artistic... or has he moved on since then? A very sad story.... Oscar White[3], at the height of his fame, made an appearance at Freddy's salon. Because Freddy was blond with rosy, pink cheeks, White flattered him with a few words... one of those compliments he was known for, something spontaneous and unpretentious... like 'You are like a marvelous white lily!' Freddy lost his head completely, realizing at once that his skinny self was the purest expression of lily-ness and vowing from that day on to live only for Art and for Beauty and to declare from time to time 'How extraordinary it is to be young!' with the utmost conviction. That was the tragic turning point in his life."

---

[2] This romantic comedy was performed in London in 1902, and starred Lewis Waller, a handsome and prominent leading man on the London stage.
[3] It's unclear whether this is intended as Mrs. Atwell's mistake or is simply a typographical error in the original, but the anecdote clearly involves the author Oscar Wilde.

"Poor Freddy. But why in the world is he on the stage? He comes from a good family and has no talent." "So true. It's an awful waste for a young man of his caliber to sacrifice his self-esteem and devote all his energies to getting walk-on roles in an operetta or a historical drama. But what can you do? He enjoys it, he likes talking about it and he sees himself as a gifted young man with a bright future who's been done in by schemers and social climbers without an iota of talent." Mrs. Atwell kept on, shifting from light-hearted gossip to angry criticism. "His family begged him, threatened him, all in vain. He had to go on the stage. And now he lives off his meager earnings and his debts, 'borrowing' money from his indulgent mother or from rich friends." "But that cottage in Mayfair and his Sunday at-homes," Maurice sputtered. "Do you think Lady Ward...?" "It wouldn't surprise me in the least. All he needed to do was convince her of his innate talent and splendid future." "Sphynx, you are incorrigible!" "As is she! I remember, around 1895 or '96 Freddy was seen in Hyde Park in a magnificent carriage, a victoria drawn by two horses, accompanied by footmen in livery. I can still picture Freddy in my mind's eye, gracefully lounging on the cushions and chatting much too loudly with a young friend, an Englishman but with a dash of Portuguese blood[4], I suppose, a charming brunette that contrasted with Freddy's fair hair. They both came to see me afterward, thrilled with the attention they got."

"Two men driving in a victoria?[5] My God!" Maurice exclaimed.

Roy managed to get in a word, after taking care of their bill. "And his clothes, Maurice! His taste in clothes!"

"I've already seen a sample."

"But that's nothing! Mrs. Atwell was kind enough to invite me to lunch with him once. My Lord, just imagine an outfit put together with exquisite bad taste, a sort of Whistlerian symphony in mauve minor![6] I'd never seen anything like it. Yes, some sort of evil spell forced him to put on clothing he absolutely ought not wear, expertly tailored by some shopkeeper in the Strand.[7] His trousers were too tight, his waistcoat too long and too cinched, and the trim on his sleeves was too showy,

---

[4] The young man with "Portuguese blood" may have been a reference to Prince Francis Joseph of Braganza, an officer in the Austro-Hungarian army who was arrested in London in 1902 for 'gross indecency.' His grandfather was King Miguel I of Portugal.

[5] The victoria, a doorless four-wheeled open-top carriage, was considered suitable only for ladies.

[6] This is a referenee to the titles of Whistler's portraits, "A Symphony in White" (1862) and "Symphony in Flesh Color and Pink' (1874) that caused a sensation at the time. Mauve was a shade associated with the Decadent movement and with homosexuals.

[7] The Strand was a less costly alternative to the chic tailor shops on Savile Row.

so of course he thought he was the very picture of the 'latest London fashion' and a perfectly turned-out dandy."

"A dandy!" Maurice exclaimed," My gosh, his wardrobe says it all, along with the chatter, the witticisms, the sarcasm, the esthetic opinions, the languid poses! He's a fossil!" "No doubt about it!" Mrs. Atwell chortled. "He's the last specimen of a dying breed. Nowadays, we're all about sport and healthy living. Those are the watchwords. But to be honest, Mr. Verdal, one does encounter more than a few of these types in London. They are much appreciated in the suburbs, and also by Lady Ward."

Closing time! The lights in the dining room were turned out and the guests solemnly filed to the checkroom at the exit. "Do you ever see Fred these days?" Maurice asked. "Oh, not anymore. I scolded him once and ever since he has held it against me and says nasty things about me." Roy laughed, "That'll teach you to socialize with impossible people."

reggie's tips
and tricks

"I NEVER LUNCH BEFORE TWO o'clock in the afternoon," Reginald de Vere announced to everyone nearby. "Actually, even with the best intentions when you have breakfast in bed at eleven in the morning, as I do, when friends stop by to smoke a cigarette and chat, when you factor in enough time to have a bath and decide which suit to wear, and which necktie goes with it, you have to admit it is hard to get these thousand and one little morning things done by one o'clock."

That's why, in principle, Reggie didn't like to be invited to lunch. He was usually late and had to take a cab, so getting to the restaurant often cost more than the lunch itself. He'd rather make his way nonchalantly to a *grill-room* around two o'clock and order a steak or a platter of cold meat. Since he almost always headed to the Trocadero, he was sure to run into someone he knew. He could easily start chatting casually with the diners at the next table and only natural that they would invite him to join them. Sometimes he took matters into his own hands and with his usual loud laugh, he would exclaim to an acquaintance at the next table, "Oh! I'm going to lunch with you." Only rarely did the person in question not tell the waiter, "I'll settle both checks, please" when they were finished.

This way Reggie got a free lunch almost every other day, and he was quite clever about it. Because he knew his hosts and the state of their finances, he was careful not to order expensive dishes or fine wines when it was clear that wouldn't do. As a result, people didn't shudder and look away when they saw him coming. They knew, too, that they would always be welcome for a drink at his rooms late at night when the pubs were closed. That hospitality was greatly appreciated, and one could always hope for an interesting and unexpected encounter at his salons.

Reggie had a peculiar status in "his" London, in the milieux that made up "Chic society[1]," that amalgam of messenger boys, minor actors and actresses, idlers, society ladies who had lost their way, foreigners who lived by their wits, and the flashy dandies who dined at the Savoy and lunched at Prince's[2] or the Trocadero when their pockets were empty, lounging in orchestra seats at the theater, strolling in Piccadilly and Bond Street during the day, rubbing shoulders with high society and even occasionally mingling with it at charity do's.

Reggie's status was unusual even in these fast-and-loose circles. Everyone knew his background was not shady, his antecedents not mysterious, and the circumstances of his birth, legitimate. He came from Jersey and a respectable family even if his mother was notoriously flighty. Clearly, he hadn't benefited from a solid education or proper role models and had become a pleasure-seeker instead of a worker bee. But he was quite comfortable in his own skin. "Chic society" knew all about his relations with Mrs. Henderson. Half of them envied him and the other half condemned him for it. Only a few suspected that there was also a Mr. Kemball in the picture. Reggie was notoriously tight-lipped about that part of his life. More, many more knew that he was intensely attracted to some of his male friends, generally the young and charming ones who didn't have dodgy reputations themselves.

Be that as it may, everyone thought Reggie was sweet and not the type they ought to shun until and unless a certain rumor would begin swirling around and he was deemed 'an absolutely impossible chap.' Then Reggie would fight back with a smile and unleash even more vicious gossip. Reggie's standing in society was terribly important to him. He knew quite well that a lot depended on the address where he lived, the funds people thought he had, and the clothes and jewelry people saw him wearing. He also knew that he had only two pounds left of the fiver he had borrowed the day before yesterday, and that he was going to have to do something about that right away.

---

[1] Translator's note: The original phrase is "Tout-Londres" or "All-London," a play on "Tout-Paris," the word for a motley collection of socialites, slightly scandalous, stylish denizens of Paris nightlife, theaters, cafes and gossip columns.
[2] Prince's was a fashionable restaurant in Piccadilly.

He considered writing to Liverpool or going to see Mrs. Henderson. These unwelcome thoughts upset him so much that he couldn't decide which necktie to wear. He tried on one after another and after the third, concluded that none would do, and the others, bunched up in a drawer, were equally hopeless. Bah! He'd get a new one on his way through Piccadilly. He had enough time. He sank into an armchair, lit a cigarette, and was soon lost in thought. All of a sudden, he leapt up, remembering that Paul had invited him to lunch! He rang the bell for the porter and shouted impatiently. "Quick, quick, call me a hansom!" He hurled himself into the cab and then stopped at a shirtmaker's where he bought two neckties, one of which was so garish he wondered if he'd ever be able to wear it. He put on the other and arrived at the Trocadero only twenty minutes late, thinking 'What in the world? I've already spent twelve shillings,' as he paid the cabbie. 'After lunch, there'll only be eight left. Dammit!'

He caught sight of Paul waiting, a frown on his face. "Sorry, my dear, to be so awfully late but I had so many things to take care of!" He shrugged. "Quick. Let's get a table…. What would you like to have?" They went into the grill-room. "No, over there. Listen, I know the waiter…. I'll have cold meat and salad, and to drink, a Hock cup.[3] Order whatever you like…. So, how are you?" Reggie smiled broadly, showing all his teeth and nodding at someone at the next table.

Paul couldn't see who it was. "Who is it?" "Maurice Verdal. I'll invite him to have a cocktail with us. Oh, I forgot. You don't like him. Bah, it doesn't matter. Not many people here today. Where on earth is everyone? Oh, there's Freddy! I'm so glad I ordered a Hock cup. He'll notice that and be annoyed. He's really something, you know. I can't imagine how he does it…. He earns thirty shillings a week, he's supposed to be on tour and he's still lunching here every day. I know it's not expensive…. He's not too badly dressed. Eh, I don't want to say anything against him, but I am curious about how he manages. People have told me, and naturally I don't believe them, that a certain member of Parliament…. I do hope that it isn't true, or else Freddy is a damn fool for not upping his standard of living. Look, he's coming over. Honestly, his outfit is in very bad taste…. That vest, *dear me*! 'How are you, Freddy? It's been ages since I've seen you,'" he exclaimed warmly. And he added, naturally, "What a chic suit!"

Paul could barely keep himself from shuddering. The man seemed to be capable of anything, even the most shocking behavior and Paul admired, liked and feared him at the same time. All of a sudden, he was struck by the pettiness

---

[3] A mixture of white wine, soda water and tart citrus juice.

of his own life and its decent, bourgeois vices. He was at a loss for words and forgot almost all his English. "It's true. Some days I can't even get a word out." "But you have a lovely accent," Fred protested politely. "Not like my French," Reggie laughed. "I've forgotten everything I knew." Since he had never learned it, he wasn't wrong. "I think that the best thing is to speak English and French with a slight accent and put words from one language into the other and vice-versa.... And then there's nothing more annoying for people who only know one of them!"

"Quite so," Fred chimed in hesitantly. His grasp of French was limited to saying 'Garçong! Eh ben garçong!' in the Italian restaurants in Leicester Square. "I missed you last Sunday, Reggie," he added. "We had a lovely time. Lady Ward said something so witty... that she was lost in an Ibsen play, or was it the fog on her way to the theater?" "Does she often come to your Sundays, Freddy?" "No, that was only the second time since I moved to Mayfair." "Well, we are practically neighbors now. You must come by some morning, very casually, and have breakfast with me.... It's a charming area, isn't it? So aristocratic." And so cost saving when one hardly ever needs to hire a hansom to go anywhere." "Indeed," Reggie agreed, "I often say the same thing" although in fact he seemed to spend his life in cabs. "I must go," Fred exclaimed. "I have a rehearsal at three. Good-bye." "Good-bye. "He's always rehearsing, but he's never onstage," Reggie said cattily as soon as Fred was far enough away. "Actually, I ought to ask him to take me to tea at the Parliament.[4] That's the height of chic and since I don't know any M.P.s well enough for an invitation. But in fact, since the Liberal party is in power, it's not so popular." "Reggie, you are so cruel. I often wonder what you say about me," Paul protested. "About you, *dear*? Nothing bad, just that you are a charming Frenchman, perhaps a touch too Frenchy sometimes, in your affections... and your wardrobe! But that's all." Paul sputtered, "But I have an excellent tailor in Paris!" "Too bad! Why not come to mine here?" "And my tailor's bills? How could I pay them, whereas my father..." "Bah! That's your business, after all. I only wished that you didn't have such... alarming waistcoats! The one you wearing today is awfully *lady-like*! You can powder and rouge your face, wear high heels like Louis XV if you like, my dear chap, but please, for the love of God, dress properly.... Your necktie, actually it's a scarf and it looks like you bought it at Horne Brothers,[5] the kind you see on display in a shop window with a sign "Latest West End Fashion" or "As Worn Now" for 2/6."

---

[4] A tea shop in the House of Lords, now open to the public. served high tea to members and guests. An M.P. is a member of Parliament.

[5] The Horne Brothers "Hosiers, Hatters and Tailors" were located in Fleet Street, Coventry Street and the Strand.

"Reggie!" "My dear boy…" Reggie had a certain way of saying critical things while sounding caring and kind. "I don't want to hurt your feelings. These are facts, pure and simple, and I'm telling you this for your own good. You'll never succeed in London dressed the way you are. First of all, why don't you shave? And your boots? They're so ridiculously narrow and pointy, like toothpicks. Why? Look at mine from Williams[6], the finest bootmaker in London. Do they look like torpedo boats? Well, well, don't fuss. Have a bit more brandy and you'll feel better. You know I'm very fond of you."

That was true. Reggie was fond of him, but not in public. Perhaps it would be better not to go around with such a ridiculous-looking boy. His showy wardrobe, very Parisian-man-about-town, the little blond moustache that was a bit too vulgar and pretty, his wavy hair. *Another idiotic affectation*, Reggie thought, *now that everyone is plastering down their hair, looking like wet seals!*

IN THE MEANTIME, MAURICE WAS finishing his tenth cigarette. He had four during the meal, savoring the fragrant Russian tobacco, and six afterward, Turkish ones. He was feeling pleasantly dreamy and lazy. He sat back, letting the sights and sounds of this enormous grill-room wash over him, watching the waiters and customers bustling this way and that, hearing the clatter of plates and cups, seeing the glare of the electric lights, feeling the jets of cool air from the electric fans.

An Indian man in a white turban and kurta circulated among the tables with plates of curry, rice and dried fish. In the corner an Arab boy brewed Turkish coffee. The cigarette vendor pushed his little cart, the Jewish orchestra conductor swaggered to his post and behind the glass divider, the grill glistened and sizzled. Maurice glanced at Reggie's table from time to time, appreciating the way he spoke to Paul, gave orders to the waiters and eyed the other diners adroitly and absolutely shamelessly. Occasionally, Maurice and Reggie happened to look directly at each other. Maurice got up and approached his table. "Oh, here comes Maurice," Reggie exclaimed smugly. "Listen, Reggie," Paul murmured, "would you be angry with me if I left now? I don't want to spend any time with that chap." "That chap?" Reggie chortled. "Do as you please." Paul mumbled a few words to Maurice as he left but managed it so clumsily that Maurice had enough time to answer. He spoke in a falsely friendly, acid tone, making it clear he understood the gesture for what it was.

---

[6] Oscar William Shoemakers on Cleveland Street, was known for 'handcrafted boots.'

Reggie commented, "He really doesn't like you, you know." "And he's quite mistaken to feel that way, but it doesn't matter. He's a sweet boy, a little silly, but apart from that…." "He's not the right sort," Reggie burst out, thinking of the lunch that was going to cost him at least twelve shillings. "You see how generous I am. I offered him a quite good lunch, nevertheless…." He continued snobbishly "I must admit that I don't like to be seen with boys who are so badly dressed, when I'm dressed well enough for two!" Maurice twisted the knife, rhetorically, "Wouldn't it have been more suitable for him to invite you, a person with such standing, and so chic! Besides, he gets a good allowance from his family." Reggie realized he had been stupid, but thought there might still be a way to wriggle out of it. "To tell you the truth," he began, "he's beginning to get on my nerves; some of his little tics are quite exasperating." "Naturally! And he's awfully moody. I'll wager that you have to do all the talking!" "No problem with that, you know!"

Both men laughed and ordered more liqueurs, more cigarettes. Reggie paid the bill and the two left together, Maurice because he had nothing to do and Reggie because he liked being seen with someone different, not one of the usual chaps. He thought about introducing Maurice to Mrs. Henderson. That might make a good impression, and if they went this afternoon, Maurice would undoubtedly pay the cab fare. So, he started talking about Mrs. Henderson. "An absolutely charming lady, and so *smart*. I enjoy dining with her because everyone's eyes are on her. I know quite well what they're thinking, but I don't care!" Maurice couldn't possibly be a rival, he assumed, so he added brightly, "I'll introduce you whenever you please. I'm sure she'll be thrilled to meet you. She admires your friend Horner's novels, by the way."

Maurice thought Roy would be quite happy to hear that… but would not care to meet her. Harold, on the other hand, would argue that Mrs. Henderson's opinion was crucially important. Heedlessly, Reggie prattled on. "If you're free, would you like to go there now? I've got nothing to do, and we can have tea there. It's in Portman Square." "All right. Let's go," Maurice said, hailing a cab. "Give him the address." "Look," Reggie began, "I'm going to be honest with you. I thought you'd hail a cab and since I only have a dozen shillings in my pocket, this suits me fine." Maurice nodded. He understood perfectly and wasn't at all put out. Instead, he admired the young Englishman's ingenuity. "What a gold-digger you are!" He laughed.

"Gosh, I am, a little." Reggie smiled ruefully. "Except that right now this gold-digger is in a fix! I ought to write to Mama because she might give me some good advice. That's all I'll get from her, though, and I do hate to write. And I'm such a bad speller. You should tell me what to say!" "All right, I will. What is this about?" "Money, of course." "I do realize that, but still...." "Do you think I ought to marry? A wealthy girl, naturally. The one I have in mind is very, very chic. She has a bit of a Cockney accent, but I'll say she's from Australia. She's quite fond of me and says that I care more about her wardrobe than anyone else does. It's true, I do give her excellent advice." "Do you think she'll say yes?" "Oh that! I hadn't thought about it... I'll find out the next time I see her.... Look! Maggie Russel just passed by in a cab.... I know her well. I met her at a *garden party*.... I know quite a few things about her. Her mother was a laundress, you know." "Reggie, are you sure?" "Am I sure about that? First off, everyone says so and, in any case, she drinks!" he concluded with a flourish.

Maurice was having a lovely afternoon. "What was I saying?" Reggie continued. "I always lose the thread. Oh yes. Well, the fact is I am absolutely fed up with the life I'm leading.... Do you think I could make a splash at the Folies-Bergères, singing in blackface? You know, wearing a big floppy hat and tight-fitting silk trousers. Gosh, that would be fabulous. But I would have to finish out the season here first! And, about Mrs. Henderson..." Maurice listened and solemnly assumed the look of a confidant as Reggie prattled on. "This can't last forever and going to Liverpool is out of the question." "Liverpool?" Maurice asked. "Yes, I have someone who cares for me there." "But, what about your mother?' "Oh, she always says she's broke. She hardly even comes to London in case her creditors here catch up with her! But for me to live in Jersey, I wouldn't consider it, and neither would she. Besides, I annoy her." The hansom stopped for a moment in Oxford Street, which set Reggie off. He fumed, "This idiot is stopping right in front of my former tailor. He'll see me, no doubt. Oh, how awful.... What a relief! We aren't there yet." He took a deep breath and laughed heartily, showing all his teeth. "There are a few streets that I avoid like the plague!"

Reggie was clever enough to realize that Maurice enjoyed this sort of patter, so he didn't hold back. With a gay laugh, he went over some of the petty inconveniences in his life, feeling that his companion was not at all shocked by them, and might even be sympathetic. "Quite often I don't go out in the evening. I laze around at home. Then at about 10:30, I put on dress clothes and go to a bar where I'm sure to run into some friends. I tell them I've just come from the opera or the Gaiety Theater. Sometimes, around 12:25, I slip into the Carlton[7] and then

---

[7] The Carlton Hotel restaurant was made famous by Escoffier, the celebrated chef.

leave with the rest of the crowd, so people will assume I had supper there!" "The key thing is, you know, being properly dressed for the occasion to give people the right impression and I must say that, thank God, I've got enough money for that, so I can fit in anywhere. I mean, I know a whole lot of tricks to make this work, to make me look good. Everybody thinks I've got a lot more money than I actually have. Let's say, this year, along with my allowance I had 250 pounds from Alec...." Reggie got tangled up in the math. "My word, you're very good at this." Maurice was impressed by his brashness, but couldn't help but think that Reggie's youth and vigor wouldn't last forever. What else could this delicate, self-absorbed butterfly do? He didn't have the stamina or the brains to be a real con man. "You said we were going to Portman Square, my friend, but we passed it ten minutes ago," Maurice exclaimed. "Always the same story, my dear chap" Reggie explained. "She ought to put Baker Street on her cards instead. But that wouldn't do! Here we are. Two shillings for the driver, that should suffice."

Mrs. Henderson greeted Maurice warmly. What an odd coincidence. She had heard her friend Mrs. Morrell mention him sometimes. Mrs. Morrell! Maurice couldn't get over it. "What a small world!" Reggie exclaimed. Mrs. Henderson turned to him, saying "My dear Reggie, you know our world is small and everybody knows each other. That's why a scandal like the one at Maidenhead...." "Very well. Mrs. Henderson is on a tear again." Reggie protested with a laugh, turning to her. "You're on pretty thin ice, Mrs. Henderson, lecturing me about decency!" She cut him off abruptly with an indulgent smile, "This child is absurd!"

Mrs. Henderson's drawing room was suitably luxurious but also quite anonymous, with no little personal touches in the decor, things that would betray her as a middle-class matron or a social climber at heart. The tea service and silverware were obviously family heirlooms. Thinking about her patronage of young men, you could say that rather than corrupting the ones she took under her wing, Mrs. Henderson gave them sound advice and costly tokens of her affection. You could not accuse her of deliberately doing harm. It was odd that this youthful-looking but obviously mature woman was especially attracted to slightly effeminate gigolos with sketchy reputations, but she certainly knew how to keep them under her wing even if she drew the line at behavior that was too compromising. She preferred to live on her own terms with her own circle of friends rather than worry about maintaining a certain standing in "society." Her personal fortune let her indulge herself and she was right to do so. Other society ladies would be better off if they were less judgmental about this woman who took such an interest in their sons.

Mrs. Henderson, draped in chiffon and perfumes, had never encountered a challenge like Reggie. She had known men with more effeminate personalities, but never one who was so feminine himself. He had an adroit way of changing course, of slipping through one's fingers or between two logical thoughts and his absurd arguments stymied her. She sensed that he was more of a woman than she was and when Reggie laughingly called himself a flirt and a tart, two of his favorite epithets, she couldn't help but agree. He was also, she thought, really a bit too outrageous and, worried about his flighty mind and his erratic instincts, she wanted to force this birdbrain to take life more seriously. But Reggie would shrug off her concerns with a tinkling laugh, exclaiming that he would be whatever she wanted, except serious, "Anyway, I think I am absolutely hopeless when it comes to anything serious. Take the time I was performing at the Prince of Wales theater …." Maurice guffawed. "Ah, I know why you're laughing," Mrs. Henderson said. "Hmm, well…. Speaking of the theater, are you going to the opening night of "His Own Way?" Everyone will be there…." "Of course, Maurice will be there with Harold Barnes and Roy Horner." Reggie jumped in, "Harold is so talented. His last novel—" Mrs. Henderson chided him, "Reggie, don't be stupid. Mr. Barnes hasn't written any novels." "That's true. I meant to say Horner and his latest novel. Harold writes for magazines. It's hard to tell the difference. If I wrote a novel, I'd want it to be so disgusting that everyone would condemn it and read it in secret!" He stopped in mid-sentence and said, "Mrs. Henderson, I've got two tickets for the premiere at the St James. What do you think? I'm going with someone charming." "Really? Reggie, who?" Reggie was at a loss for words. "I don't know yet." He bristled with pride at this witty remark. "So, we'll all see each other there," Mrs. Henderson said gaily, with an air of pleasant anticipation. "I'm going with Mrs. Morell."

Maurice was quietly thrilled. Dear Mrs. Morell! He hadn't seen her since last season. Charming memories came to mind. They had had some lovely times together in London and in Richmond before going their separate ways. No doubt, when they met again, it would be with a neutral "How are you?" and no undercurrents of emotion. Still in all, this was an amazing coincidence. Maurice asked, "And what has Mrs. Morell to say about me, Mrs. Henderson?" "My Lord! Nothing special…. You were charming and conceited, and you met at someone's…

someone's house. I don't remember who." Maurice smiled. "True enough." Reggie had been fidgeting and distracted for a few minutes now. He announced that he had to leave, he was waiting for an important message and had to go back home. Maurice left with him. As soon as they were outside, Reggie burst out laughing. "Another one of my tricks! I want to upset her a little… and prepare the ground for the letter I'm going to send her." "My compliments!" "I was an actor, my friend. So, tell me, about Mrs. Morell. Did you know her well?" "Yes, rather well." "No more than that…? Oh, you are tedious. You won't tell me. Because now, you know, she's living with Mrs. Adam. They're both very intellectual and irritating, though, because they're always using words I don't understand! Where are you going? Can I drop you somewhere?" Maurice declined the offer since they were already in Portman Square, and he could easily look up Frank Mattison who lived nearby. "Who is he?" Reggie asked. "A man who's obsessed with waistcoats," Maurice explained. "Then you ought to introduce me," Reggie smiled. "Would you mind lending me a pound till tomorrow? I'm sure I'll get a check tonight, but it will be too late to cash it…. Don't worry. I'll pay you back. I'm not foolish enough to want to get on your bad side… for one pound! Thanks. So long." "Bye!"

Maurice grinned and walked on while. Hoping to hail a cab, Reggie flailed his walking stick in the air. There were no hansoms in sight and for five long minutes he seemed to be threatening to punish the sky or flinging a fishing line in an invisible body of water with no luck. He walked a few blocks further and, exhausted, flung himself into the first cab he saw.

BACK HOME, REGGIE TOLD THE porter: "Pay the cabbie. I haven't got any change. And call a messenger boy for me." One of Reggie's hard-and-fast rules was to have servants pay cab fares and all small bills. "They put it on my tab," he once explained to Fred. "It's a good to get them used to it, and an awfully handy dodge when you're broke."

Reggie, ensconced in his dressing gown, labored over the letter that the messenger would bring to Mrs. Henderson's, where he would wait for a reply. And this reply, he fervently hoped, would include a check for twenty pounds. He explained, in deliberately rushed handwriting, that he absolutely needed the money, he had so many pressing bills, he had sought help everywhere and didn't really know where else to turn. The loan would get him back on his feet, tide him over and enable him to pay the most urgent creditors until he got his allowance and some more breathing space. Reggie was quite pleased with the result. The letter intimated that there was a serious confession to come, enormous bills to pay and a set of circumstances to make right. He calmly waited for the messenger to return with the check.

He dressed even more carefully than usual, and was in a stunning suit and tie, impeccably turned out, when the boy arrived. The check was inside the envelope. Ah, a sigh of relief. A shilling for a tip. A few sound pieces of advice and a hint of annoyance were in the envelope too. *I've got to be extra charming from now on. I'll send her a lovely bouquet of Malmaison daisies tomorrow or maybe a Japanese bonsai tree. That will do. Dear Mrs. Henderson! I will miss her terribly when we break up! I can only hope that won't happen too soon! I must remember to pay Verdal back too.... He's nice.... I wonder if he wants to get to know me better? In any case, he finds me amusing, that's for sure. Eight o'clock. Right! I'll head to the Empire Theater[8] and then have late-night supper at the Savoy. I can afford it, and I think I've earned it!* Reggie powdered his nose, filled his cigarette case, and folded an overcoat lined with rustling silk over his arm. He felt very satisfied with himself. He had a pound to spend, a check in his pocket, life was beautiful and London, especially so. Never had the season looked so *smart*.

---

[8] On Leicester Square, the "gallery" or balcony of the Empire was a well-known cruising spot.

C H A P T E R   V I

memories and photographs

BACK AT HIS ROOMS, MAURICE felt strangely agitated. He opened his trunk, pulled out some packages and carefully unwrapped the photographs and other personal mementoes. *Mrs. Morell! Dearest Lillian with her precious smile! A close friend of that notorious Mrs. Henderson.* He sorted through the photos and found some of her. He was soon lost in a daydream where pleasant memories were mingled with fantasies surging from the deepest recesses of his heart. Gazing at her portrait, he felt a wave of incredible passion and indescribable joy. The magic power of memories! A chance remark brought back the full force of emotions that had been buried and forgotten for a year. Her physical presence seemed so close now. He could hear the sound of her voice and smell the sweet fragrance of her skin. These tantalizing illusions excited him even more.

He remembered what attracted him. Everything about her fascinated him, from the careful way she spoke French, translating word for word, to the childlike boldness and shamelessness in other matters that he found so refreshing. He could recall every detail of their affair. How marvelous! He first met her at a very 'continental' American woman's salon[1] where she immediately started talking

---

[1] This "very continental salon" would resemble the ones in Paris. hosted by the expatriate American lesbian writer Natalie Clifford Barney. Her lover, Liane de Pougy, wrote the novel *Sapphic Idyll* (1901).

about Paris and French literature with a seriousness that seemed out of place but somehow added to her charm. She brought up Liane de Pougy's latest novel and the poems by Verlaine that she had read in translation in the *Savoy*[2] exclaiming, "Honestly, French literature is so exciting!"

Maurice knew she was a widow and apparently kept to the straight and narrow, so he made no effort to seduce her. Whenever they met, which was fairly frequently, they chatted about the things that interested them both. They ran into each other often, at the theater, at tea parties, or in Hyde Park. At first, they simply spent time together, talking about Art. After that, they moved on to heartfelt discussions about their tastes, their lives and their deepest thoughts about love. In an amazing coincidence they discovered they were very much alike, emotional soul mates in fact, who suffered from bouts of melancholy, experiencing setbacks and frustrations in love. They were the kind of people who quietly kept their distance from the social whirl with a bitter smile on their lips. Mrs. Morell forthrightly confessed, to Maurice's eternal gratitude, that all the erotic variations she had explored so far disappointed her. Yes, she had admitted to 'variations,' and Maurice urged her to tell more, hiding his intense curiosity behind a psychologist's bland expression. She explained that one or two intimate lady friends, whom she had dearly loved, had barely reciprocated her affections.

Poor Mrs. Morell! Her common sense told her to live a celibate and secluded life instead, barricaded in her ivory tower against the cruel world and harsh reality, with only a few good books for company. Her thoughts were so cynical, and she seemed so lonely that Maurice, an inveterate contrarian, felt obliged to argue the other side, take advantage of the situation and have a taste of these tender green shoots.[3] He described his own disappointments in love but insisted that suffering was not an end in itself. Though it was inescapable and taught us mortals valuable lessons, we ought not succumb to despair. Instead, we should do all we can to make ourselves happy. Maurice reminded her that our emotions, our feelings, are critically important, so it's only logical that we ought to follow our instincts and avoid sentimentality, which was a dangerous illusion, and a scourge of the gods. Maurice proffered one contradictory theory after another as Mrs. Morell listened intently, looking bemused. He concluded with a flourish, asserting that all passions are noble and allegiance to duty was a sham. As they continued probing these

---

[2] *The Savoy* was a literary journal founded by Aubrey Beardsley and Arthur Symons in 1896. Like *Akademos,* the journal that published Boulestin's serial novel, the *Savoy* only lasted for a year.

[3] This is a reference to LaFontaine's fable, "The Animals Sick of the Plague" about inequality, temptation and divine justice.

theories and debating these high-minded questions, Maurice decided to press his case and started to flirt with the young widow. She didn't object to or resist his attempts, but she seemed utterly detached, as if her motto was "My kingdom is not of this world."[4]

Their vague, undefined courtship continued for a while through many twists and turns. Maurice maneuvered her ever closer with clever ruses and ingenious strategies. After all, he was a man of flesh and blood. One day, he urged Mrs. Morell, whom he now addressed as Lillian, to join him in more earthly pleasures. 'Have I wasted my time with her?' Maurice wondered, as he lit another cigarette. "I've been ignoring all my friends." Remembering their encounters last year, Maurice leaned back in an armchair and closed his eyes, replaying the film, watching reel after reel of their affair. Once, in a deserted room at the National Gallery, in an exhibition of English school painters, he made a frank and open declaration of his feelings. Mrs. Siddons in her portrait by Gainsborough must have turned beet red behind the protective glass when she overheard them. Maurice went on eloquently for ten minutes, offering variations on "I love you, I want you, you must be mine."

Lillian seemed to be in agony but finally after countless circumlocutions and even excuses, she managed to tell Maurice in so many words, "My God. I would like nothing better, I love you so much."

However, as a widow, she was in a delicate position. She was so afraid! That was holding her back. Maurice would have to swear that he would not be reckless. He agreed and swore a binding oath by the water of the river Styx, as the ancient Greeks did, that he would do whatever she asked. Her reluctance seemed amusing to him then and her confession sent him into raptures. She promised to come to his rooms the next afternoon; she sighed, she balked, she ginned up her courage, she wilted in the National Gallery, protesting "We are making a mistake. Just remember I told you that." And then she abruptly changed the subject and discoursed on early Italian primitive painters in the Renaissance.

Twenty-six hours after their conversation in the National Gallery, Maurice tried his best to convert words into action but their first encounter didn't go especially smoothly. Moving from Maurice's drawing room to his bedroom was a bit awkward since the flat wasn't designed for a quick and easy passage. The prim, proper and bland English decor made Maurice long for his sumptuous apartment on the avenue Montaigne where each stage in a seduction seemed to fall into place naturally, from the first cup of tea to the final movement to the bedchamber.

---

[4] A Bible verse from John 18:36.

In this case, dampening their ardor further was the quasi-medical discussion Maurice and Lillian had to have. Lillian, as a widow, needed to ensure she would still appear chaste. Still, after the first stumbling, awkward moments, they enjoyed themselves admirably. Maurice descended "treacherous byways" that fortunately weren't "painfully obscure" with "her dear hands as a guide."[5] They made practical use of *La Bonne Chanson*[6] and varied their pleasures, keeping strictly to illicit embraces which satisfied partners, but were especially reassuring for her. A critic or a busybody might dismiss their lovemaking as no more than flirting stretched to the limit. The couple's love affair lasted for a month.

"A little more than one year ago!' he sighed, as even more explicit images floated in his mind's eye. The memory film continued. Now, it was time for Miss Ellen Wallis to step into the frame. Though Miss Wallis was an actor, her pretty face counted for more than her acting talent. Maurice had met her by chance at Roy Horner's and one evening shortly afterward, Maurice found himself embracing the lovely and accessible Miss Wallis. He hardly knew how it all had come about.

But Lillian's delicate nature and sweet caresses attracted Ellen too. One day, Lillian arrived at Maurice's rooms, looking thrilled by a secret. "You'll never guess what happened to me!" she exclaimed with a smile. "I'll be frank, an affair. I met and seduced a lovely actress, Miss Wallee. You know, the one who performed at the Garrick Theater and other places…. But don't worry, as you would say, it's one of those passing flings that don't matter." This coincidence infuriated him, though, and left him feeling very, very resentful. 'It's immoral… a scandal!' he fumed. 'They'll tell each other everything, and no doubt I'll be the butt of their jokes!'

He imagined the two of them caressing each other, the tender gestures Lillian enjoyed so much, the ones forbidden by the Church. He sat up with a start. "I'll be damned!" The scenes he imagined were pleasing, actually. "And they're fine without me? Could I possibly be jealous?" he fussed. Was he jealous? Yes and no. In any case, their affair put a dent in his self-esteem, but his sensual side longed to share in their embraces and kisses. He decided he had to bring them together and make the duo a trio. He could, he thought, guide these two poor frail young ladies with his years of experience; his savvy approach would satisfy them both.

"All three of us will savor the ecstasies of mutual understanding, through a system of flawless cooperation and an intelligent division of labor. If this works out, it will be stupendous! Love that is well-organized, sensuality given its due,

---

[5] The words are from Paul Verlaine's 1870 poem "J'allais par des chemins perfides."
[6] *La Bonne Chanson* is a collection of poems by Paul Verlaine, written in 1869-1870, and later set to music by Gabriel Fauré.

all in a nice, neat package…" Maurice, still lost in his memories, had to laugh at his rationales and the way he fooled himself. He was caught up, obsessed, with complexity. He pretended that his perversity was motivated by genuine affection. Now, a year later he looked back at the ruins of this love affair and marveled at the efforts he had made to keep that house of cards from collapsing.

Oh, he would never expend so much energy nowadays. His heart was colder and better defended. He took the cowardly option of taking life as he found it without ever trying to discover the secret of happiness. He smugly and selfishly enjoyed his emotional numbness, his indifference and passivity. Being a voyeur, a mere onlooker, would protect him from any more reckless adventures and he could easily satisfy his taste for sensual pleasures at the Hotel Continental[7] or somewhere like that. Now Maurice felt a mixture of satisfaction and regret, of contempt and envy as he remembered the days when his life was unpredictably stormy.

The film continued to the final, crucial scene, just before the catastrophe. Maurice saw it all again. He had finally brought Lillian and Ellen together in his rooms. They were sophisticated ladies and he soon realized that he had a difficult task ahead of him. He would need a lot of tact to bring this off successfully. He decided it would be better to leave them alone at first so that they'd feel more comfortable, so he pretended that he needed to go out and buy some cakes for their tea. Just for fifteen or twenty minutes, no longer than that, he said, stressing the "no longer."

When he apologized for having to leave them alone, they smiled graciously and told him not to worry. He actually did walk to a bakery to while away the time, and checking his watch every three minutes, wondered why the quarter-hour was going by so slowly. "I wonder what they're up to?" he muttered, without feeling overly concerned. He was sure that when he returned, their desires and their warm relationship would overcome any scruples they might have. He came back, a little nervous, crept up the stairs and listened at his door. No noise at all, a good sign. He opened the door and saw no one. He gasped; had they left? Actually not, he caught a glimpse of them in his darkened bedroom, so he tiptoed toward the two bodies entwined on his bed. He was filled with gratitude and felt a wave of tender emotion. He loved them both, and wanted them both, equally. "How charming you look, my sweet, and how I love you!" He took hold of their heads, stroked their hair gently and brought their faces together with his own. They shared a deep, long kiss….

Maurice sighed deeply several times and shivered. This was one of his most precious erotic memories! He brought the picture into clearer focus, mentally

---

[7] This hotel on Regent Street was known as a haven for high-class prostitution.

framing it in words that were vulgarly explicit. Shortly after this encounter, however, he stumbled. He should never have tried to recreate the perfect harmony of that lovely afternoon. But one can always hope…He wanted the three of them to enjoy the country charms of Richmond together in a retreat that was perverse, poetic and gave at least the illusion of privacy. Lillian agreed, "That would be lovely." Ellen laughed, "This is madness!" But they both accepted the invitation. Madness indeed. Maurice rushed to Richmond-upon-Thames to find a suitable love nest. He rented a charming little furnished house in the upper part of town, near Richmond Park. He paid the rent, which was exorbitant. He was mad, no question about it. The drawing room had floor to ceiling windows that opened onto a spectacular view of the famous terrace, the sloping gardens, the deep green valley and the Thames with its rowers and canoes.

Their tranquil and loving entente lasted two days and nights before things boiled over. On the morning of the third day, Lillian took Maurice aside and told him she had had enough. She felt neglected, she was jealous and seeing Ellen making love to Maurice upset her "because you know she loves you!" She trembled, burst into tears, and got angry. "I couldn't help but notice, you see, that last night I did everything I could, but she wasn't satisfied until you kissed her," she sobbed. She threw her arms around Maurice's neck, told him she adored him and didn't want to see him with anyone else. Maurice bristled, "That's a bit much, Lillian, really! Such feminine frankness! Such female logic!" He tactfully left her alone so she could finish dressing and make up her tear-stained face, but when he came back to the house for lunch, the love nest was deserted. The two turtle doves had flown away in feminist unity. And, truth be told, after he got over his astonishment and his anger, the surprise ending to this tale piqued his "*sense of humor,*" something he valued above all else. For one thing, he mused, the situation was actually very funny. For another, he knew even his stamina wasn't inexhaustible and that purely perfect happiness doesn't exist on Earth.

The bizarre Mrs. Morell, he thought. Was she sincere or a schemer? He wouldn't mind seeing her again, but he worried that she would hold their past encounters against him. He had, after all, walked out on her that fateful morning. How would she react now? He gazed at the photograph for such a long time that his vision blurred, and he could no longer recognize her face. What the devil had become of Ellen Wallis? he wondered. Truth be told, Maurice did have fond memories of Mrs. Morell. She was so sweet. She made him laugh with her bad French when one day she said, "You know. As soon as I saw you, I thought I'd like to be 'screwed'[8] by you. You must want to 'screw' me." Maurice shrugged, shook himself awake and stopped mulling over his special memories. He stopped mulling over his affair with Mrs. Morell and put the photographs away.

---

[8] The mistake is the verb "baiser," It means "to kiss," but is also used in French to mean "to fuck."

in lady ward's salon and mrs. atwell at home

I F YOU ARE LUCKY ENOUGH to be invited to Lady Ward's salon, you will find a lovely collection of sofas; one is upholstered in brocade, in Genoa silk velvet, another in printed Liberty cotton, another in chintz and another in faux tapestry. The extraordinary number of sofas in a room of ordinary size is as stunning as it is awkward. Maurice had a difficult decision to make: ought he ignore the sofas or talk about them? Lady Ward was being very… Lady Ward.

"Well, Monsieur Verdal," she began, "are you enjoying yourself in London? My word, it's hard to believe that anyone would love London when they have Paris." Maurice smiled. "I don't like living in Paris, Lady Ward. I'd much rather settle down in London permanently. I'd enjoy Paris if I were just a tourist. I would take a hotel room on the Champs-Elysées for six weeks in the spring, and one day I might even decide to visit Napoleon's tomb!" Mrs. Hallet chimed in, "When I was in Paris for the last World's Fair,[1] I found it quite changed." She was wearing a magenta-colored frock with a wide white lace collar covering her shoulders and décolletage and a gray tulle choker around her neck. "My dear Caroline," Lady Ward exclaimed a bit cruelly, "don't you think Paris found

---

[1] The World's Fair was the Exposition universelle in 1900.

you changed also?" Shifting her weight on one of the sofas, Lady Ward squinted in the sunlight and asked her maid to close the shutters. Mrs. Hallet, shaking her false curls, began explaining to her friend. "Agatha, nothing on Earth is eternal. What I meant to say is, in my day—"

She was interrupted by Fred, who arrived with another nice-looking, shy young man. "How are you, Lady Ward? I've brought along my friend Guy Gregory who really wants to be an astrologer… in our matinee." He surveyed the guests with a practiced eye and seemed content with what he found. "Because," he continued "we might as well announce it right here and now. We are going to organize a charity do and..."Maurice jumped in, "Who are 'we'?" "Well, Guy, Miss Rising and I. Lady Ward is our sponsor and we're going to perform *Herod's Niece*.[2] My costume is green and violet, inspired by a mosaic in the British Museum." Mrs. Hallet was overcome with enthusiasm. "How interesting!" Maurice murmured, "Sounds charming, absolutely charming," and looked a little bemused. "I mean, a capital idea. You will make a perfect Herod." Fred nodded. "Yes, I think so too. I'm mad about the role. Just think, my big break in London!" Lady Ward chimed in "Fred has convinced me that this play is vastly superior to *Salomé* and so much more artistic." Fred added casually, "The end is gripping. I rise from my seat on the throne, where I haven't budged till then, and cry out 'Kill that woman.' It makes quite an effect." Lady Ward and Mrs. Hallet simultaneously shivered at the thought.

"And let's hope this charity do brings in a lot of money for our poor folks," Mrs. Hallet opined piously. "And who are your poor folks, Mrs. Hallet?" Maurice asked. "Actually, we haven't any idea yet. Probably the 'flood victims on the East End.'" Lady Ward disagreed. "Caroline! I think 'Our Dumb Friends League" is more worthy. These little creatures need the hospitals, the doctors, as much as your poor people in Whitechapel!" Mrs. Hallet bristled, "Really, Agatha. You cannot compare the two!" "But of course I can! My dear, we've tried so hard to solve the problems in the East End with film showings, horticultural exhibitions, and whatever else. But if our charity matinee is dedicated to "Our Dumb Friends," we are guaranteed to have at least four duchesses and perhaps one Royal Personage in our organizing committee. Then all the morning papers will cover it and we might even get a paragraph in one of the weeklies.

"Monsieur Verdal, do you think you could invite Mr. Barnes to the performance?" Mrs. Hallet sighed reprovingly at her friend, "You are hopelessly

---

[2] This imaginary title might be an ironic reference to Oscar Wilde's scandalous play *Salome*, performed in Paris in 1896.

in the thrall of high society, my dear!" Lady Ward moved to another sofa where the pink brocade seemed to revive her. She appealed to Maurice. "Aren't I right, Monsieur Verdal? In London nowadays, the press is more interested in reporting on society news than on a reshuffle of the Liberal party's cabinet. For instance, do you know what made that perfectly banal play, *The Politician*, a success? It was simply the bridge game in the second act where the duchess cheated. Once everyone understood that the cheater was meant to be the duchess of Harland, we all flocked to see the play, we London society people as well as our suburban neighbors. The play ran for over two years because of that." Mrs. Hallet protested, "My Lord, what times are we living in?" Fred and his friend eagerly and vociferously agreed with Lady Ward. Maurice said that he too saw it her way, and politely took his leave. "What a charming boy," Lady Ward exclaimed once he was gone, "And such good manners." Fred added generously, "And quite well-dressed for a Frenchman!" The silent Guy piped up, "And even for an Englishman!" taking his friend by surprise.

AFTER HE LEFT VICTORIA STREET, Maurice walked across the park to Mrs. Atwell's. He was fairly sure he'd find her at home in the tiny, overstuffed house on Connaught Street, immersed in laying out her cards. "Harold just left," she reported as she offered him a Russian cigarette. "We were both in good form, quite brilliant! And now I feel a little done in, as tired as if I'd done some vigorous exercise. I'm afraid I've run out of steam. You must excuse me…. Would you like me to read the cards or your palm?" "Do you really believe in all that, Mrs. Atwell?" "Only when I see happiness, good luck or a handsome dark stranger who'll love me to death. I feel quite affectionate at the moment." "Toward whom?" "How indiscreet! A person you don't know. But we never see each other, and we never write. We only declare our feelings for each other by telephone. It keeps me busy for twenty minutes before dinner and entertains me." "But you have no need of distractions!" "I most certainly do. My husband came back from South Africa unexpectedly and stayed here for three weeks. That was terribly upsetting! I'm just beginning to feel like myself again now that I know he'll be gone for another ten months." Maurice laughed, "Such tender feelings!"

"Indeed. Not every woman can be a widow. Anyway, I have no doubt there are some good husbands… somewhere in Kensington, near Prince Albert's monument? You can tell by the look of the flats there with red velour curtains at the windows… My word, where have you been, so dressed up? Surely, that wasn't for me." Maurice shrugged, "I've been to tea at Lady Ward's." "My poor chap! Who was there?" "Your friend Fisher, a very shy, handsome young man, and Mrs. Hallet in magenta silk." "Really?" Mrs. Atwell chortled. "I'm convinced she's the last woman in London to wear magenta silk to one of her friends' at-homes. I imagine she had a bonnet tied under her chin and a cameo brooch fastened on her dress. Or was she wearing all her pearls?" "No, neither one. She had a plain gray tulle choker—" "My Lord, a tulle choker! That's the limit! I can picture the salon as if I were there, the ribbed drapes, the red velvet, the crocheted doilies, a mahogany pedestal table holding a 'keepsake album.' A museum of all things Victorian. In the foyer, engravings. One of them of a Highlander romantically gazing over a gloomy valley, standing between a boulder and two trees! Oh, the memories of my youth! I wonder if that choker…." Mrs. Atwell dissolved into fits of laughter. A puzzled Maurice asked, "The choker?" "A long and complicated story, my friend. I'm not sure I even know the half of it." "Could you try?"

"Well," she hesitated. "Even for a Parisian… this is a bit much! Poor Mrs. Hallet had a nephew, the son of her deceased sister, if I understand correctly, a young man who was quite free-thinking and not at all conventional looking either. He was neither a romantic nor an esthete but was thoroughly modern in a way that was interesting, though hard to pin down, exactly. Mrs. Hallet sent him to Paris to learn French and there he got into a relationship with a gentleman known as…'le bel Ernest.'" Maurice exclaimed, "'Le bel Ernest? I've heard of the fellow, a pimp who spends all the money his girls make… on boys." "Exactly." Mrs. Atwell continued. "And one girl in his stable at the time wasn't a professional. She was simply a seamstress. Ernest introduced Mrs. Hallet's nephew to her, pretending he was a client in order to save face, or for some other reason. The nephew felt he ought to buy something from her, so he purchased six chokers and gave them to his aunt for Christmas, saying they were 'the latest Paris fashion'! If the poor lady knew where they actually came from…." Maurice agreed, "No doubt, she would shudder and toss them all in the fire. But how did you learn all this?" "Oh, from a journalist who lost his way." "What do you mean, lost his way, Mrs. Atwell?" At that point, the telephone rang, interrupting their conversation.

She left the room saying, "Excuse me. That's my latest crush, no doubt. Yes, yes. What? No! Oh, it's you, Harold. Mr. Verdal, it's Harold, with some very important news." She listened, at first smiling and then stunned. "Who is here with me? Oh, Verdal. He's sorry to have missed you. He says he's pretty well settled in London. He bought five geraniums in pots for his windowsills. That's confirmed? As far as you know.... What? What? No? That's impossible.... Naturally. Good-bye." Mrs. Atwell came back into the drawing room and took a seat next to her visitor. "Harold just told me that George Trait—you know who I mean, the one who writes those charming plays, one part Ibsen, one part Bernard Shaw. Well, Trait just got married in secret to a woman who's twice his size and not even rich. Her only goal in life is to discover the exact dimensions of the pyramids in Egypt. What a fresh and absolutely marvelous piece of gossip!" "Indeed!" Maurice said genially. "Tell me, do you know George Trait?" "Not at all, only by reputation." "A wonderful man," she chirped. "I'm awfully fond of him. He's such a talented playwright and also the last English author to write epic poetry. He has the poems printed specially in limited editions: 150 for his closest friends, two for the general public and one for the United States.... Still, I don't know why but he always looks like a hotel manager who's in love with the head chambermaid.... *Dear* George. We get on so well together!"

CHAPTER VIII

at the premiere

THE FIRST ACT OF *His Own Way* had just ended. The audience was thrilled with Madame Le Bargy's[1] costume. "She's rather hard to understand," Harold Barnes commented to Roy Horner. "She speaks too quickly." "And in French," Maurice added. "But I do like George Alexander's performance. It's so powerful," Harold continued. "He's a paragon of conventionality onstage. The contrast between his performance, so forceful, so apparently natural and Le Bargy's, makes her look over-the-top. One hardly ever sees a play where the two leads are this terribly mismatched. It's awfully interesting. Let's find our way to the bar and toast the "entente cordiale"[2] of the dramatic arts. You know that *Pelléas et Mélisande* is going to be performed by your greatest tragic actress, speaking in English, and our... best actress speaking in French?" "And who is England's best actress?" Maurice asked "That is yet to be decided."

The bar was crowded with men smoking and drinking; very few were talking about the play. A man came up to Harold. "Hullo Harold!" Astonished, Harold called out "Frank! You've grown out your moustache?" and gestured toward a

---

[1] Madame Le Bargy was the French actor Pauline Benda (1877-1985), married to the actor Charles Le Bargy at the time.
[2] This is a joking reference to the diplomatic alliance of France and Great Britain in 1904.

few short blond hairs visible on each side of the man's nose, an excrescence that ended in two almost invisible points. Frank Mattison[3] looked hurt. "All right! Tell me, Verdal, " Frank began, "don't you think Harold's judgement and his usual perceptiveness are a little off? No and no. I am not growing out my moustache. It's already grown. Here it is, the finished article in good condition, the smallest and least offensive moustache anyone could possibly have. If I were Roy, for example…." Roy shot him a look. "Mattison, please. Don't add to my confusion. It's already been a month that I've been wondering whether I should trim my moustache, shave it off or leave it as it is. Honestly, I had just started to forget about it…." Frank said decisively, "Either trim off nine-tenths or shave it entirely." Frank's advice was worth its weight in gold as he was the most well-informed man in London on this topic. He had strongly held opinions on moustaches, sideburns and waistcoats that livened up any conversation though he might seem terribly annoying to those who didn't appreciate his very special sense of humor. He had published two very clever novels which, not surprisingly, dealt exhaustively with moustaches, sideburns, and waistcoats. But his favorite topic was sideburns and he could talk eloquently about them for hours. He was also responsible for the now famous joke about Bayswater[4] and how to get there. One popular magazine dubbed him "the Kipling of Bayswater" although people living there cursed him, with some justification. He was also a lawyer, but no one knew whether he was a lawyer who enjoyed writing novels or a novelist who occasionally pleaded cases. The fact that he rode in Hyde Park every morning did nothing to clear up the matter.

Harold confided to his friends, "I had a most surprising experience the other day. I was invited to lunch with some friends who know Madame Réjane [5]quite well. Since she was performing in London at the time, I thought they wanted to introduce me to her. And at the luncheon I was introduced to a French actress whom everyone was treating with the greatest respect…. 'May I introduce Sir Harold Barnes, the drama critic for *Tragedia*, one of our…etc. etc.' We were seated together at lunch and had a lovely conversation. I praised her perfect English, lauded her talent, congratulated her on her triumphs, her art and so on. Afterward, I thanked my friend, naturally, for introducing me to Madame Réjane, and told him how charming she was. He was dumbfounded and the look on his face made me wonder if he had lost his mind. I probed further. " Réjane?" he chortled. "You

---

[3] In his memoir, *Myself, My Two Countries,* Boulestin recalled that his friend Frank Richardson was the model for this character.
[4] Bayswater became popular with artists and writers after a rail station opened there in 1868.
[5] The dramatic actor Gabrielle Réjane (1856-1920) was considered the equal of Sarah Bernhardt in France.

mean, Madame Yvette Guilbert!"[6] That's when I understood why my luncheon companion looked so different in person from the way she looks onstage and in publicity photographs!" "That was rather embarrassing, wasn't it?" Roy asked sympathetically. "No, not a bit. That's the funniest thing about it. She didn't catch on at all. When I was going on about 'art, theater, triumphs,' she had no idea I wasn't talking about her specifically. It was all so general that it could have applied to any actress." Harold's friends chuckled appreciatively, naturally.

Maurice changed the subject. "What will you say about *His Own Way?*" Harold, the drama critic, said casually, "Nothing much. But I will include a few incisive insights and clever remarks about the two leads." Frank laughed, "That's why Harold's reviews are so fascinating. He writes about everything but the play itself. That way, he avoids the appalling banality of most reviews and readers can easily go see the play without any preconceptions or spoilers. It's impossible to enjoy watching a play if you already know what's going to happen in the third act. Harold's articles are the epitome of theater criticism and will be forever! Besides, he doesn't even like plays…. By the way, my dear Harold, I saw the original version of this in Paris, and I swear to you that Guitry[7] had a thick black moustache. But here George Alexander is clean-shaven. In my opinion, if you're going to play a Frenchman onstage, you ought to have a thin, slightly curved moustache that's a little lighter color than your hair. I mean, for example, a reddish henna tint…." But at this moment the bell rang, and the intermission was over, cutting short Frank's crucial insights.

The audience was stunning, breathtakingly elegant, the brightly colored gowns, the ladies' bare shoulders, their diamonds glittering against the somber backdrop of the men's evening dress. Celebrities were spotted here and there in the audience and there was even a Royal Highness seated in a loge on the right. The second act ended with a polite smattering of applause. Maurice left his friends to their cigarettes and went to speak to Mrs. Henderson, who was sitting with Mrs. Morell. "How are you, Mrs. Morell?" Maurice said. They exchanged friendly smiles, but Mrs. Morell's behavior spoke volumes. Her firm handshake, forthright gaze, and neutral words conveyed the message that she remembered nothing at all. It was a classic case of partial amnesia. Maurice decided to take a chance and asked a few questions. "So, have you been traveling a great deal…? And Miss Ellen Wallis, how is she?" Mrs. Morell seemed totally indifferent, making a pretense of vaguely recollecting the name. "Miss Wallis. Oh, yes, yes. I hardly know her."

---

[6] Yvette Guilbert (1865-1944) was a well-known music hall star.
[7] The French actor Lucien Guitry (1860-1925) was aa famous as Sarah Bernhardt at the time.

Visions of their encounter in Richmond suddenly flashed in front of his eyes, but he kept a poker face. This was not the time for more questions. "Of course." He couldn't forget their time together nor would he bring it up in any way now. He would have to learn to forget. Mrs. Morell ventured in a friendly tone, "You've lost weight." "So much the better, Madame! Gaining weight means getting older." Mrs. Henderson, bored by this superficial chat, launched into a commentary on the play and its leading lady. "Isn't she positively charming, Monsieur Verdal? I think I like her even better in the second act." Maurice was taken aback by her enthusiasm. "And that lovely tunic of unbleached lace, and her hair." She turned to Mrs. Morell. "My dear, did you notice her coiffure? Oh, my goodness, these Parisian ladies!"

Mrs. Morell offered a literary analysis. "It's not much of a play." "Clearly," Maurice agreed. "Not worth discussing. "Ah, Mrs. Henderson" he exclaimed "there's our friend de Vere, coming toward us, with a big smile." "Ah ha, for a change! Tell me, who is he talking with?" Reggie, seated in the orchestra next to Paul, had been turning this way and that like a contortionist, giving as many cordial nods and smiles to his acquaintances as possible. "Look, there's Verdal, with Roy Horner, and there's Lord Joyce, and there's Fred Fisher in the stalls, my dear! with Adolph Jones. My word, the balcony must be sold out! I say, Paul, if it's all right with you, I'm going to say hello to Mrs. Henderson. I won't be five minutes."

Reggie didn't want to introduce Paul to anyone even though in his dress suit he looked more acceptable and less vulgar tonight. As Reggie's eyes swept through the theater audience, he froze suddenly, exclaiming, "Dammit! There's Mama. That's too much. I didn't even know she was in town. This is just like her!" He then stood up and went to shake hands very warmly with a woman, remarkably youthful looking and quite elegantly dressed, seated in the second row. Paul watched his friend laughing, chatting and gesturing animatedly. Then, Reggie left her and joined Mrs. Henderson's party. "How do you do, Mrs. Morell?" he said suavely. "Listen, Mrs. Henderson, this is unbelievable. Can you guess who I was chatting with?" "That attractive lady…" Maurice laughed, "We were watching you, de Vere!" "Well, to tell the truth, that's Mama!" Reggie enjoyed their surprised looks as he stood next to Maurice and watched the two women. Mrs. Henderson looked back at him, gaily but with a touch of melancholy, thinking 'this boy is really quite elegant, weak and utterly useless!' He exclaimed, "My mama! I had no idea she was in London…. She didn't have time to let me know…. I understand that, given all the things she has to take care of, dressmakers, designers and all that! She's invited me to lunch tomorrow. She's at Claridge's. That's a little straightlaced for her, but so *smart*! I must say, she's even more of a snob than I am!"

"*Smart* may not be the right word, Reggie." "All right. Let's say it's exclusive and very respectable. Speaking of which, I'd prefer lunching somewhere else; Prince's would suit me better. There'd be more chances of being seen by my friends there." Mrs. Henderson chided him gently, "Being respectable wouldn't hurt for once!" He smiled, "But Mama is hardly that!" Some people turned around and stared at them, shocked at hearing this loud rude comment. "Tell me," Reggie continued, "are the ladies' jewels *smart* enough tonight?" *Smart* was his favorite adjective; for him it meant the ultimate in chic. Mrs. Henderson pointed out another lady in the audience. "Who is that woman, the one whose face is more purple than her gown? Sitting next to the duchess of Harland?"

"Why, that's her Grace's sister," Reggie prattled on. "She started out as a laundress in Brooklyn and then got rich. She doesn't know how to make conversation but blurts out whatever is on her mind in a horrid accent. The duke finds her gaffes amusing so he took her under his wing and the duchess goes out with her because the contrast makes her look aristocratic. In addition to that, she's a handy person to run the household. She tyrannizes the servants, who detest her." "Of course!" Mrs. Morell agreed. "I'm sure she knows all the kitchen drudges by name and asks about their love affairs." Mrs. Henderson grumbled, "I don't care for American ladies. They look like they're always acting a part, especially the ones who've married English dukes, pretending to be as high and mighty as the Empress herself." "They're only empresses in their dreams, my dear! All these Gibson girls get on my nerves!" Reggie interjected cautiously, "She's wearing a very chic gown." "No doubt," Mrs. Henderson replied impatiently, nonplussed by the young man's obvious admiration. "With her fortune, if she didn't dress spectacularly, that would really be the limit! Besides, she's awfully eccentric." Maurice said snidely, "She has a lot of taste though I'm afraid to say, it's all bad!" "Ha! No doubt about it!" Both women agreed with him, so Reggie quickly changed the subject. "Are you going to dine after the theater? No, that's fine because I would have been shattered not to be able to go with you. Paul Haret is taking me to Hurlston's where there will be a lot of people…" Mrs. Henderson sniffed, "A lot of extraordinary people, I imagine?" "Of course. That's why I'm going…. May I come to see you tomorrow, Mrs. Henderson? Are you lunching at home? Then, I'll come around three o'clock. And you know, if you do have to go out, don't worry. You can take me with you. I adore electric autos! Are you coming, Maurice? I insist that you have a drink with me before the intermission is over. Can I bring you ladies some ices? Or would you prefer chocolates?" He smiled radiantly at the two women.

AT THE BAR, HE TOLD Maurice that he had kept to the straight and narrow, paid off his back rent, given the cigarette vendor a little money and hardly spent a penny on himself. "It's only that, you know, all these friends who stop by after closing time and drink my whiskey…. It may seem like a trifle, but the bills add up. And my God, the cost of my rooms! Four pounds a week, and everything else is extra, naturally. I can't move again. I'll only be there till the beginning of the season. And moving is a bad sign for your creditors. They think you're leaving because you can't pay. The truth is, in one place I had to leave my trunk as security! But those crooks will never see any money. I only left a pile of old clothes inside!" Maurice grinned, "Another one of your little tricks, de Vere." "Yes, but you mustn't use that one too often!" Maurice stepped away, saying "The third act is starting. Good-bye. I'll see you sometime soon. I'll come to you. It's number 44, isn't it?"

The play ended to waves of applause. It was a hit. The third act was electrifying, and the actors were called back onstage several times by the enthusiastic audience. Mr. George Alexander led Madame Le Bargy by the hand, presenting her graciously to the crowd as if to say, "It's thanks to her that we're a success tonight." She stepped back and urged him forward, as if replying, "No. It's thanks to him." Then a few voices chanted "Author! Author!" and "Translator," but neither came onstage. The show was over. Harold, Roy, Frank and Maurice strolled over to the Reform Club for a nightcap. Frank took Maurice aside, asking, "This de Vere you were chatting with earlier. He's Mrs. Henderson's young protegé, isn't he?" "I think so." "If I were you," he cautioned Maurice, "I wouldn't be seen with him too often. He's terribly compromising." "That's nonsense! My dear, I don't live in London and besides, a bad reputation doesn't concern me." Maurice quickly changed the subject, "What did you think of the translation? It was a literal one, not an adaptation." Frank shrugged, "All translations are useless. For example, this *His Own Way*…."And the four began discussing the play, the actors and a book written by one of their friends that had just been published. On the subject of books, Roy gave them a preview of his next masterpiece and Frank confided solemnly, "I'm also writing a novel. It's the height of idiocy; it's all about sideburns." Finally, Maurice excused himself, claiming he felt a migraine coming on, but when he reached Pall Mall, he walked briskly towards Buckingham Palace instead of his rooms on St. James Place.

C H A P T E R   I X

in mixed company

O N THE WAY TO ARTILLERY Row, Reggie de Vere crowed to Paul Haret, "I turned down two dinner invitations tonight. One was at the Savoy. I do hope Hurlston will be flattered. Is it going to be fun there?" "Without a doubt," Paul said enthusiastically, "At least in my opinion.... A fabulous house, always full of people, dinner and drinks, a wonderful spread that's beautifully presented, guests that sneak off somewhere and never reappear, others that suddenly pop in, no one knows how." "Oh really!" Reggie was enthralled. "Still, if I were him, I wouldn't choose to live on Artillery Row," he frowned. "It's not at all chic." Paul bristled, "His flat is magnificent, you'll see. But if I can give you one piece of advice, Reggie, it's to—" "To hell with your advice," Reggie interrupted. "I know how to behave in society, especially that sort!" The hansom stopped in front of an attractive building, one of those sprawling *mansions* that were being built all over London. They took an elevator to Hurlston's floor and followed the sound of people laughing and shouting behind the thick wood-paneled door of his apartment. When Hurlston himself opened the door, he and Reggie greeted each other rather stiffly. "I've heard a great deal about you, Mr. de Vere," he said. "Likewise, my dear Mr. Hurlston. Everyone in London knows about your dinners."

Once inside Reggie casually stretched out in an armchair, laughing. Five or six people in the room gave him unfriendly looks. There was Arthur, a dancer at the Empire, two young actors from the St. James Theater, also Claude Colwyn, the well-known designer, and Harold Berkey, who did something vaguely literary. A very handsome brunette barely said a word. All the guests silently exchanged glances. It was obvious Reggie's arrival had put a damper on the party for them. A few minutes later, Maurice came through the door and smiled as he took in this drama without words. Paul glowered when he saw him arrive and Reggie was astonished, "What, you here, Verdal?" "Does that surprise you?" "Rather! But then again…." Maurice and Reggie sat together in a corner. "So, tell me why, Reggie. Are you a prude? Why wouldn't I socialize with a different crowd, not my type, I admit, but one that intrigues me? I don't care what people say about me, and I don't pretend to be the arbiter of virtue. If I pursued my curiosity even further, would you blame me? We shouldn't judge our pleasures so harshly. It's moralists who invented the category of 'vice' by proclaiming that one kind of embrace is permitted and another forbidden. Actually, I'm more of a voyeur than an active participant. Being disinterested, for me, takes the place of value judgements."

Reggie began, "Then, there are times…." "There are times, Reggie! *You never can tell*' as George Bernard Shaw demonstrated in four acts.[1] Nevertheless, the spirit must be willing and the flesh up to the task." "Up to the what?" Reggie mumbled. Just then, Hurlston called out, "That's it. No one else is coming. Let's go into dinner." The party reassembled in the dining room, taking seats around the table. Reggie ended up sitting between Paul and Hurlston. Everyone else scattered, choosing their own seats. It was a spectacular meal with lobster "à l'Americaine"[2] that the host himself heated in an imported *chafing dish*. There was a stunning array of cold meats and salads too, and to top it off a fine selection of expensive pastries. Crystal carafes of wine and bouquets of enormous carnations stood on the table. Two of the guests served the meal and refilled the carafes since Hurlston never allowed servants at his evening parties. Perhaps he was worried about gossip? Still, as the dinner began, the men's conversation was quite banal with nothing compromising about it.

Reggie did his share of talking, naturally. "Everybody was there," he burbled, "and Madame LeBargy had the most gorgeous costumes, very Parisian of course…. You should go and see, Mr. Colwyn…" Someone interjected drily,

---

[1] "You Never Can Tell" (1897), a comedy by George Bernard Shaw, premiered at the Royalty Theatre in London. The plot hinged on mistaken identities.

[2] This dish, lobster cooked with wine and tomatoes, is a specialty of French cuisine, despite the name.

"Colwyn doesn't need to see French fashions to create his fabulous frocks." Colwyn demurred modestly. Reggie, unperturbed, continued, "As you wish, but for a woman, nothing beats Parisian fashions. That's my opinion. For instance, Mrs. Henderson, who dresses very well..." Someone snickered. "She orders all her dresses from Paquot.[3]"

The host, uncomfortable with the direction Reggie was taking, changed the subject back to the play and started asking about the audience. "Who did you see there tonight, de Vere?" "Who? My word, I can't recall. Everyone who is anyone in London, and even some nobodies... Fred Fisher was there, in the stalls.... No doubt he has an evening session at Parliament, and next to him.... Can you guess? Adolph Jones! I didn't know that they were acquainted.... But sitting in the stalls, how absurd!" Harold Berkey chimed in, "The stalls are often more interesting than the orchestra seats. I've had some fascinating encounters there." "Maybe so," Reggie nodded. "But the stalls are so bourgeois and proper. Though, for me, balconies are never much fun! And that Jones chap. When you're in his flat, you can never tell which is more badly painted, his portraits or his friends!" Maurice chided his friend, "Reggie, you *are* malicious," as he savored the angry looks of some other guests. "Me! Not at all. I didn't invent that cruel joke, nor would I ever willingly repeat it." He laughed and sipped some champagne. Expensive champagne was, of course, the wine he liked best.

One of the actors from St. James said, "Well, I've been in Jones' flat, and I assure you..." Reggie cut him off, looking ashamed, "Have you? I didn't know. Please forgive me." At the other end of the table, Colwyn was chatting with Arthur, "A little minx, my dear, and quite a rogue to boot. His mother has run up a bill at my shop that worries me a little. She hasn't got a penny... lives in Jersey off several gentlemen, I think. What a fine mess! As for the boy himself, he goes everywhere with Mrs. Henderson, and that's all one needs to say about that! I don't think he even has any vices. He adores everything that's chic and expensive... spends money like water, too. Poor Mrs. Henderson. It wouldn't surprise me if he had someone waiting in the wings...." "And that young Frenchman with him?" "Oof. Nothing special. Naturally, Reggie has had a few affairs. People have named some names, but, in my eyes, he loves nothing so much as luxury and money." Colwyn's judgement was a little too harsh. In fact, poor Reggie didn't love money; he loved the things money could buy, and he wasted his own money as easily and thoughtlessly as he did other people's.

---

[3] A reference to the French couturière Jeanne Paquin, who opened a shop in London in 1896.

ONCE THE DINNER WAS OVER, the men chatted in twos and threes, claiming separate corners of the drawing room, absorbed in their private conversations. A few poems were recited, a few chords were played, and then Harold Berkey disappeared with the handsome, silent, brunette, who hadn't uttered more than three words during the dinner. Two of those words were enough for Reggie to detect a Cockney accent. He bristled, "I don't like people who don't say anything, and I like even less those who can't utter a word without destroying the King's English. What a horrendous accent that boy has!" He turned to his host, and asked "Who is he?" "A very sweet boy, a chauffeur." "Oh, well, uh…." Reggie was flabbergasted and for once, speechless. Hurlston, in a dressing gown that was a touch too flamboyant, sat quietly smoking, leaving his guests to entertain themselves. Then Reggie caught a glimpse of him standing at the window signaling to someone who was standing on the sidewalk and then going to the front door. "What now?" Reggie joked. "Is it a police raid?" "Not at all," Hurlston quickly replied. "It's just the local bobby coming upstairs. I waved to him, to invite him up. I'm going to give him a whiskey and soda. He's a good sort, just a young fellow, quite young." He walked into the foyer. The door opened, a voice or two was heard, and another door closed. Silence.

"IT'S AWFULLY LATE, PAUL. I'M going," Reggie yawned. "Are you coming?" "Good night, Mr. Colwyn," Paul said. "Will you tell Hurlston that I'm terribly tired and I'm so sorry that I can't wait…. Please thank him for me, all right? Good night." He left, trailed by Paul and a volley of nasty commentaries. One of the actors muttered, "What a phony. I can't stand him though…" Outside on the street Reggie exploded, "See here, Paul! You're mad! Why spend time in such sketchy company? And, most of all, why invite me along? I didn't enjoy myself one bit and besides, it's awfully dangerous. Tomorrow everybody who's anybody will know that I dined at Hurlston's with a chauffeur, a policeman, and that nasty piece of work Colwyn, who's been dunked in the Thames twice for his indecency…. No, no, it's a fact. He's even been banned from Windsor.[4] Do you know that they kicked him out? I have to admit Hurlston is very nice even though he is annoying, flashing his diamonds and showing off the family silver that he probably picked up at an auction! I wouldn't want to be seen talking with his guests for all the money in the world! Paul, you're a complete ninny to spend time with people like that. That, and your Parisian clothes, take the cake! I will never go back there, and I am extremely sorry that I came tonight."

---

[4] According to historian Jacques Dupont, Windsor was a private boarding school that operated from 1854-1967.

He ranted on, "Why compromise yourself so thoroughly, I ask you. It's not worth it. Hurlston isn't worth it. And his vulgar, common guests aren't worth it either. I'd rather dine at the Trocadero all by myself, ten times over, than have one dinner with those no-talent actors who are going to tell everyone where they met me. I'll never live this down! And, as for you, my dear, if you keep seeing those people, you've lost my friendship forever, that's for sure. I don't want to jeopardize my status and tarnish my reputation.... Yes, I said 'my reputation.' It's bad, I admit. People call me a gigolo... and other things! But until now, no one can accuse me of fraternizing with riff-raff. That is always risky.... And do you realize that those boys despise me because they're flat broke with no one to help them out. Oh, I can just imagine what they'll say about me now. It'll be worse than ever. And it will be your fault! And, what a neighborhood! Not a cab in sight. Do you think we'll have to walk all the way to Victoria Station to find one? What a wasted evening! Ah, I can finally see a hansom. Not a moment too soon." Reggie smugly gave the cabbie his *smart* address, 44 Clarges Street, Mayfair. "Hullo, Reggie!" a familiar voice hailed him. It was Maurice. "I've had my fill of the limp-wristed little so-and-sos.... I'm off to bed while those chaps strike poses from naughty Italian photographs[5] and make nasty comments about us." "Let me drop you at home," Reggie offered. The two drove away, waving a casual "Good night" to Paul, and leaving him standing on the sidewalk, with a bitter taste in his mouth.

---

[5] This is a reference to Baron Von Gloeden (1856-1936) and his homoerotic photo portraits of young men, taken in Italy, at Taormina.

reggie de vere's reputation

REGGIE DE VERE ATE HIS morning eggs and sipped his tea, cozily propped up in bed. On the tray next to him was a stack of envelopes that he wasn't ready to open. He knew perfectly well the envelopes contained only one thing: bills. But first he was going to smoke a cigarette, enjoy this lazy relaxed feeling as long as possible and look at nothing more serious than the blue-gray smoke swirling up toward the ceiling. *My lord, life was exhausting,* he thought. Still, he had to get out of bed. "Oh, these letters!" Of course, the tailor wanted to be paid, the shirtmaker sent his bill, the florist asked when it would be convenient to stop by.... "Too too annoying!" He lit another cigarette, all the better to take stock of his situation. He picked up a pencil, did a few sums and arrived at a frightening total. He tried again, cutting the charges by a third, by a half, and then gave up, tore up the paper and threw down the pencil. He decided he couldn't pay anyone at present. He barely had enough left of his allowance to make it to the end of the month.

Reggie had a unique and entirely personal definition of the word "loan." He absolutely had to have 300 pounds before the end of the year. And then what? But he wasn't worrying about next year. That was out of the question. He lived for the moment. He had always managed in the past, so there was no reason why he couldn't keep on that way. If Mrs. Henderson or the man in Liverpool got tired of him… well, there are other fish in the sea, and Reggie knew how to find them. That would do until he brought off his great coup, a marriage with a wealthy woman to set him up for life. His thoughts turned to Miss Houston. Would she marry him? He didn't have a title or a fortune, only a meager allowance and an unspeakable number of expenses. Bah! She might actually love him. Reggie felt supremely confident. He knew that kings' daughters fell in love with shepherds and married them, at least in fairy tales and that in London, some rich ladies married personable young men. These precedents gave him hope. And then, what was the point of worrying? Worrying caused wrinkles and it was crucial not to have any. He decided to live in the present and let the future take care of itself.

He was going to lunch with his mother. She had invited him to Claridge's. He'd go to the theater this evening and tomorrow he'd dine with Maurice. On Sunday he'd go boating on the river with Mrs. Henderson. Things are going well! He dressed more carefully and less flashily than usual, with a sober dark tie, jacket and trousers, a waistcoat in a lighter shade and boots with an impressive glossy shine. He tucked a bright red carnation, kept fresh in a glass of water overnight, into his buttonhole; his necktie was perfectly tied. Reggie was quite superstitious about neckties. They were holy, almost divine objects that were sometimes animated by a vengeful spirit that wouldn't cooperate, no matter how many times he tried to knot them. But today the tie seemed to knot itself, neatly and gracefully. His mirror reflected back an image of a chic and svelte young man… though the sight of a few lines on his forehead and around his eyes gave him pause. After lunch, he would get a manicure and see his esthetician for a facial massage. He was always up on the latest techniques and the hottest gossip about the city and the royal court. It was going to be a lovely day. The only thing missing was a fortune teller who could study the lines on his palm and reassure him about his future.

OUTSIDE IN PICCADILLY THE JUNE sunshine glistened on shop windows and brightly polished hansoms. The dust floating in the breeze was tinted gold. On Bond Street the jewelers' display cases sparkled and the florists' bouquets looked fresher than ever. At the fishmongers' the salmons and lobsters slumbered peacefully on their mounds of ice and ferns. Carriages passed back and forth, carrying ladies in bright-colored frocks with piles of neatly wrapped packages and little dogs wriggling by their sides. Uniformed doormen standing in front of fashionable shops whistled and whistled for cabs. Some men, like Reggie, were strolling down the street, gazing at shop displays and smoking cigarettes. Bond Street in the morning, in high season! Everywhere you looked, you saw charm, elegance and luxury. Reggie felt as if his money was begging to be taken out of his pocket and spent on something. These shops are so alluring. Here you see the latest fashion in neckties, and there cigarette cases more attractive than yesterday's models. And tie pins! And buttons! He couldn't tear himself away. In Asprey's[1] window he admired a charmingly simple, tasteful flower stand made of white porcelain surrounded by tiny diamonds. It was the sort of trinket you paid a fortune for but couldn't resell for two guineas. "I absolutely must have someone buy this for me!" Reggie said with conviction. He felt calmer once he turned into Brook Street and mulled over his marriage plans. His mother had been the first to suggest that he marry for money. Miss Houston wasn't an extraordinarily wealthy heiress, but her income would at least cover an appropriately chic residence in town and a little country house somewhere, with a month at the seaside in the summer and a month at Monte Carlo or in Rome in the winter. Even if she married a man with no money of his own, any husband of hers wouldn't have to earn a living. And, as Mrs. de Vere always said, "Reggie, when I die, everything I have will go to you." He snapped back once, "You mean, whatever you have left, Mama!" knowing that she didn't have much money of her own and that her men friends would most likely have no interest in her son's welfare.

While he waited in the hotel lobby, he fantasized about his inheritance and Miss Houston. He got along quite well with her even though they didn't see each other often. Strolling around the lobby with its somber, pricey atmosphere, he suddenly felt a surge of optimism. He felt lucky. His mother must surely have some money now, he reasoned, so he ought to ask for a loan right away. He was even working on his lines, when a porter accosted him with unwelcome news, "Mrs. de Vere is not in her room." "Are you sure?' Even though he knew his mother well, he was astonished. "Very well, I'll come back later" he said nonchalantly. *This is too much!* he fumed silently, but the anger faded away quickly. He was, after all, his mother's son, and had to laugh at this turn of events. This is so like her! *Since it is lunch time, I might as well go have lunch,* he thought. Where? He hailed a cab and went to the Bristol in Piccadilly to mull everything over with a cocktail. Then he had three choices: eat alone at Scott's[2] and order a nice lobster, pick up a friend to

---

[1] Asprey and Garrard was a "luxury emporium" on Bond Street.
[2] A well-known seafood restaurant, then located on Coventry Street.

dine with him, or find a friend who would invite him. Why not Verdal? But Verdal knew a lot of people; he might not be free. Maybe he should go directly to Mrs. Henderson's since he had already arranged to see her today. He ordered another cocktail, decided on Mrs. Henderson's and hailed another cab. Along the way, he stopped at a florist. Ten minutes later he was sitting opposite Mrs. Henderson at her table, and she was thanking him for the lovely flowers.

MAURICE WAS HAPPY TO BE in London, even if, as Verlaine wrote, he was a man *sans amour et sans haine*.[3] Free from romantic entanglements, he spent his time cultivating his very special *sense of humor*. He wasn't eager to start a new love affair that might interfere with his easy-going routine and bring him no joy. He enjoyed the odd encounters he was having in London, getting to know all kinds of people in all kinds of places. He had friends to suit every mood, and could look to Harold for stimulating intellectual conversation, chat with Roy who was always good for a laugh, smile at Frank's outrageous jokes and be entertained by Reggie's shallow blather. Every now and then Maurice would look up a few duller, more conventional acquaintances. Wandering through the city alone, he would occasionally jump onto any double-decker bus that came along, ride to the terminus and explore a new neighborhood. That's how he got to know London, where there was always something more to see: the pretty red houses and quiet squares in Kensington and Chelsea, the bustling City, the streets crisscrossed with train tracks, choked with cars, buses, trucks and busy people, the crowds of men with not a woman in sight, the wide sleepy avenues near Regents Park, the glittering streets in the West End, the sketchiness and grime in Soho.

Once or twice on drizzly, overcast days he even ventured as far as Whitechapel. Setting the scene like a talented director, reluctant to taint his memories and shatter his illusions, Maurice never visited a certain type of picturesque neighborhood on a sunny day if he thought it would look better in the mist and fog. Hyde Park was made for brilliant summer days when the carriages sparkled and the horses' reins shone. But the Thames or Whitechapel required hazy, filtered light and clouds of mist. He wandered through the East End's Jewish quarter when the streets were illuminated by the waning light at dusk, when pubs lit up one after another and a cloying musky smell filled the air. He walked down High Street when the grocers'

---

[3] A line from the 1874 poem "Il pleure dans mon coeur" in the collection *Romance sans paroles*.

gas lamps flared, lighting up the signs written in Hebrew letters. He ambled along slippery sidewalks with gutters teeming with bones, rags and rotten fruit. A motley crowd of nocturnal idlers and exhausted day laborers surged through the grayish fog and funky odors to the wheezing sounds of a Barbary organ. One night he got lost and had to ask for directions. A helpful policeman led him though narrow, deserted alleyways, taking a shortcut. When Maurice commented on the quiet atmosphere of this clearly impoverished, but, to him, not particularly dangerous area, the officer chuckled, "Yes, sir. But where you're standing now is the very spot where Jack the Ripper cut up two of his victims!" Maurice enjoyed his walks. He usually took the District Railway back to the center of town, and in twenty-five minutes, almost all of it underground, he would be in the middle of Piccadilly, with its glaring lights and snatches of music filtering out from restaurant doors. An endless stream of carriages passed by, carrying men in evening dress and women in gorgeous gowns, draped in jewels. Omnibuses disgorged suburban passengers dressed for an evening out, in town to join in the brilliant tumult of the London Season.

WHILE REGGIE LUNCHED WITH MRS. Henderson, his ears must have been ringing. At that very moment he was the subject of a conversation, perhaps closer to an argument, between Maurice and Roy. They were eating together at the Café Royal.[4] Roy was warning his friend against being seen with the compromising de Vere, but Maurice shrugged it off, explaining that he didn't go out in society, or at least not much, and intended to keep doing what he pleased. "Listen, Verdal, this doesn't matter at all to me personally. I can't say I've never had any contact with him. He's amusing but I can do without his nonsense. If I can't socialize with him in public, I'd rather not see him at all. I won't tolerate secret, hypocritical arrangements." "He's not as bad as all that," Maurice protested. "I know, Mrs. Henderson has taken him under her wing, and he has some unusual friends. I do recognize that. But how many people we admire, especially in the theater, for example, aren't just as compromised?" "You're right, but his behavior is beyond the pale, his recklessness, his big mouth, the rumors about him…." "The rumors are overblown." "Granted, but you know in London, Maurice, it doesn't matter what you do or don't do. It's what people say that counts. And people tell horrific stories about de Vere… as if he's actually guilty."

---

[4] The café was popular with writers like Oscar Wilde, George Bernard Shaw and Max Beerbohm.

"That's stupid. And unfair!" "Indeed. But what can we do about it? Besides, I'll wager that de Vere is thrilled by that sort of talk. Being a nobody that no one cared about would be too painful. He's always demanding attention!" "Roy, I think he is well aware of that and admits it openly. He is disarming. Even when he speaks badly about someone, he does it in a comical way with so much enthusiasm and so little real conviction that one can hardly hold it against him.... He slags someone every time he takes a breath, and he only breathes in scandal. No one can do anything about it now or in the future. He enjoys people shooting him angry looks when he walks into a restaurant. Instead of being intimidated and afraid, he relishes stirring up controversy and showing himself off. He'll sashay around the tables, pretending to look for a friend who isn't even there in order to give everyone a better view of his elegant self, the way an expensive whore might. You know, at Armenonville[5] he stood in the entryway for a long time, to give everyone a good look at his get-up, before he found a table that he liked. He doesn't simply come inside or go out. He makes an entrance, he makes an exit and tries to make them as spectacular as possible.

"If you've noticed, he isn't especially handsome and he dresses well, without overdoing it... Yes, I mean it. He's always dressed in the latest fashion but never with the kind of excess that detracts from a man's style. If you realize that there's nothing special about him, except for all those rumors, well, I'd say he's succeeded in making a lot from very little! It's true! He's notorious for no particular reason except for living on his scandals, his debts and other people's money." Maurice continued with a flourish, "You're wrong, Roy, to criticize de Vere. He deserves our admiration. Conmen are everywhere, but Reggie's little games are in a league of their own. Think about it. With neither brains, nor money, nor a job, he lives quite comfortably. He's reckless enough to be constantly short of cash, he's always spending and never saving, even though in his heart of hearts he knows his good luck can't last forever. Still, he doesn't put anything aside for a rainy day! I must say that I find his self-confidence, his fantasies, and even his supreme carelessness endearing, and his superficiality is so profound that it's become a sort of masterpiece. I do think none of his gaffes and outrageousness are deliberate. He operates on pure instinct. As for the way he sees the world, it's worked out splendidly so far. Reggie only knows two types of people: those he likes and those who are or can be of use to him. His relationships have to turn a profit. He has to benefit in some

---

[5] This was a fashionable restaurant in the Bois de Boulogne in Paris. The Belle-Époque-style Pavillon d'Armenonville, is still open for business.

way. He applies this rule diligently and is right to do so! Whenever he visits Mrs. Henderson, he comes away with a check in his pocket. When he meets a friend, he leaves with a new necktie or a handkerchief that he discreetly admired. He trolls for free lunches at Trocadero and free dinners at the Savoy. On top of that, he's not stingy. When he's with friends who have less money than he does, young men who are having a hard time making their way, for example, he always picks up the tab if he can afford it. His calculations are perfectly all right and, to my mind, not at all exploitative. I know that all the talk about him is exaggerated, and I really don't care. He's my deplorable acquaintance, if you will, but I have no qualms about being seen with him.

HONESTLY, HOW COULD YOU NOT like this chap? The other day I ran into him as I was leaving the National Gallery. I told him I was surprised to see him in Trafalgar Square at that time of day, and he explained that he had just come from his pawnbroker's. 'Yes,' he added. 'I always go to the same man in the Strand. He knows me very well and gives me the maximum…. And you, where the devil have you been? A museum? What are you doing in there? Don't you feel a bit like a Cook's tourist?' "When I told him I enjoyed looking at the Gainsboroughs and the Turners" he pouted and said, 'Oh, for me, you know, all these old paintings! They don't do a thing for me. I only go to a gallery once a year, to the opening at the Royal Academy. The ladies look so fabulous, you run into absolutely everyone and it's always fun to see the celebrities' portraits there. Except, you know, I don't recognize any of them. And the artists are all dead.' Then he shrugged and made a sweeping gesture, dismissing the National Gallery, all the masterpieces, the elegant architecture, and even Trafalgar Square." Maurice laughed, "I can't tell you, Roy, how much I enjoy such nonsense."

a charity matinee

BECAUSE FRED FISHER HAD PERFORMED at the Apollo a week or two ago, he could proudly put on the charity matinee publicity: *Herod, Mr. Fred Fisher of the Apollo Theater*. But the auditorium was only half full, so after the benefit performance the "Flood Victims of the East End" could probably only expect heaps of regrets, not tall stacks of pounds and shillings. At least, they got some free publicity. When it was time to start, however, the stage curtains stubbornly remained closed and three ladies seated in a loge exchanged worried looks. Lady Ward was overdressed for the occasion, Mrs. Nordon was too elaborately coiffed, and Mrs. Hallet was overloaded with jewelry. "Caroline, just between ourselves, the box office sold hardly any tickets." "I warned you, Agatha, you'll not get back your advance. But you never listen to me. You're so foolish, my dear! I'm beginning to think that young man, Fred Fisher, is a little too bizarre. At the last rehearsal, I overheard a few words he exchanged with Guy Gregory, and that made me wonder...." "Ah, then, what? What were they saying?" "Agatha, I couldn't quite hear it, but still...." She shook her curls worriedly and reached up to make sure her necklaces and brooches were still in place. One particular coral brooch seemed awfully recalcitrant. Mrs. Nordon tried to lighten the mood, exclaiming, "What a lovely hall! My word, look how elegant!"

A party of three took their seats in the opposite loge. Mrs. Henderson wore a superbly eye-catching hat decorated with expensive feathers and a gigantic rose, the kind of hat the best hatmakers in Paris designed for their wealthy American clientele. Mrs. Morrell looked quite distinguished, and Reggie was all smiles and gardenias. Scrutinizing Mrs. Henderson's gown through her lorgnette, Lady Ward erupted with a disdainful, "Ugh, that creature. What a get-up!" Mrs. Hallet loyally chimed in, "A lady of the evening, one might say." In her mouth, the word "evening" took on a terrifying significance. In their box, Mrs. Henderson turned to Reggie, asking, "Well then. Is chic London here?" He replied sadly, "No, Mrs. Henderson, it's quite a hodge-podge…. My goodness, who is that fat lady in the satin gown looking like a daguerreotype? She's sitting with a blonde lady who must be… yes, it's Lady Ward! Gosh, that's extraordinary… in a loge? Herod must really interest her…. As long as it isn't too boring…. Are there speaking parts? I see the program calls it a 'dance drama.'" "Look, Reggie, your friend Verdal is here." "With Horner, I think, and Flint, a Cambridge man I met at Freddy's." Mrs. Morrell smiled and said cattily, "That poor Lady Ward is dressed in awfully bad taste. I can only imagine she's very proper matron." "Lillian, she has exclusively platonic passions. She suffers from unrequited love for Sidney Martin," Reggie snickered. "She saw him seventeen times in *Monsieur Beaucaire*. She admires actors for their talent. Speaking of which, I wonder how Freddy will do…. Smashing, I hope…I mean, I'm afraid. Ah ha!" Reggie shrieked so loudly that some people in the audience turned around. Lady Ward shot nasty looks at the trio making such a disturbance. "Quick, quick, Mrs. Henderson," Reggie gasped, "look at the fifth row in the orchestra. Do you see?" "Yes, perfectly. I see Mrs. Atwell, who wants to pretend she doesn't see me." "No, further on. Next to the young lady in blue tulle." "Yes, and…?" "But that's Lord Chetwoode. This must mean he's been released from prison." "Lord Chetwoode? That's impossible." "No, just wait a moment." Reggie did some calculations, "He was in for six months. Yes, that's it. He looks quite good…." The women examined him through their lorgnettes. "A bit pale. I guess it must be tiring to rest for six months. Would you like to be in prison, Reggie?" "Oh no!" He stopped to think it over for a minute and then said slowly, "Well, it depends. If I had to choose between fifteen days in jail and paying a tailor's bill of 150 pounds that I didn't have, I believe I would prefer prison though not during the Ascot races or the Henley regatta, of course!" "I hope you would always be able to find 150 pounds to pay off a bill, Reggie!" "Dear Mrs. Henderson, that is my most ardent desire!"

MRS. MORRELL PRETENDED TO BE lost in thought as she inspected the audience. Most of them seemed to be ordinary-looking middle-class women, the kind who throng to matinees. She noticed a handful of jauntily dressed young men who were friends of Fisher and Gregory, and a few poor relatives and honorary members of charitable organizations. The press was glaringly absent and her Royal Highness' box was empty, though rumors circulated that in a gracious gesture it had been reserved for the matinee. The orchestra began playing an overture heavy on harps and flutes, and light on actual music. A terrible fog of incense wafted under the curtain into the theater. The curtain rose and the audience saw Herod, immobile on his throne, dressed in sumptuous yellow robes, wearing an Assyrian-style beard. The play began. An astrologer gazed at the moon, incense smoldered, Miss Rising performed a belly dance with a vaguely mystic and Biblical theme, Herod declaimed a few verses in a refined manner, softly and indistinctly. An invisible crowd screamed in terror and the curtain fell, after barely thirteen minutes. There was a round of applause, some "Hurrahs" and even a few laughs but also a blizzard of puzzled looks: Was it over? Or was this just the prologue?

Reggie was overjoyed, standing up briskly to leave immediately for his tea with Mrs. Henderson at Rumpelmayer's.[1] In his dressing room, Fred regally accepted compliments and congratulations. Mrs. Atwell made her way through the excited crowd of friends celebrating his triumph, telling him. "You probably didn't expect to see me after all this time! But when I learned that you were going to perform as Herod, I couldn't resist." He seemed touched by her gesture. It's easier to forgive when you're on top than when you're down and out. "How kind you are, Mrs. Atwell, " he murmured. "And how did you like it?" "Charming!" she said with a smile. "And your family? Are they here?"

ROY, CYRIL AND MAURICE STROLLED to the Bath Club. "What a pity that Harold couldn't come. That was one of the funniest things I've ever seen," Roy smirked. Maurice mused, "This sort of performance is an entertaining sort of trifle, a mish-mosh of pantomime, tragedy, ballet and music. At first, I thought it was a parody, not too broad, rather clever, of other plays on the same subject, but now I'm convinced that it's a retelling of *Salome* and is actually a serious and original piece of art. No doubt the author thinks so, as does Fisher." Cyril shuddered, "I'm going to avoid him for the next three months. I really wouldn't know what to say

---

[1] The famous tea room was located on St. James Street in London.

if he started bragging about the play and his performance. And honestly…." Roy interrupted, "Yes, honestly, that's the word." He lectured his companions, "How can you spend any time with a chap like Fisher? He's so predictable, so boring. You know all his phony poses. Leave him to those sham society ladies, his admirers, and don't compromise your own reputation." Maurice laughed, shrugging his shoulders. Cyril was speechless. Roy continued, "I mean it." "Well, I'm leaving for Germany tomorrow," Cyril said, "so that solves that."

They sank into the enormous leather armchairs in the Bath Club library and chatted idly for a while before going into the baths. The clear water sparkled in the big white porcelain swimming pool and the water spray kept up a monotonous one-note fizzle, occasionally interrupted by the thump-thump of a diving board and the splashing sound of a diver. A trapeze swung gently back and forth. As his two companions got ready to swim, Maurice said, "It's the Turkish bath for me. I think I'm gaining a little weight. A cup of tea after that will be perfect. What a wonderful place this is. Just the way I imagine a chic bathhouse in ancient Rome."

CHAPTER XII

a sunday at maidenhead

WHEN MAURICE VERDAL STEPPED OUT of the train at Maidenhead, Roy Horner was waiting in his motorcar to pick him up. The crowd flowed around them in front of the station. It seemed as if the whole of London had taken the 10:55 express that morning. The station was a sea of white flannels, filmy summer dresses, Panama hats and embroidered shawls. Maurice was fascinated by London society's customary Sunday exodus to Taplow[1] and Maidenhead. He wouldn't want to stay in London on a summer Sunday either; restaurants were only open a half day, theaters were closed, shops were barricaded behind their shutters and the streets were deserted. A depressing sight. It also seemed as if the sun beat down even more fiercely on a summer Sunday on those empty streets. On the other hand, not far from London the river was delightful, very sham countrified, very elegant and very festive. Roy turned to Maurice and exclaimed, "I've never seen such a crush!" Then he brought his friend to the cottage he had rented for June and July. It was a tiny house at the top of Cookham, shaded by tall trees and set in a garden that was even more charming because it was slightly overgrown. "I had an awful time reserving a table for dinner at Skindle's

---

[1] Taplow is a village on the left bank of the Thames, connected to London by rail.

Hotel.[2] They were all booked, but I managed after all. I didn't want to offer you dinner here. It's too gloomy in the evening. But we'll have lunch here. Would you like to have it outside on the lawn?"

Maurice was thrilled. What a peaceful and charming spot. He thought he could quite easily imagine living there for a while, alone with his books. Or not quite alone. Birds chirped in the trees and other sounds of the countryside filtered in through the open windows. Church bells began ringing nearby. Roy sighed contentedly, "I am perfectly comfortable in this lovely cottage… and I can get work done here. No one comes by to interrupt me though I must admit I've spent almost every evening in town until today, either taking the train or my car. But I do always come back here to sleep, and I've had some wonderful wanders in the mornings…. I mean wonderful ideas for my work…. I just thought of an excellent idea for my novel."

Maurice joked, "A very moral novel, I suppose, if the thought occurred to you here. You're breathing air that's not contaminated by either too much noise or too much vice!" "Bah! The river is about a mile away. I deliberately took a cottage not so near it so that I have a good distance to walk to get there. I could have found something right on the river." Maurice mused, "How I would love, Roy, to have the Thames at the bottom of my garden. I always dreamed of spending a few weeks in the country but then I end up only coming here on Sundays in the season!" "It is charming but also terribly gloomy. The locks on the river are so crowded with boaters on Sundays but they hardly ever have to open for a passing boat during the week. For me, the thought of the Sunday crowds makes the sight of the empty river so depressing the rest of the time. But today will be gay, I'm sure of it. You won't leave till tomorrow, of course. I insist on it." "Does Harold ever come to see you?" "Never!" Roy replied. "I invited him to come on different days, at various hours, whatever suited him, but he always refused. I think at heart he's only happy in London. He's a dyed-in-the-wool city type. Even the delicious vegetables in my garden couldn't lure him all the way to Cookham Dean. Do you know that the gooseberry fool you just ate was made with berries from my own garden? I'm very proud of it and the cream is from..." Maurice interrupted, "From your cows!" "No, the local dairy. But I still feel a bit proprietorial about it all, even though I only have the cottage for two months…." "And, after that?" "Afterwards?" Roy said dreamily "I'll indulge my cosmopolitan footloose side. France, with its casinos and

---

[2] At the time, it was a fashionable hotel in Maidenhead. Later in the century, it became notorious as a site for assignations.

miniature horses, is calling me." "Me too, Roy, naturally. We'll make our way to Dieppe and then Biarritz. And Harold will say that he's going to explore Paris, as he always does." "But he'll stay in Dieppe, as always."

AFTER LUNCH, THEY GOT IN the car and headed to the river where they rented a punt, hired a man to steer it and settled back comfortably on cushions, lazily watching the water flow and smoking cigarette after cigarette. The view was stupendous; the narrow waterway sparkling in the sunshine and crowded with boats looked like a busy street between the two banks of the river. On the shore rows of villas with beautifully tended gardens sloped down to the water's edge. Ladies in light summer frocks stretched out on boat cushions and dangled their bare arms in the water. The bravest among them stood up in their punts and holding onto a long pole pushed the punt forward in a slow graceful motion. Young men in flannels rowed vigorously. A few had a dragon or snake tattoo on their forearms, in the latest fashion. The crowd on this part of the river was quiet, true to its aristocratic nature, with no loud voices singing or calling out. From time to time an electric launch passed through, making a purring noise. Swans were paddling tranquilly under the willows. The boats all clumped together at the locks, and someone could have walked across the river from one bank to the other without getting their feet wet. Then, the boats were guided one by one into the narrow channel, the lock was closed behind them and the water drained down slowly. The lockkeepers made their rounds, collecting the fee in little pouches attached to long poles. Finally, the upstream barrier swung open, and the boaters were free to go on their way.

There were so many boats on the river on Sunday that Maurice, Roy and their boatman had to wait a half hour or more to pass through a lock. Everyone waited patiently though; no cutting ahead in line or angry shouts spoiled the mood. Most of the Sunday boaters were, it seemed, not working people who had to make the most of their one day off. Instead, they were idlers relishing the sensation of doing nothing and savoring a day without theaters, concerts, or ceremoniously scripted visits. They were still surrounded by London Society as they enjoyed the fresh country air with their friends. They were seeing and being seen. The day after, the same crowd would be back in London at the Savoy, meeting and greeting the people they had just seen at Covent Garden or Hurlingham.[3] That's why the crowded river traffic, paradoxically, seemed so tranquil. The boaters felt they were

---

[3] Hurlingham was a fashionable sports club with polo fields, a golf course and croquet courts.

'among family.' They were guests at an enormous, very chic *garden party* and for once didn't feel obliged to preen or play a role.

The two or three little hotels along the river had the same peaceful, familiar London atmosphere. At Ray Mead, for example, where Roy and Maurice stopped for tea, a gypsy orchestra on the grassy lawn played some of the same tunes you'd hear in Piccadilly: 'My Venetian Daughter,' Mimi's famous solo in *La Bohème*, Delilah's aria from *Samson and Delilah*, some slow waltzes. The service was pleasantly smooth, and not at all clumsy or rustic. A constant stream of boats landed, and slim athletic young men leapt out, going in to order tea for the ladies who were staying behind in the punts and canoes. These courtly fellows didn't bother to put on a jacket over their thin shirts and sun-bronzed arms. On the roadside motorcars and carriages deposited another steady flow of customers at entrance to the hotel. Some of the guests were clearly foreigners out touring for the day. The American women invariably dressed in silk frocks and wore fussy hats decorated with feathers or they had motoring costumes that were entirely inappropriate for the site and the season.

But in the evening Skindle's hotel restaurant had higher standards for looks and style. You could even imagine you were at a hotel on the Riviera then, hearing the orchestra playing and seeing guests in evening wear, though they were still a bit less formal. Dinner was served in the spacious dining room and out on the lawn sloping down to the Thames. As it got later, the river became even quieter, reverberating only with the splashes of a few late boaters. The windows of the villas along the shore gradually lit up, the swans were bright patches floating on the dark water, and church bells rang in the distance. Night fell softly on this English watercolor painting. Skindle's dining room was sparkling that night. The table Roy had struggled so hard to reserve was next to an enormous table for fifteen guests who seemed to be quite wealthy, to judge from the large electric canoe that brought them to the landing. Only one table, on the other side of the room, was unoccupied. It was obviously reserved because the host kept turning away latecomers who thought they might have a chance. Ten minutes later, a party of three, two women and a young man, made their entrance, showily. Mrs. Henderson looked lovely in a very simple but exquisite linen frock that more than one casually dressed young woman noticed, admired and filed away in their memory. Mrs. Morell followed her in, and then Reggie appeared, putting on a nonchalant air, dressed in charming pale green flannels with a blue stripe. Two women sitting behind Maurice started gossiping about Reggie and Mrs. Henderson, but disappointingly, they stopped short when they noticed Reggie gesturing a greeting to Maurice from the other side of the room.

After dinner, Roy, who absolutely did not want to be introduced to the Henderson party, left to see if his chauffeur was in a fit state to drive. He told Maurice he would pick him up at the hotel in half an hour, so Maurice strolled out to the lawn to join his three London friends. Mrs. Henderson greeted him warmly, saying, "What a perfect day we've had." They chatted about the river, the sights and the train they were taking back to London. "You'll come with us, won't you?" "Why no," Maurice demurred. "I'm staying at Cookham, at Roy's place, in a cozy bedroom shaded by Virginia creeper." "My word, that must be fabulous. I love the countryside!" Reggie said enthusiastically. Then he abruptly changed the subject to gossip about people they had seen. "You know, Verdal, we've got one of the chicest electric launches on the river... and came across Kays in a punt... also Miss Houston with a boy I don't know. I'm going to make a scene about it tomorrow." Mrs. Henderson interjected, "Reggie has the oddest sense of humor." Scanning the crowd for celebrities, she exclaimed "Why look, there's Maud St. Denis.[4] She's wearing too much makeup for a day in the country." Maurice was curious, "Maud St. Denis?" "Well," she continued "you know that dizzy Lady Barthe met her and wanted to invite her to dinner. Luckily, I was able to tackle it before it happened." "You dissuaded her?" "Easily. I told her 'Just because Jesus Christ spoke with the Samaritan woman doesn't mean you ought to invite Maud St. Denis to dine.'" Reggie giggled, "Too funny. I'll try to remember that, but I'm afraid I won't get it right. By the way, how do you like my new outfit, for casual country wear?" "Charming!" "Exquisite!" Reggie said complacently, "Yes, it'll do for excursions on the river."

Maurice teased him, "For boating on the river in a musical comedy, perhaps. But it's lovely. Your necktie coordinates nicely with your socks, your tiepin is casually fastened sideways, but the color matches your cufflinks perfectly. What time did you get up this morning, de Vere? I'm worried about you." Reggie was thrilled, "Don't go on. You're killing me!" Mrs. Morell changed the subject. "Did you hear about the dinner party an American hosted at the Savoy that cost 3000 pounds?" Reggie sighed, "The hotel courtyard was transformed into a lake, floating gondolas were filled with flowers, a real live baby elephant carried the dessert tray

---

[4] The name is a combination of Ruth St. Denis, the American choreographer, and Maud Allan, the Canadian dancer. St. Denis had a successful European tour performing "Oriental" and "Indian"-inspired dances in scanty costumes and Allan was known for her "Dance of the Seven Veils" and "Vision of Salome."

on its back." He laughed. "Right up my alley."[5] Mrs. Henderson complained, "But even Skindle's is awfully expensive. I paid three pounds tonight and we hardly ate or drank anything! They're charging Monte Carlo prices!" "But not Monte Carlo quality though it is chic to have dinner here on Sundays, so...." Reggie chimed in, "What snobbery!"

The party got ready to leave, and while the two ladies retrieved their coats and touched up their makeup, Reggie burbled, "Verdal, I do like you, you know. You're absolutely charming. And I'm not going to criticize your wardrobe. We have the same tailor." Then Reggie launched into some apparently unrelated gossip. "You know Fred Fisher, don't you? Dear old Freddy, he's going to play Romeo. Gosh, too funny! Actually, it's a special event, a matinee that's half amateurs, half professional actors... but still! He hasn't a clue about acting. Knows even less than I do, I think. If you had seen him playing Herod.... Really? You were there? What did you think, eh? Don't you think his cottage in Mayfair is a bit much? Awfully sketchy. Even so, it costs something. He must pay at least eighteen shillings a week. I imagine Lady Ward gives him a little help because a week after that matinee, he was seen around town in two different new suits. "Tell me, did you see any actresses here tonight?" Maurice tried to interrupt. Reggie droned on, "Speaking of Fisher, I went to see him the other day. He was in the middle of writing a letter and I saw a coat of arms on the stationery. 'Those are my father's' he told me, with the most serious look on his face. His father's! But he was born somewhere near Clapham Junction, and I've heard that he was a porter in a hotel! I know quite well that Fisher knows an M.P.... and all the rest... that's his business. But it's too infuriating when he takes that superior attitude with me.... The other day, for instance, I asked if he was related to the Fisher who is a moneylender on Shaftesbury Avenue. He got all dignified and said, 'No, my dear, there's only one Fisher family and we are not moneylenders, thank God! That doesn't surprise me because they probably don't have any to lend....'" Maurice, deciding it was a wasted effort to stop this torrent of words, stood and listened patiently. Reggie abruptly rushed off to the lavatory to primp a little before taking the train.

MRS. HENDERSON'S PARTY WENT BACK to London, the river was deserted, and the roads were empty. Horner's driver took them quickly back to Cookham with its

---

[5] The Savoy hotel hosted a notorious "gondola party" in 1905 for the American millionaire "champagne king" George Kessler.

views over less sophisticated hills and valleys. *My word*, Maurice mused, *against that sort of Riviera backdrop, Reggie wasn't at all shocking and his gossip was a fine way to end the evening. It reminded me that the river towns close to London are just another Piccadilly and when one goes to Maidenhead, one isn't leaving London!*

a mother's love

For an entire week Reggie de Vere had forgotten that his mother was in town. Between two visits to dressmakers, however, she suddenly recalled that she had a son living somewhere in the West End. As soon as the thought struck her, she sent a messenger boy to invite him to come and see her the next day in the afternoon, preferably not too early because she had a luncheon date at Prince's and not too late because she had to put in an appearance at a friend's salon. Reggie decided to wear the new suit his tailor had sent, one in a flattering greenish-brown shade, and went to Claridge's where his mother greeted him with a mixture of gushing warmth and worldly politeness. She was so terribly, terribly sorry not to have contacted him sooner, but she had so little time in London and so many things to do, shopping and errands that couldn't be postponed." "I understand that perfectly, Mama," Reggie commiserated, as a loyal son would.

Mrs. de Vere continued, "But I am so eager to hear all about you, what you're doing, how you're living, my dear boy. How are things with Miss… Miss what's her name? Miss Houston, isn't it?" "She's fine, thanks. Still has her Australian accent," Reggie smiled. "But, actually, your marriage plans?" He had to laugh, "Really, Mama, that's in the distant future." Mrs. de Vere bristled and said in a serious tone, "I'd rather focus on the present and the near future, Reggie." "All right," he sighed. "Miss Houston always asks me for advice about her wardrobe. That's a good sign, isn't it?" "My poor child, that tells me she isn't taking you seriously. Hmm… I only met her once, but I'm a pretty good judge of people. I think she's the ambitious type, a social climber. She's looking for a husband with a good position. What can you offer her? She'll make you earn a living. You'll have to work." Reggie trembled and exclaimed "My lord!" horrified at the thought. He added calmly, "She'll soon realize *that* won't happen." His mother insisted, "She's strong-willed, I'm sure of it. The iron fist in the velvet glove…." "Oh yes," Reggie agreed. "The iron glove, as they say, on a velvet hand, or something of the sort. Very true!" She pressed the point, relentlessly, "She's headstrong. She won't be docile. She won't be led around by the nose." "As if I'd even try! I have enough difficulty leading myself. But that's not the only thing we need to talk about, Mama. Listen, I can't go on like this. I need an allowance, a regular one, not just the pocket money you send me now and then," Reggie whined. "My dear boy, if I could, I would," his mother murmured tenderly, as if she had no choice in the matter. "You must," Reggie said firmly, exhausted by the effort.

Mrs. de Vere strategically chose to act insulted, replying in a high-pitched, strangled voice, "My God! Reggie, you are so selfish. But you always were…. You don't realize how much this hurts me. When I think of the way I had to scrimp and save… and all the sacrifices I've made. Don't you remember how I sold my jewelry to pay for your piano lessons?" "Yes, indeed. And you told me to stop after three lessons because I was too lazy to keep it up!" "Ah," she continued mournfully, "my pathetic, horrid expenses." Reggie retreated, "Oh, Mama, this is not the place. I think Claridge's…" She recovered her aplomb, "Reggie my dear, my bill here doesn't concern you. I mean, don't worry about it for my sake. I spend so little time in town." She tried to smooth things over with a display of motherly affection. "Honestly, Rex, if I could, I would do whatever it takes to support you, but my income…" Reggie interrupted brusquely, "How much is it, actually? I'm your only son, so…."

She protested, "What a cold-hearted creature you are, Reggie. You bring that question up so casually." She dabbed at her teary eyes with a tiny lace handkerchief, or, more precisely, raised the handkerchief to her forehead, taking care not to smudge her mascara. After a short pause, she sniffed once or twice, pretending to hold back her tears. Then she took out her compact and examined her face in the mirror. Luckily, her makeup was intact, and her eyes weren't bloodshot and her face puffy. Reggie, diplomatically, looked concerned. "Have I hurt you terribly, Mama? Don't hold it against me. Talking about money is so annoying. I hope your weak heart...." Mrs. de Vere hesitated, surprised, "My weak heart?" She had forgotten that she used the excuse of heart trouble the last time he asked for money. "I see you're fine now. I'm so glad," Reggie ventured. "I'm all better? Hardly! But I was so upset I forgot all about it. My memory is getting so bad...." He laughed, "Mama, you're a worse liar than I am." She snapped, "Oh really? Your jokes are atrocious, Reggie." He fought back, saying, "Oh, that one barely missed the mark. You're getting old, Mama." "True. And how old are you now, my dear boy? I can never remember. Twenty-one, isn't it?" "At the very least, I should say! But you don't look any more than twenty-nine yourself, Mama." She shrugged off her feelings of anger and resentment, appreciating his obvious attempt at flattery. Shaking her head skeptically, she said, "Well, I hope you're happy living in London. You never tell me anything about yourself." "Yes, Mama. Things are all right. Mrs. Henderson—" "Not a word about that woman!" she exclaimed, playing the role of the aggrieved mother. With that said, she added "I hope you act properly, decently." "More like 'strategically,'" Reggie replied. "Reggie, please, let's not discuss it any further." She thought the word 'strategic' summed it up neatly. "Let's talk about something else." "All right, mother. Let's talk about money!"

SHE REGRETTED TRYING TO CHANGE the subject. She might have ended the conversation without having to hand over any cash. *Money! The only word in his vocabulary! That's all he thinks about,* she fumed. Did she have any? In fact, she had never before been in such straits; she had only a few miserable pounds in her purse and nothing at all in the bank. She had just enough to cover her hotel bill, and now she truly regretted staying at such an expensive one. But she hadn't been able to find another room. And she couldn't bear to think of the other bills she had run up. There would be a blizzard of them delivered to her door soon enough. And Reggie chose this moment to harass her about money. *No, a thousand times no. He'd have to manage somehow,* she thought bitterly. *At the age of twenty-three he should be supporting himself. But he never had the slightest inclination to earn a living. This son of mine was simply toxic.... Money!* And, she protested, she didn't even know how she would get through the summer. Perhaps she could get a special rate at

Eastbourne or Bournemouth at that time of the year, staying in a small hotel or even a guesthouse. She'd live there, under a false name, wearing three-year-old frocks and pinching every penny. She couldn't even bear to think of Trouville! This would be a sacrifice, but she knew how to scrimp and save. She was used to it! Reggie was only half listening to her plotting out the summer. He knew only too well how it would end; his mother would conclude that living expenses were not a penny higher in a fashionable resort anyway. He was also well aware that she hated to waste money, and to her "wasting money" meant spending it on her poor son. "Listen, Reggie, I shouldn't be the one suggesting this to you, but couldn't your friends…?" his mother's voice trailed off.

Reggie was shaken but he was determined not to leave the hotel without at least a little money. "It wouldn't do, at the moment," he answered, shrugging his shoulders. "Really? I don't understand. Couldn't you ask for a short-term loan?" She emphasized the word "loan." Reggie was relentless. "So, will you give me the money when it's time to repay the loan?" They kept going back and forth, and Mrs. de Vere soon used up all her arguments and her store of advice. She said whatever came into her head, not worrying too much about logic or credibility. Finally, he wore down her resistance and managed to get five pounds. Mrs. de Vere became a little sentimental after she handed them over. "Farewell, my little Reggie, take good care of yourself and don't spend it all in one place!" "Not to worry, Mama!" he replied in a sprightly tone, feeling that this was a job well done. He began prowling around her room, looking into open hat boxes and pulling out a new hat to examine it more closely. "Very nice," he purred, in the voice of a connoisseur. "You are truly stunning, Mama," he cried admiringly. "Do you have any new jewelry?" She hesitated and then admitted, "Oh, I did manage to make a few good deals. I exchanged some old bits of gold for a ring and a rather attractive bracelet." She opened her jewelry box, took them out and left the box half-open.

Reggie swooned, as he was meant to, and poked around the treasure chest. "You have lots, Mama! Goodness, have you pawned something?" He recognized the little square envelope, a familiar sight. "At the pawnbroker? Are you mad? Oh, what I mean is every year I give them my furs, they take very good care of them, it's the law, and it's cheaper than storing them at the furrier. I reclaim them at the beginning of winter. This way, everybody wins." They both giggled at this idea, approvingly. Reggie thought the time was right for another sortie. He kept examining the contents of the jewelry box. "Ah, you still have the cufflinks I sold you, Mama. When I think of you benefiting from my misery…." "Oh, I only did it as a favor to you, Reggie. Of course, I never wear them." "Well then, I'll have them back." He leaped over the sofa, and got to the door, ignoring his mother's protests. "I have them in my hand, and I'm going to keep them. You can certainly afford to give me a little gift. My birthday is coming up. They're not worth much, you never wear them, you're not being deprived of anything. Don't scold me, Mama. I'm not going to change my mind. They have a sentimental value for me. Good-bye, Mama. See you soon!" He left, feeling very pleased with himself, as Mrs. de Vere's curses rained down on him. She hated being cheated. That was an unwavering principle. Her son had so little respect for her that he was probably laughing at this very moment. But Reggie wasn't laughing. He was simply glad that he hadn't wasted his day.

C H A P T E R   X I V

the theories of monsieur verdal

WHEN HAROLD BARNES ARRIVED AT Maurice Verdal's rooms around 9:00 in the evening, Maurice was hard at work on a letter. He seemed to be terribly amused. "I'm writing to a former mistress of mine, a provincial lady. I do it every three months. 'The daylight is not purer than the heart' [1] of this sentimental spinster." He went on, "Our souls, nothing more, mated two years ago when I spent my vacation in the countryside. Ever since then, I nurture her illusions of our love. She's the only woman I've ever led on in this way." "That's good of you, Maurice." "Even more than you think. Because I don't even have the excuse of her not replying much or at all. My lord! She sends me eight pages every week, written in violet ink on both sides of very thin paper, and to make things worse, she fills every margin too." "But surely you don't read the letters." "I glance at them and that's enough. Then, every three months I burn them and write one of my own. Today is my deadline. I'm in the midst of composing my letter. Here, take a look at this."

Harold scanned the page. "But this is truly eloquent, Maurice; you've combined great passion with the most refined gallantry and even a few touches

---

[1] He borrows a well-known line from Racine's play <u>Phèdre.</u>

of French *politeness.*" "Thank you." Harold continued, "I've always believed the French—" "See here, Harold," Maurice interrupted. "Please don't say 'the French' or 'the English.' We're all just people with our own specific strong and weak points. Nationality has nothing to do with it." "True. Our friend Roy, for instance, raises grave social and political questions in his novels but he himself is just a charming, frivolous chap. In his latest, a virtuous Englishman will be corrupted by a devious Frenchman, no doubt, but to you they're just people with their own unique characters." "Seriously," Maurice asked, "what exactly is his new novel about?" "You see, an Englishman inspired by the *Entente cordiale* goes to France to learn the language and the customs. He decides to live in a hotel in Boulogne but discovers that the owner, the waiters, the chambermaids, everyone there speaks English. Roast beef is on the lunch menu and the smoking room is actually a pub!" "So, does he decide to go back to Folkestone?" "No, he decides to visit every hotel and guesthouse in Boulogne. Eventually he finds a little cafe with rooms to let. The clientele is French, of course. So, the Englishman keeps dropping in and ends up renting a room there, hoping to live like an ordinary Frenchman. He begins drinking two glasses of absinthe a day and smoking strong dark tobacco. One day, he is introduced to Monsieur Georges, a man who spends all his time in the cafe and has his meals with a young person who wears flashy dresses and disappears for a few hours every day and every evening. The Englishman and Monsieur Georges become friends and soon they are very Parisian!"

Maurice chuckled, "That's quite an English idea! But ingenious nonetheless." He said jokingly, "I suppose Monsieur Georges has a brown finely trimmed moustache, wears trousers that are a little too tight with pockets in the front, 'coin pockets' the Paris tailors call them. He keeps his hands in his pockets, is always dressed in an alpaca jacket with 'hard-wearing heavyweight front panels' and wears a white canvas cap with a stiff brim to protect his face from the sun. This is the classic get-up of men like Monsieur Georges when they're rusticating in the country, I think. Though a green houndstooth checked suit would be even better. In any case, Roy's young man will acquire, along with his experience of cafes in France, a bad reputation."

"Bah!" Harold scoffed. "I think Roy will bring him safely back to England so that he gets married with a clean slate. I must say, however, in London, a bad reputation doesn't necessarily hurt...." Maurice smiled, "Harold, I'm glad you brought that up.... The other day I had quite an argument with Roy about Reggie de Vere." Harold cautiously weighed his words. "Reggie, people tell me, is rather compromised, but I don't think he'll compromise you very much. Let's grant that some of his crowd will sneer at you because you're an outsider, but what does it matter? Roy really astonishes me at times with these incomprehensibly prudish impulses. There will always be a Reggie de Vere in certain social circles in London. And in this town where truly first-rate gigolos are rare and most are second class or worse, it's inevitable that some people will hire 'private secretaries' or other young men of that ilk instead. A society that tolerates this has no right to be shocked by it and in fact, is really not shocked at all. Most people would rather close their eyes or simply pretend it's not happening. This is what Anglophobes call 'British hypocrisy.' When no one sees anything, there's no public scandal. I have to add that for our Reggie in particular, unfortunately for him, people associate him with Mrs. Henderson. She's gone down in the world, lost her position in society, I mean. She's *déclassée* and goes about with some awfully sketchy companions nowadays. If you factor in Mrs. de Vere's past, the way Reggie acts and the company he keeps, you start to understand why people gossip about him. He's scandalizing rather than scandalous, I'd say. He was made for scandal, but I know you, Maurice, are savvy enough to avoid being entangled in it." Maurice said thoughtfully, "The truth is I don't like to cut anyone or pretend I don't know them, especially someone who's always welcomed me with open arms and sees me as a friend. Since I didn't turn him away when we first met, it would be hard for me to start snubbing and avoiding him now. Also, I really don't want to. I'm fascinated by his life. It's quite a juggling act." Harold laughed, "And you're waiting for the slip-up." Maurice protested, "No, certainly not. I'm not that cruel. I'm just curious about how it will all turn out and I enjoy seeing him, in small doses, say, once every two months. This is how I deal with his bad reputation." "But if he didn't have one, no one would notice him." Harold said thoughtfully. "He'd be crushed!"

"Yes, he adores stirring up gossip and scandal. Oh, reputations," Maurice sighed. "No one can escape them, Harold. Even I, in Paris…. Even you! Do you realize how besmirched your reputation is, how cynical and nasty people think you are? Even when you're simply expressing an opinion, people take it for either a veiled insult or a profound philosophic observation. I remember last year in Dieppe you said, 'The sea is stormy today,' and several people snickered, as if they had decoded a secret message." Harold burst out laughing. "I suppose I should be flattered, at the end of the day." "Of course. It always works that way. People only gossip about someone who deserves the attention. That's why I never blame anyone who gossips about me," Maurice concluded. Harold stood up. "I'll leave you to your love letter. I'm going to finish writing my article. I plan to write at least fifteen sentences today and I've only got three more weeks before the deadline. Here's another rumor! Who says that I'm working too slowly now? You know Frank's new book is coming out soon. It's called *The World Out of Whiskers*." "About whiskers, naturally." "But a bearded lady plays a big part in it too. If you go to see him, he'll tell you all about it. With great passion! Lawyers beat every other kind of author in caring about their fictional characters. And, I forgot to mention, the other night I saw your greatest actress in a play she herself adapted.[2]" "And?" Maurice prompted him. "She was wonderful and revealed a talent for comic timing that I never knew she had. Thus, during a terribly tragic scene she was playing the piano with a hitherto unsuspected talent, and her shawl began to slip off her shoulders. Sarah gracefully adjusted it, taking her hand off the piano keys, and the piano kept playing all by itself! Then in the last scene, which takes on the third floor of a house because one can see trees and a hazy moon through the open window, she takes her final breath, of course. Awfully touching! The audience called her back for six encores and the last time, she came through the open window and seemed to be miraculously suspended in the air, arms outstretched as if ready to fly up to heaven. I'll never forget the sight. I fell back in love with the theater for a whole week after that," he laughed.

When he was alone again, Maurice picked up his pen and added to his letter, waxing eloquently on the theme of "But for you...." Then he dreamily smoked a few cigarettes, feeling a bit lonely. He missed human connections. His tender heart was troubled. He mused vaguely about love and affection. In fact, there were times when he ached for a grand passion, a shared passion. But these feelings soon faded away. Later that evening, he was caught up in a different sort of revery. A few snatches of conversation came back to him; a few memories of things he had seen floated before his eyes. He stood up abruptly; it was ten o'clock and a little theater would soothe him. Pleased with the thought, he decided to see a comedy to lighten his mood. Since he wasn't dressed in evening clothes, he would buy a ticket for the balcony.

Coincidentally, the balcony of the theater he chose was the preserve of a special kind of spectator. Walking away from his flat, Maurice breathed in the lukewarm humid night air and enjoyed the sight of the bright moonlight. At the

---

[2] This is probably a reference to Sarah Bernhardt, who performed the tragedy *Adrienne Lecouvreur* in 1908 in London.

end of St James Street, the palace's bulky silhouette loomed[3] and the enormous, illuminated clock was visible between two towers. He crossed the silence of Jermyn Street, headed toward the glaring lights of Piccadilly Circus, and then hurried on to Leicester Square. He hesitated for a moment at the theater entrance and then went inside, walked up the stone steps, smiled at the ticket booth clerk and handed over a shilling. He got a token in return accompanied by the gruff announcement that there weren't any more seats. He shrugged and found a spot in the pitch-dark balcony, standing in the midst of poking elbows and stertorous breathing. He leaned against the railing and started watching the play. The actors, far away under the glaring lights, looked like oversized marionettes.

Gusts of warm air and traces of different scents assailed his nostrils. He vaguely noticed that someone next to him with his elbow propped on the railing began caressing him, gently and hesitantly at first and then insistently. Maurice didn't react at first nor did he change places and the stranger took that as an encouraging sign. Maurice eventually took evasive action and subtly but firmly, pushed the man away. Everything was quiet for a few minutes until he noticed the same man caressing his neighbor. He could vaguely see the motions that became more and more urgent. He heard faster and deeper breaths. Maurice was determined to ignore it all and keep his eyes on the stage, but his thoughts were as agitated as the shadowy figures next to him. When the play was over, the lights came back on. He glanced at his neighbor, a middle-aged man, very proper looking, who was hiding his evening dress under the turned-up collar of his overcoat. Maurice left the theater quickly, feeling disturbed and on edge. The moonlight greeted him as gently as it had before, and he took a long deep breath. *Oh, those bad reputations!* he thought with a brief smile. He automatically headed toward the Continental hotel. He was upset and fidgety. He had to satisfy his soul by cleansing his body, surely. And an immediate plunge into sensual pleasure would be more effective than "spiritualizing his sensuality by calling it Love.[4]" He walked into the hotel lobby where rather elegant looking women waited for their clients. He sat next to a young woman who smiled warmly only with her lips while her cold eyes surveyed him in a business-like manner. She suggested going to dinner. "Afterward!" he said roughly. She followed him upstairs obediently.

---

[3] This is St James palace, once a royal residence.
[4] This is a reference to Oscar Wilde's novel *The Portrait of Dorian Gray* (1885) and the notion of 'spiritualizing the senses.'

C H A P T E R   X V

photographs, confessions,
and the end of an encounter

REGGIE DE VERE'S DRAWING ROOM was crammed with dozens of photographs. Some were framed and signed with affectionate messages, showing that he had many acquaintances from different walks of life. French and English celebrities shared wall space with less well-known faces. There was even a portrait of his friend Paul by a photographic studio near the Gymnase Theater on the Boulevard de Bonne-Nouvelle in Paris. Paul looked charming and faintly ridiculous. There was a snapshot of Maurice too, somewhere on the shore, dressed in casual outdoorsy clothes and strolling with a few dogs. But Reggie was clearly the star of the show, and more than half the photos were of him alone. He was awfully proud of his collection, bringing it along to decorate every new flat even though some of the elaborate frames were heavy and difficult to pack. Admirers had quite a variety to choose from: Reggie dressed in blue serge, looking sultry; Reggie standing, one foot perched on a chair, wearing evening dress and a top hat, looking masterful; Reggie in a nice suit, looking like an eager fiancé; Reggie in traveling gear, looking tired; Reggie in a nightshirt; Reggie dressed as Pierrot; Reggie as a harlequin; Reggie in a riding habit trying to look very manly, with his gaiters fastened backwards; Reggie with an open book on his knee, looking thoughtful, very much in the "Artists at Home" genre; Reggie onstage in *The Magic Slipper* looking more natural than theatrical. His visitors could feast their eyes on a variety of photographic processes on his walls: carbon print enlargements, platinum prints and color miniatures, from the most basic gelatin silver bromide prints to the most up-to-date techniques making a photo look like a charcoal sketch. He wasn't showing all his teeth in his familiar practiced smile in only two of these portraits.

Only one of his many photo portraits didn't really please him: a retouched picture where his eyes were made bigger, his mouth smaller, his wrinkles smoothed out and a real "professional beauty" expression pasted on his face. This look was the specialty of a particular photographer on Bond Street, one of the most expensive in London. His particular talent was to turn all his subjects into a specific type of pretty English boy, no matter what they really looked like. At first Reggie was thrilled to buy a dozen prints for ten pounds from his studio. He fantasized about his image being featured in *The Tatler* or *The Bystander*[1] with a flattering caption; unfortunately, no reporter ever called. One evening Reggie noticed a young man gazing at this portrait on his mantelpiece, who asked, "Who posed for this?" and Reggie replied with a laugh, "Why, it's me." To prove the point, he added, "Don't you recognize my brown suit and my smile?" Just so. That was Reggie. A smile and a suit.

A hairdresser came regularly to shave and style this mannequin. A weekly manicure and pedicure kept his nails looking their best and a skillful masseuse pushed, prodded and smoothed his face. Reggie was a prime example of "a tool-using animal," although he most definitely had never read *Sartor Resartus*.[2] If he ever came across a picture or description of the author, he would have been astounded that Carlyle, who was so obsessed with clothing, was so poorly dressed himself. Reggie lived surrounded by images of himself and surely had a secret desire that even though he was past twenty and getting older every year, his portraits would work their magic on his aging face and keep him looking young. On the hottest days of the year Reggie would take a nap just before dinner; that refreshed him. One day Paul knocked on his door and no one answered, so he wandered into the bedroom. Reggie was sleeping peacefully sprawled on his bed, wrapped in a Japanese dressing gown. The room was rather messy. Piles of neckties spilled out of a partly open drawer, collars bulged out of a box, and boots on their stretchers crowded the carpet. His valet would put everything back in its place every morning

[1] These are two weeklies that published criticism, short fiction and illustrations.
[2] Carlyle's novel was published in English between 1833 and 1836 and was translated into French in 1899.

but since Reggie was always late and always in a hurry, so he would yank open the drawers, pull things out willy-nilly and turn the neatly organized closets and shelves into a jumble. He liked to color-coordinate his outfits, and with so many suits, shirts and neckties to choose from, he usually had to try on several things before anxiously settling on the right combination.

His dressing table, his altar to Beauty, had pride of place in front of the window where it was bathed in natural light. The dressing table was covered with mysterious bottles, strange flasks and much-used boxes of powder. So many accessories littered the table that one had to wonder how Reggie ever found the right one when he needed it. His collection of magic potions included Glycerin and Cucumber, Achilles Lotion, California Poppy, Ideal, Listerine, and a handful of discreet little vials with labels identifying them as Number 203, Lotion 2B, or Milk 86. Those were compounded and sold for extravagant sums by a consultant on Bond Street. Reggie had a habit of announcing to one and all that, "Special lotions are so tacky. I make do with a touch of powder after my shave, and that's all!" Well, really? A set of brand-new golf clubs in a shiny leather case was leaning against the mantelpiece. This was an odd sight in his boudoir, but the clubs were ready to be brought to the course and put to use by his manly arms. As an avid sportsman, he claimed to adore golf and loved hearing anecdotes about the game though he barely understood it. Unfortunately, or perhaps "Thank God" there were no golf courses near Piccadilly, and he rarely went to the country.

After looking around the room, admiring much of what he saw and feeling surprised by the rest, Paul shook Reggie's shoulder gently to wake him up. Apparently napping had a particular drugging effect on Reggie. He looked up at his visitor with glassy eyes, staring so blankly that Paul thought he had temporary amnesia. He turned over, ready to go back to sleep, but Paul was insistent and shook him awake. Reggie sat up indignantly, sputtering "What? What's this? I'm exhausted. Why are you waking me up? You'd better get out…. I mean it." Paul stood his ground. "Wake up, Reggie. I've got to talk to you." "Later, later. Can't we do this some other time?" "No, I need your advice." Reggie gave up any thoughts of sleep. "Hmm, my advice." He got up, poured himself a small glass of whiskey and lit a cigarette. He realized it was time to get dressed for the evening and began looking through his wardrobe. "Go on, I'm listening." But Paul was upset that his friend seemed so distracted. He got all tangled up in his words and thoughts. He wanted Reggie's undivided attention, he said petulantly. Reggie bristled at the implied criticism and shot back, "As if I can't even get dressed!" "Uh, well," the Frenchman continued hesitantly with his confession. Reggie interrupted him brusquely, wondering out loud in the most urgent tone whether he ought to wear pumps or patent leather shoes. "What do you think, Paul?" "I always wear kidskin boots with buttons," Paul replied. Reggie gave him an acid look whose message was clear: *I guess I'd better let you tell me about your problem. That way I won't have to hear any more of your fashion tips.* He did say out loud, "Your collar is too high, my dear friend." Paul sighed. "As I was saying—" Reggie said impatiently, "Excuse me. You still haven't told me a thing!" "Well, it's about—" Reggie crowed, "Money! I knew it. I can certainly give you some very good advice there. First of all, ask for more than you actually need. Done!"

Paul groaned, "It's not about money, Reggie. It's Maurice Verdal." Reggie's jaw dropped. He was astonished and stood stock still, his suspenders dangling from one hand. "What in the world do you mean?" He stopped assembling his outfit and threw himself in an armchair, so he could listen more carefully. Paul began, "You know, Reggie, that I told you I didn't like him. I have a good reason for that. We knew each other in Paris and, unfortunately, he knew a lot about me, more than I thought. Whenever we met, he unleashed a torrent of jokes, innuendos, things that annoyed me intensely. But I have to admit, I enjoyed the attention. One night during Mardi Gras I ran into him at the Bal Wagram,[3] naturally. He was there with a journalist friend, looking for interesting subjects. I was a bit out of control that night, though. The two of them said they'd invite me to dinner if I agreed to tell them scandalous stories. We went to Verdal's apartment which was very secluded and awfully well furnished. They offered me a drink and I don't know what demon possessed them, but when I started talking, they kept laughing and interrogating me, asking for more juicy gossip and more explicit details."

Reggie smirked, "Poor boy! I know how much that must have disturbed you." "Verdal was appallingly entertained by it all, even the grossest confessions didn't faze him. But that's the last time we met. I expected more, after everything I told them. I'll never forget being led on that way." Reggie laughed, "No doubt! Given your proclivities…. He would have had you *on toast* for breakfast, my dear little Paul, with a smile on his face!" "Don't you think that was awful?" "No more awful than you are! You ran into each other; their curiosity was aroused. I know about that!" "All right. Wait… the other night I was in a theater balcony, standing a little apart from the crowd. He came in later. Yes. I'm sure he couldn't see me, but when

---

[3] The Bal Wagram was a dance hall in Paris..

the door opened, I recognized his silhouette. He was coming in from the stairs which are well-lit. What was he doing there?" Reggie shrugged, "Just passing the time." Paul protested, "It looked suspicious to me. I leaned on the railing next to him and started touching him up, very lightly at first." "And then?" "My dear, I could have lifted his cigarette case and his handkerchief, easily. He pretended not to notice a thing. After that, well, I left him alone, but I got the distinct impression he knew what was going on in the balcony. But he just leaned on the railing and was absorbed in watching the play. When it ended, he left immediately without a backward glance!"

Reggie said teasingly, "He was afraid of being turned into a pillar of salt," pleased with his Biblical witticism. "So, do you think he would be interested, in the right circumstances?" "What? You're still going on about this? My sense is that he wouldn't give a damn about his reputation or about anything else, if word got out." Paul continued, "So, do you think I should discreetly bring it up, the next time I meet him?" Reggie shrieked, "My dear Paul, that's insane. He'll simply laugh at you." "But still…." "My dear friend," Reggie started to lose patience, and his mood turned ugly. "Don't be so stupid. And frankly if this is why you came to see me…. This blather doesn't interest me at all." Paul stuttered, very put off, "I thought my feelings—" "What? You're a minx and a very foolish one at that! You need to learn how to attract people, at the very least. But you! You spend all your time looking for complications. But I can guarantee you, you aren't going to distract me any more with your idiocy. So, if you please, let me get dressed. I can't tie my necktie properly with you here. You're getting on my nerves. Honestly! You interrupted my wonderful, restful siesta and now I'm exhausted, absolutely played out for the rest of the night. And when I feel that way, I look a fright!" Paul left, feeling dejected.

What an idiot! Reggie thought. *But I'm not going to waste time worrying about his nonsense…. My lord! I feel sorry for these trolls. Crowded balconies where you're stifling hot and squeezed in an uncomfortable position, no thanks! And where you meet up with people you wouldn't recognize the day after if you passed them in the street. Really! What is attractive about it and how in the world is it profitable? Also, it's absolutely guaranteed to give you wrinkles…. Oh, that Maurice, though. What brought him there? Curiosity, no doubt… and he's not worried about the consequences.* When Reggie came back from the theater that evening, there were four letters waiting for him. The first was a charming short note from Paul, apologizing for having left so abruptly. Reggie shrugged. The second was from Mrs. de Vere. This model parent informed her son that she had to leave London immediately since she was being pursued by her creditors. She didn't say where she was going and that made Reggie laugh. The third letter was from Mrs. Henderson, just two sentences asking him to come as soon as possible to "explain himself." Reggie rolled his eyes. The last letter, stamped in Liverpool, brought a frown to his face. Mr. Kemball, writing in an unfamiliarly distant and unfriendly manner, let him know he would be coming to London. Reggie started to fret. Suddenly, a fist banged on his windows. Fred and several other men had come to see Reggie, and he, gayer and more wrought-up than ever, left his cares at the bottom of a glass or two of whiskey.

ONE MORNING, MAURICE RAN INTO Mrs. Morell in Hyde Park. She cheerfully invited him to sit with her. It was the first time they had been alone in quite a while, and they had a friendly chat. "I've been left on my own today," she explained. "Mrs. Adams is in the country. I was going to have a bachelorette lunch at my club." Maurice smiled, "Have lunch with me at Prince's instead, Mrs. Morell, and then we'll have time to catch up." She didn't have to be asked twice. In the restaurant she was in high spirits and was a charming companion until Maurice suggested taking a drive to Richmond. He actually didn't have an ulterior motive. *Richmond!* There was a sudden chilly pause in their conversation. The name brought up unpleasant memories. Mrs. Morell decided to attack them head-on. "No thank you! Too many uncomfortable feelings." Maurice protested, "Uncomfortable? Say delicious, rather." "All right, delicious!" She hesitated for an instant. "So, you don't hold it against me?" "Not at all. That's absurd! I was the clumsy one. I should have realized…." "Not at all. I assure you…." This extremely polite discussion began to seem ridiculous to both of them, and a little champagne encouraged them to laugh about it.

Maurice said casually, "In any case, we can't really talk in this restaurant. Will you offer me a cup of tea at your house, Mrs. Morell?" She stumbled over her words, "Well, it's … I…to tell you the truth, Mrs. Adams isn't out of town, but we had a little tiff, and I don't want to go straight home today." "Well then, come to my place." "Your place?" "Why not? You came often enough in the past." She looked at him a bit suspiciously for a moment but then said, firmly "All right. I'm not afraid." Maurice swore to himself then that he would be the epitome of a proper gentleman, but he soon changed his mind. They settled down comfortably in the drawing room, sipping liqueurs and smoking cigarettes. Mrs. Morell didn't discuss literature as she had in the past. Instead, she glanced around the room, smiling, laughing shrilly and chattering about this and that. She was obviously nervous but started talking about their past in an almost nostalgic, regretful manner. He responded coyly, begging her not to pity him, assuring her that the past was indeed dead and buried and that he hadn't really suffered. This made her more agitated and emotional. When he noticed that her eyes avoiding his and her lips were tightening into a thin line, he realized she was his, if he wanted. He didn't, not then. He was expecting more of a challenge but he savored the moment, enjoying her surprise at his lack of interest or his dullness at reading the signs. She stood up and strolled around the room, brushing past him to examine his etchings and gesturing at this or that. She kept talking, getting drunk on her words, perhaps helped by the champagne at lunch, but she finally wound down and, settling into an armchair, sighed deeply. Maurice looked a little paler, but he was still smiling. Silence. Feeling discouraged and a bit put out, she went on the attack. She smirked, "You have some nice friends."

"So do you" he snapped back. Then he decided to make his move, standing up and coming alarmingly close. He then wrapped his arms around her despite her indignant protests. "Let me go! Will you let me go! You cur! I trusted you. If you think this is why I came here…. You brute! I hate you. No, let me go… no!" She struggled but his grip was too strong. He closed her mouth with a kiss, murmuring "This is my revenge, Lillian." She pushed him away, but also felt a wave of intense desire. Confused by her conflicting emotions, she kept protesting in a husky, passionate voice as they began making love. Their encounter was short, uncomplicated and not at all tender. Maurice discreetly disappeared into the adjoining room afterward. When he returned, Mrs. Morell was sitting in an armchair, neatly coiffed and powdered as if she had just arrived for afternoon tea. She looked directly at him, calmly, as if nothing had happened, and chatted for a while. Then, she stood up to leave. "It must be late…. I have to go home to see what's become of Mrs. Adams. The poor dear, she must think I've gotten lost. Good-bye, Mr. Verdal. Thank you for your kind invitation." She said all this and left with a *proper handshake* as if there were no hidden emotional undercurrents. Maurice almost convinced himself he had been dreaming.

C H A P T E R   X V I

the anonymous letter

THE LETTER WAS WRITTEN ON ordinary stationery, on cheap paper in fact, in ordinary English. There were no gross mistakes in spelling, which was the usual ploy to throw off investigators. Every letter was carefully shaped and printed, not in cursive, and the letter did not end with the usual salutation: *From someone who wishes you well.* "How awful it is to receive an anonymous letter," Mrs. Morell shivered. Mrs. Henderson, dressed in a too-elegant day gown, lifted the paper up to the light for the twentieth time, turned it this way and that, as if these fruitless gestures would reveal the sender's identity. "I can easily imagine," Mrs. Morell continued with a flair for the dramatic, "someone being poisoned by an anonymous letter. Just think of a prim and proper bourgeois wife whose husband is exposed by something like this. At first, she shrugs it off and puts it out of her mind, but instead of burning the letter as she ought to, she reads and rereads the vicious accusations until the venom seeps into her veins and her naive happiness is gone forever."

Mrs. Henderson chided her, "My dear, we're not talking about my husband. I am a widow. This is about Reggie. How ridiculous! What on earth does it mean?" Smiling sweetly, Mrs. Morell explained, "Oh! People know that you know him and the two of you spend a lot of time together, so, don't you see…." They reread the letter together, in which the overly discreet accuser mentioned a dinner at Mr. Hurlston's where Reggie behaved badly and spoke about Mrs. Henderson with complete contempt. That poor woman protested feebly, "I really think Reggie…" Mrs. Morell interrupted firmly, "My dear, I no longer trust anyone…. At least, not any men. And de Vere knows a lot of people, Mr. Verdal for instance. I'm not accusing him of anything. He's charming and…." Mrs. Henderson asked, "Do you know him well?" "Uh, I mean, I used to know him rather well, years ago. We went around together sometimes," she added more emphatically than necessary.

Mrs. Henderson already knew about Maurice and Mrs. Morell. She always found a way to know everything she needed to know about the people she met. She didn't like virtuous people with stellar reputations, and she would never want to socialize with someone who was free from any whiff of scandal. She even felt uncomfortable in their presence. So, she didn't react when Mrs. Morell tried to deflect attention from or lied about her past. Mrs. Henderson's tact and her lady-like good manners were her personal version of a moral code. Still, both women were reluctant to speak freely about their love lives despite having lost their standing in society. "Of course, Mr. Verdal flirted with me in the past and tried to seduce me," Mrs. Morell continued, "but after that we lost touch. I see so few people nowadays." And she let Mrs. Henderson know, in so many words, that she was a lot happier now that there were no men in her life. They were so pushy and fickle! A dear friend like Mrs. Adams was so much better. Mrs. Morell gave Mrs. Henderson a meaningful look. But Mrs. Henderson didn't take the hint, and even if she understood, she did nothing to show that she agreed. Instead, she said brightly in the forthright manner of a person who has a clear conscience, "You know, I'm not afraid to admit it, I adore young men's company, whatever people may say about it! They tell me their little troubles, I give them sound advice and I enjoy doing so. I'm awfully silly, aren't I?" Mrs. Morell smiled, "No doubt!" She didn't add, "and it costs you a pretty penny!" though she thought it. Both women had firm beliefs and definite preferences about how to live their lives, but each could understand the other's choices perfectly well. To top it off, they continued playing their roles as 'respectable ladies' in this comedy of manners. This made them admire each other even more.

"I do believe," Mrs. Henderson said after a pause for thought, "that at least part of this letter is accurate. Reggie has some abominable friends…. I don't mean Mr. Verdal, my dear, whom I like very much." She emphasized the word "like" and took pleasure in doing so. Mrs. Morell frowned prettily, ambiguously. "Yes, I like him too, but honestly, he has no morals. He mocks everyone and everything and one has no way of knowing when he's being serious." She delved into her memories for a minute, looking pensive, and concluded, "I really cannot hold anything against him, and I don't mind meeting him now and again. He is entertaining." Mrs. Henderson deduced that their love affair must have been brief and not particularly serious, if they were now on such good terms. Mrs. Morell concluded that Mrs. Henderson knew something about the affair, but none of the awful details. *Richmond, really, was the last straw for me*, she thought. "Ahem! To go back to this horrid anonymous letter—"

BUT THE FOOTMAN INTERRUPTED HER to announce Reggie's arrival. He was elegant, perfumed, and totally superficial. Mrs. Morell realized she should leave the two of them alone. She suddenly remembered a rendezvous with Mrs. Adams and left with a tiny sympathetic smile. Reggie exclaimed, "Goodness, I hope *I* didn't make her leave like that." He added, "Don't you like my new waistcoat?" Mrs. Henderson was flustered. "Yes, that's what we need to talk about—waistcoats. No, what about anonymous letters?" "They should be burned," Reggie replied in a ponderous, dignified manner. In fact, that was the last thing he would do, but it seemed to be the appropriate response. After stating his general principles, he asked curiously, "Did you receive one?" Mrs. Henderson nodded. Reggie was very excited, "Really? From whom?" "But it's anonymous, so…." "Ah, I see. No signature. Any clue as to who…?" "None, except for the tales they were telling about you, Reggie." "About me? Well then, it must be from one of my friends!" He looked thrilled. An anonymous letter! "May I see it?" He examined the handwriting from every angle and shook his head. "Mrs. Henderson, I haven't the slightest idea…" She exploded, "Reggie, really! How can you be so naive? You must tell me where this came from! Or at least, about the accusations they're making." He was genuinely astonished. "What? Did you ask me here to have an argument? Or to scold me? All this because of a stupid letter that you ought to burn, and never think of again. First off, these sorts of letters are never true, and if they were, they're only meant to make you suffer. You ought to trust me, Mrs. Henderson," he protested, looking dignified. "The fact is, Reggie, I don't trust you anymore. I care a great deal for you, but that doesn't mean…" He shook his head sadly. "Oh, well…." "I can only hope," she continued haltingly, "that you haven't stooped to talking about me with these people?" He countered, "Don't even think that. I'm not stupid enough to speak badly about you." "But why didn't you tell me about this dinner? And why did you go in the first place?"

Reggie exploded. If he couldn't go out to dine with friends! And they weren't even friends and he certainly regretted going. That little idiot Paul took him there. Not at all acceptable, that place and those people. But he thought he was a free man and could do as he pleased. No one had ever ordered him around, not even his mother, and he certainly wouldn't start being a dutiful son now. The whole of London would be laughing at him. That's all there is to it, he snapped. Then it was Mrs. Henderson's turn to explode. She was fed up with all the gossip and that's a fact. She woke up every morning worrying if the other shoe was going to drop. After everything she had done for him, she expected a little more consideration, but instead Reggie was making a fuss. Now, she could see everything clearly. The scales had fallen from her eyes. She was wrong to have gotten involved with him, to have cared for him when all he cared about was his own miserable self. A plaything, a flirt, with no dignity and no manliness. "Ah, I can see very well that you'll never grow up," she ended her half-hour tirade. "But I'm warning you. This cannot go on."

Reggie had exhausted himself after his ten-minute speech, so he sat quietly listening to her tirade, smoking cigarette after cigarette and looking as impertinent as possible. Meanwhile, Mrs. Henderson, shaken by her own vehemence, waited anxiously for a kind gesture, a heartfelt apology, but the way he ended their conversation left her speechless with shock, anxiety and rage. "Mrs. Henderson," he said in an icy tone, weighing each word as if it were a gold ingot, "believe me, I regret having spent every penny you lent me. Otherwise, I could have brought the money to you tonight." And he swept out of the room without shaking her hand or even turning his head.

C H A P T E R   X V I I

future plans

Aᶠᵗᵉʳ Reggie de Vere left Mrs. Henderson reeling in shock, he congratulated himself on a brilliant exit. In fact, he was so excited that he didn't even think of hailing a cab and walked all the way to Bond Street, immersed in an intense dialog with himself. Yes, his exit was dramatic but, he began to wonder, wasn't it perhaps a little over the top? As he went over her complaints and arguments once more, he thought he could detect a note of exhaustion in the midst of all the heat and light. That worried him. Obviously, she was getting fed up. He vowed to be kinder and cleverer in the way he handled her. If he was especially attentive, she would forgive his missteps. He decided to send her a humble note with his apologies and invite her to dinner tomorrow night if she were free. Yes… looking at it that way, he felt he had nothing to worry about.

And Mr. Kemball was arriving in two days! What more bad news awaited him? Had Mr. Kemball also received an anonymous letter? Reggie sighed. His life was becoming so complicated! He would have to make up with Mrs. Henderson as soon as possible in order to save all his strength for the next attack he sensed coming his way. My god! He was feeling vulnerable. Was bad luck on the horizon? It couldn't happen at a worse time with so many bills coming due and not a penny in savings.

He was depressed. He felt he couldn't depend on himself or anyone else. He needed a new interest in his life but couldn't imagine what that might be. He decided to turn into Hanover Square and visit his tailor to look over the new merchandise. He was welcomed in the way a young man who purchased a lot and paid irregularly would be: with the disdainful attitude characteristic of the finest London merchants. "I absolutely must have something new," he called out as he entered the shop, "a suit, a waistcoat, an overcoat… I don't care which, but I want something unique!" He strolled around the shop, closely examined one or two articles on hangers, ready for their clients' fittings. "My word, how ridiculous that embroidered vest looks. I wouldn't want one!" The tailor agreed, adding with a smile that there was no accounting for tastes. Eventually Reggie ordered three waistcoats in white piqué and a long tight-fitting jacket with a cinched waist that harked back to the era of Mr. Pickwick. But the tailor insisted it was the latest fashion. They had just finished one for the Duke of Harland.

Reggie was walking on air when he left the shop, having been assured he'd be able to try on his new purchases very soon. The ugly scene with Mrs. Henderson receded into the distance, and he felt calm and happy with the visions of a young dandy dressed in a fabulous new jacket dancing in his head. All of a sudden, he felt an urge to unburden himself to someone. Perhaps wise words from his friend Maurice would help? He hurried toward St. James Place. Maurice was at home experimenting with perfume essences, mixing two exquisite scents together but coming up with a nasty smelling potion. He was just about to add a third essence to change the equation. "I've concocted some superb perfumes at my place in the country," Maurice explained, "using plants that I picked myself. I'm fascinated by this, especially after visiting Piesse Perfumery.[1] I watched them blend a wonderful combination of amber, patchouli, and khus, which is a kind of vetiver from Japan. When I left the shop, I had a migraine for two hours and lost my appetite for any dish except salad with a sharp vinegar dressing."

Reggie said dreamily, "How economical! I only use Ideal which I know is the most expensive scent." "Of course, you do!" Reggie laughed and launched directly into his favorite topic, "My dear, I'm having a new frock coat made," gesturing wildly to help his friend picture it. Maurice stopped mixing his potions and listened closely. Clothing interested him tremendously and he never tired of discussing styles, fabrics and wardrobes. He joined Reggie in praising their wonderful tailor. "What a fine man! I'll never forget the first time I ordered a suit there. He asked if I

---

[1] Piesse and Lubin was a luxury perfumery located on New Bond St.

wanted two pairs of trousers, one for wearing with pumps, and the other for shoes with laces; the trouser length is different depending on the thickness of the leather and the height of the heels. That's it; I was sold!"

"Maurice!" Reggie burst out. "Give me a whiskey. I missed my tea today and it's too late now." "You must have been awfully busy to miss that." "Awfully! Thanks, that's enough soda. Now, I wonder if you can give me some advice. What do you think of anonymous letters?" Maurice said jokingly, "I think they're usually written by close friends and that one ought to burn them to purify one's soul." Reggie began, "Well, Mrs. Henderson got one yesterday and still hasn't burned it. If only I knew who sent it!" He described the tense conversation they had, sighing "She's going to dump me one of these days." "Poor Reggie! You'll have to find a job." "Never!" Reggie said adamantly, as if his vehemence could keep such a fate at bay. "These money problems are a real bother," he muttered.

Maurice teased, "Money isn't everything, Reggie." "Oh, that's what the people who have money say!" he burst out. "If they only knew all the hardship I go through and the hustling I have to do to keep my head above water. I've managed until now. I have a nice life, as *smart* as possible, but I'm always broke." "Maybe you are a little too spendthrift." "Indeed, but there are people who don't understand the value of money. My mother, for example. I must take after her." "Speaking of Mrs. de Vere, where is she at the moment?" "Someplace at the seaside, I guess." "She didn't stay long in London." "Only a few days, because of her creditors. Poor Mama! She loves the season so!" "Aha. She's a spendthrift too." "Without a doubt. Her dressmaker won't let her order any more gowns until she pays off her bill. Then, she starts threatening to enter a convent, or says it's more chic to wear last year's fashions at Trouville! I do worry about her."

Maurice interrupted, "I think she lives quite comfortably. She knows how to manage, doesn't she?" "Certainly. She's got the touch. I'm quite proud of her. She's not your common or garden mother; she's extraordinary!" "Well, Reggie, you're a good son. Why don't you try to get rich and help her out?" Reggie's eyes almost popped out of his head. Then, he burst into uncontrollable laughter. "Oh hell, that's too funny! Me, make a fortune? I can hardly make a joke. All I can do is live off other people as best I can and run up debts. And also speak badly about my fellow man from time to time. Get rich? I thought you knew me better than that, Maurice!" he protested bitterly. "Reggie, I wonder sometimes if your brain—"

"My brain! Mama often says I don't have one. But luckily, I've got style.

Believe me, I wish I knew how to make money since I know quite well how to spend it. If we're going to talk about disagreeable people, listen, that chap Smith who made millions in mines or some such, he invited me to dinner at the Criterion and do you know he offered me a rotten red wine, not even a glass of hock! How awful! My word, some people will be good-for-nothing for their entire lives." Maurice pretended to lecture him, "My dear Reggie, duty is…" Reggie cut him short with the sort of pithy phrase a cynical worldly character might deliver in a play, "Duty is the moral code of others and the annihilation of the individual." Then he burst out laughing, pleased with his quick wit. Maurice was stunned to hear this from him. "Really? Where did you pick that up?" "Oh, I don't remember. Maybe I read it in a French magazine at my hairdresser's. It struck me. Anyway, that was the only thing I understood in the whole article. It was full of strange words. There were so many quotations in Arabic or Greek, one of those languages, in any case, neither French nor English…." "Now I see. I appreciate your precision, Reggie. In any event, whether you are under salutary or unsalutary influences…." "Sally or unsally?" "Don't distract me. I'm scolding you." "It suits you!"

Ignoring the interruption, Maurice continued, "I must say that the life you're leading, my dear boy, is unacceptable for someone of your pedigree." "But something done chicly is always chic!" "Absurd!" "That is Mama's pet theory. She would know." "An extraordinary idea!" Reggie smiled, "So you aren't pretending. I'm impressed!" He shook his head sadly. "For instance, I don't understand anything about playing cards. That requires too much attention. I chatter all the time, don't I? Once, at Dinard, I almost collected my cousin's winnings. Luckily, someone recognized me, I mean luckily, I recognized my mistake in time…Still, it was a nasty incident. And yet, my word…." Maurice smiled. "All right. My lecture is over." "But don't you have any advice for me?" "What about?" "About what I should do about Mrs. Henderson." "Go and see her, be nice and manage her diplomatically since you need to keep her on your side." "Oh, I need a great deal of niceness and a good strategy! I'm going to have some awful bills to pay…without even factoring in some difficulties on the Liverpool side." "Liverpool?" "Yes, an uncle I'm afraid to disappoint." "Ah, family troubles!"

Maurice's smirk made Reggie burst out laughing and he soon abandoned the pretense of family ties, but he didn't want to give away anything more. "The fact is," he continued, "I'll find out this week what I can expect and if he doesn't want to give me any more, well, we'll see!" He nodded his head decisively. "Go slowly,

Reggie," Maurice warned, "or he'll write you out of his will." "Including me in his will, what a dream come true. But his wife..." Maurice corrected him gently, "You mean, your aunt?" "My aunt? Which aunt?" Reggie blinked. "How stupid I am!" "How well do you get along with her?" Maurice pretended the answer was important and listened attentively. Reggie was unfazed. "We are no longer on speaking terms, after a few unfortunate incidents," he explained glibly. He looked terribly sad, drowning in a vast sea of depression. Fatigue and anxiety were taking a toll. His eyes were blank and empty and his usually smiling face was drawn and tense. Still, he perked up after another whiskey. "Let's imagine," Maurice muttered thoughtfully, "that your uncle in Liverpool is done with you and Mrs. Henderson leaves you in the lurch all of a sudden. What would you do?" "Such a charming thought," Reggie protested. "Just thinking about it is going to bring me bad luck." He knocked briskly on a wooden armrest. "Let's see. I have my mother's tiny allowance and what else... well, I could marry an heiress!"

Maurice exclaimed, "Miss Houston! My poor Reggie, I honestly don't think you are the right sort of fellow to win over a woman or at least to satisfy and hold onto one for a long time." "But I do have a chance with Miss Houston." "You have neither a bright future, nor a serious position now." Reggie laughed, "And not to mention my past." "Yes, a young man with a sketchy past is hardly encouraging. Neither is your present situation or...." Reggie protested, "I'm very well-versed in women's fashions. I've given her wonderful advice about gowns, about home decor, the way I do with Mrs. Henderson. Yes, the situation will be just the same, plus the sacred bonds of marriage!" Maurice chided him, "My dear Reggie, it's completely different! The women one marries are much more demanding. A wealthy and ambitious Miss Houston will want a man... a man, Reggie, that she can mold or that she believes she can mold into a superior being. If she's a virtuous young lady, she might in a pinch take a notorious sinner for a husband. His aura of sinfulness attracts her, and she wants to rescue him. But you can't even give her that illusion. You have no vices. You're actually better than your reputation." Reggie's pride was hurt, "So you say!" Maurice chided him, "I'm not saying you're a paragon of virtue." "Not even my worst enemies have stooped so low. Nor has anyone dared to say I dress badly." "True. But you are hardly deviant; you're a mere beginner. Vice has never motivated you to perform an evil act, nor have wayward desires led you to any... malicious actions. You never act impetuously, burning with passion. Your indifference and your ignorance lead you into certain situations or actions, that's all."

Reggie was stunned. "What in the world?" he exclaimed. "Mama doesn't think so, in any case. She says I'm terribly immoral." Maurice smiled, waving a hand dismissively. "Maternal pride, Reggie. Mothers are prone to exaggeration." Reggie smiled with secret satisfaction. "I do think that in her heart of hearts Mama admires me a little. And she knows I don't want to be too much of a burden, so she wants to see me in a secure position, one way or another." He made his remarks lightly, carelessly, without recognizing the double meaning of his words. "But I do have another idea," he continued enthusiastically. "A better one, I think, than marrying for money. I'm going to Paris to try to get a job at the Olympia or the Folies-Bergères.... Which is more chic? Do you suppose I'll be successful?" Maurice thought there was no point dousing the young man's enthusiasm with cold water. It was obvious he already imagined himself on stage, hearing the applause and stepping outside the theater to see his name in big letters on giant posters. "You know, I was really good in *The Magic Slipper*. I can sing and dance a little and I could work up an act with two or three songs, a line of dancers, girls to sing the choruses, something very English.... For the first song I could be an 'Eton Boy' with a wide collar and tight pants and a few funny stories or maybe a messenger boy.... Then, I absolutely must have one number in blackface, with me wearing a big hat, a silk shirt open halfway down my chest and short striped trousers. I'll sing something about the moon that's silly and sentimental like 'Oh! the moon is shining bright and the river in the night...' and the girls will join in the chorus from the wings at first and we'll have colored lights and images projected on the stage. It'll be fabulous and something new for Paris or even London. People will be talking! 'Mr. Reginald de Vere at the Folies-Bergères.' And of course, my dressing room will be overflowing with flowers, and we'll go out to dine in fashionable restaurants until 3 in the morning." He was totally caught up in his fantasies. He continued, "Here, you can help me. You know an awful lot of people... journalists...."

"Of course," his friend said mildly. "We'll talk about it again. We're not there yet. For now, you haven't broken up with anybody!" "That's right!" But Reggie was wound up. "You know, I could still try it. I'm sure Mrs. Henderson and my uncle would be thrilled to see me accomplish something." "Fine! In the meantime," Maurice suggested, "come and dine with me at Earl's Court, all right?" Reggie was thrilled. It would be lovely. And after dinner they could take in the entire exhibition.[2] He left at a trot, he was so eager to dress for the evening. He

---

[2] Earl's Court Exhibition Grounds opened in 1892, near the site of today's Earl's Court underground station. It was known as a cruising spot.

hailed a hansom at the corner of St. James Street anyway since he was too tired to go home on foot. He had, after all, walked all the way from Portman Square to Piccadilly. When he got out of the cab, he saw Fred waiting on his doorstep. "Come in, come in, Freddy! But I must dress. I'm dining at Earl's Court in a little while, and I have to get ready." Fred unceremoniously asked, "With whom?" "Verdal. I do like Frenchmen, at least the ones who spend every season in London and have a tailor in Hanover Square. He's not at all like Haret, thank God! And I have big news for you. I'm leaving for Paris. Yes, my dear, I'm going to be signed up by the Olympia to perform in blackface, to sing with eight chorus girls and the whole shebang. It's a big deal, isn't it? If you come to Paris this winter, I'll make sure you get complimentary seats in a box, so you can lead the applause!" He was so excited that he forgot, for once, to tell Fred all his news. He passed over the distressing arrival of the anonymous letter.

At Earl's Court Reggie was enthralled by everything, even the so-called French cuisine at the only decent restaurant in the exhibition grounds. He enjoyed the roller-coaster that made a hellish noise, and he didn't even mind the crowds of clerks and other working-class types milling around, stepping on his patent leather shoes. He almost had a butterfly tattooed on his forearm, but Maurice's comments and his own fear of the painful procedure stopped him. "Reggie," Maurice warned, "in your position this might not be wise. What if, in the future, the police identify you because of it?" At least the two took advantage of the fresh air and the opportunity, so rare in London, of having drinks outdoors. After a few cognacs, Reggie was tipsy, saying, "I'm going to tell you something I shouldn't. Paul Haret—" Maurice cut him off, "That little idiot!" "Paul told me a few things…. You treated him abominably." "His own fault!" Maurice shot back. "But if you had done that to me?" Reggie protested. "Reggie, that makes no sense. Haret is a little minx, and a very clumsy one." "It would take too long to explain it to you, especially since I don't know exactly what he told you. What did our friend, the denizen of Whitechapel and the West End,[3] actually say?" Maurice asked impatiently. "Ah, Paul lets off the smell of the Docks when we're strolling through Piccadilly. It's not done…." Reggie murmured philosophically, "One never knows!" He struggled with contradictory ideas and settled on the anodyne, "You're no better than I. I am quite moral, you said so." Maurice replied reassuringly, "I am too, and I have no vices though I don't make a clear distinction between good and evil. My moral compass isn't working well; it's gotten rusty…. Facts don't matter much,

---

[3] Boulestin mentioned these well-known gay cruising grounds in letters to friends.

it seems," he added, unsure if he sounded convincing. The next day, after a good dinner Mrs. Henderson and Reggie reconciled, though they hadn't made up all their differences. She thought Reggie was more egoistic than ever.

the end of the season

REGGIE DE VERE SAT DOWN next to Maurice Verdal and moaned, "What awful heat! I'm sure my nose is shiny." They were sitting in the shade in Hyde Park, but the air was still, the sun shone fiercely and even the leaves of the plane trees overhead gleamed like overheated zinc roof tiles. "I've had enough of London," he sighed. "Either the pavement is sizzling or it's melting; one never knows what to do in the daytime or where to go at night. I'd give anything for a bit of real countryside though I'm absolutely broke at the moment." Maurice chided him, "Again?" "Yes, again and I'm drinking a lot now and the more I drink, the thirstier I get and that is expensive. Anyway, I'm leaving for Liverpool tomorrow." "Ah, ha." "But it's just for the day. My uncle can't come to London. So, at least I'm going somewhere." Maurice mused, "Well, I'm off too but I'm not exactly leaving for a village in the country. I'm going to Dieppe." Reggie smirked, "How awful! It's full of cut-price English tourists." Then he asked nervously, "What do you think of Ireland? Is it too terrible?" "It's very green," Maurice replied soothingly. "Should I go there for a little while?" Reggie continued. "I'll stay with one of Mama's friends." He dug his walking stick into the ground, traced out one, two, three circles, and then pulled a green and blue handkerchief from his pocket and dabbed at his forehead. "Gosh, what weather," he said impatiently. "You know, I'm using a different brand of face powder. It's Gypsy number 2. It's a bronze tint, more seasonal. Well, toodle-oo!" He strolled away, a light gray silhouette, trailing Ideal scent in his wake, and a comically short shadow sketched on the gravel by the noonday sun.

AFTER LUNCH MAURICE HAD NOTHING to do, so he went to the cottage in Mayfair to look up Fred Fisher. He found him in the midst of packing, with Guy Gregory's help. "We're going to the Lake district," Guy said. "It will be so deliciously romantic," Fred exclaimed. "We'll read the poets there." Maurice asked curiously, "Who are the poets?" "The 'lakeists' of course, and maybe Walt Whitman too.[1] I'm imagining the scene, me reciting 'The Prairie Boy' on a deserted riverbank, with a friend," Fred said dreamily. Maurice laughed, "It sounds wonderful. I'm jealous. Give me something to drink as consolation. A whiskey, a brandy, it doesn't matter. No thanks, no cigarette for me." He exclaimed in mock surprise, "My goodness, a cigarette stuffed with rose petals? What a luxury!" Fred smiled, "They're what I usually smoke. A cigarette made of rose petals is the only link between nature and art." Maurice murmured, "Hmm, I've heard something like that before, worded a little differently." Fred, annoyed, shot back, "I don't think so."[2] He had already given his valet time off, so he went out to a shop to buy the soda he needed to mix drinks. Maurice and Guy were left alone, feeling awkward, sitting side-by-side on the sofa. Guy said admiringly, "You always have such lovely suits. I adore clothes." "Fisher dresses well, doesn't he?" "He has his own style." "It suits him." Silence. Then Guy asked resolutely, "Verdal, why have you never invited me to dinner?"

MAURICE WAS STYMIED. HE COULDN'T think of an answer, so he simply continued gazing pensively at the cigarette smoke swirling up toward the ceiling. Though he said nothing, Guy kept on. Forgetting his usual shyness, he said bluntly "I would have been very pleased. I was attracted to you right away." "But my dear Gregory—" "Have you been having many affairs here?" Flattered and wanting to demonstrate some polite interest, Maurice searched for a few friendly evasive words but found

---

[1] The Lake District Romantic poets included Wordsworth, Coleridge, de Quincey and Ruskin. Freddy refers to Walt Whitman, the American poet's *Leaves of Grass* and the line "O tan-faced prairie boy."
[2] This may be another reference to Oscar Wilde and the fad of wearing green carnations.

nothing to say. "My dear boy," he began. The dear boy felt encouraged by this, and grasped Maurice's hand. Maurice shook him off, feeling terribly uncomfortable but at the same time clear-headed. He noticed he had broken out in a sweat and decided not to contradict the young man. It was certainly warm in here! "Why should I take you to dinner?" Maurice began, "You're leaving London and so am I—" "Meet me tonight, won't you?" Guy interrupted, "At midnight. Quick, let's agree on where. What about the corner of..." At that moment, the door opened, and Fred came in with soda, interrupting this attempt at seduction. Maurice sighed with relief. *This makes everything easier*, he thought. The three sipped their drinks and Maurice took his leave with a friendly, "I'll think of you while I'm in Dieppe," nodding vaguely at the space between the two young men, Freddy thanked him and Guy, though tormented by regret, smiled bravely.

FOR THE NEXT TWO DAYS, Maurice prowled through the shops looking for things he thought he would need for his vacation at the shore. One evening, half-drunk and exhausted, he started leafing through the piles of magazines littering his flat. All of a sudden, Reggie was standing in his doorway, unannounced. Pale and out of breath, he made a sublimely theatrical entrance. "Maurice, I'm going bankrupt!" he cried. "Mrs. Henderson has gotten a second anonymous letter. It's disgusting!" Maurice started to console him, "My dear friend—" "I don't give a damn! All of a sudden, she sent me a letter along with 200 pounds in a little wallet from Vickery's.[3] And she's leaving for the continent." Maurice prompted him, "So? What then?" "So, I haven't seen her since! I haven't even tried!" The older man friend said cautiously, "Perhaps you're making a mistake." Reggie scowled, "Too bad! I've had enough, even with the little gifts and everything. It burns me up to... you understand.... She was right. I'm too effeminate to be a good lover. She wrote that she's tired of my passivity, and I'm tired of all the activity. Oh, well. *That's all right.*" Now that he had brought off his spectacular entrance, he relaxed into his old self. He didn't look at all anxious. Instead, he was smiling. Maurice asked, "What are you going to do, Reggie?" "I'm leaving for Gort in County Galway." "What?" "It's in Ireland," he explained. "It might be very boring there, but if so, I will plunge into the simple life, and what's more, let the climate do wonders for my skin. Tomorrow I'm going to try on my travel wardrobe." His friend wanted more details, "And it is...?" "A

---

[3] Vickery's was a luxury leathergoods store on Regent Street.

light, beige tone, awfully *Sport and Country* in Irish homespun."[4] "Perfect! Reggie, you can never be completely serious, can you? Speaking of serious matters," Maurice asked, "what about Liverpool?" "Oh, that went very well. I think I'll get a regular allowance now. It's small, but that won't stop me from asking for more." Reggie abruptly changed topics. "Fisher is a bastard! Can you imagine, he's been saying terrible things about me, and he's owed me five shillings and five-and-a-half pence for months? I can't possibly ask him to pay me back. Such a miniscule amount, you see, but it's the principle of the thing." Maurice smiled, "No doubt, Reggie. One must uphold one's principles." Reggie continued, "So, the other day I wrote him a nasty letter, saying 'I'm appalled at your behavior, etc.' I alluded to Lady Ward because you know, she's the one on the hook, at least she coughed up all the money for the matinee even though Freddy sold thirty pounds' worth of tickets himself. He had the checks made out to him personally. I'm not surprised the box office didn't bring in a penny.

"AND HE'S USING THAT MONEY to go to the Lake District with Guy Gregory! Ugh! Gregory, that little worm," he exclaimed. He paused to catch his breath. "Where was I? Oh, yes. He sent me a stupid and pretentious letter and enclosed five shillings and six pence worth of stamps! I got a receipt and returned a half-penny stamp to him since he had overpaid, but he sent it back, claiming it was mine! So, we each spent three pence in postage sending and resending that damned half-penny. At the end, I told my valet to hand-deliver it, and we haven't spoken since. I will cut him the next time I meet him. He's an impossible chap, so badly dressed, like Paul Haret. And *that's* another one I'm glad to be rid of. He's finished his English course, thank God! Considering how long he spent here, without buying a decent suit of clothes or learning to pronounce his 'th' properly!" he fumed. "Why so bitter?" Maurice asked teasingly. "Are you getting old?" "No, not at all! I only live in the moment, so I ignore my age completely. There are chaps like Freddy, who's been twenty-nine for three years in a row, and someone like Lord Chetwoode, who sent a correction to *Burke's Peerage*, shaving off a year or two.[5] I'm just glad to forget the whole thing!" "That's very wise and after all, you're only as old as you look," Maurice replied, soothingly. Reggie smirked, "That depends what

---

[4] "Irish homespun" could be cotton, linen or tweed. The color and fabric are Reggie's salute to upper-class country attire.

[5] This lists the titled aristocracy, or peers, of Great Britain and Ireland, and was first published by the genealogist John Burke in 1826.

night it is!" "In any case, some people are too ridiculous." "Absolutely! You know Berkey," Reggie continued, "the fellow at Hurlston's dinner party? Of course, you do...the one with a narrow tie and big fat hands...Well, Berkey, when I first met him three years ago, he said we were the same age, and now he says he's younger! But he's aged so much. I think he's going bald because he's changed his hairstyle twice." Maurice sighed, "Oh, all this talk about age!" Reggie protested, "But Miss Houston, you see, she told me the other day that she thought I was too young, not mature enough for marriage and that I ought to wait a year or two. That certainly proves I don't look old! Anyway, I want you to know that next season I'm going to be quite respectable. I intend to be welcome everywhere."

CHAPTER XIX

at the seaside

MRS. ATWELL SET UP TWO chairs side by side as she did every morning on the esplanade in Dieppe. They were a little to the left of the stairs to the bathing pavilion. She took one chair; the other was reserved for the book she wasn't reading. From this perch she could keep an eye on the bathers and strollers who passed by. The sea sparkled, very calm and very green, and the outlines of tall bluffs stood out sharply against the sky, sketched so precisely and purely they looked like part of a stage set. The bulk of the old castle looming over the town added a banal, picture postcard touch. Maurice Verdal and Roy Horner already damp from an early-morning plunge, climbed the steps toward her. Harold Barnes came up behind them, perfectly dry since he shunned all things oceanic. "Is the water nice?" Mrs. Atwell called. "Excellent." "What lovely weather!" "Getting a bit warm already. It'll be awful by this afternoon." Harold seemed irritated by this chit-chat. "For the love of God, Mrs. Atwell, is this all you can talk about when you haven't seen us since yesterday?" "My dear Harold, I enjoy chatting about nothing by the seaside. I'm perfectly content not having to think." "Granted, that's all right on a beach. But not on the boardwalk in front of the casino! That's the outer boundary of Dieppe's civilized society. The Café des Tribunaux is its center."

Maurice looked around, musing "I've always thought of Dieppe as a French town, but I'm wrong. The railway posters say 'Dieppe, four hours and a half from London' but not 'five hours and a half from Paris.' I think all of London society is out on the boardwalk this morning, painters, writers, actresses and the anonymous hordes who buy six-shilling seats at the theater. The only Frenchmen you meet here are the ones coming back from London after they've learned English. Just look at that lady. Isn't she the picture of English respectability? I suppose she lives somewhere in Berkshire and only spends a week in London during the season." Mrs. Atwell agreed. "Yes indeed. And when she comes to town, she wears a gray skirt, a jacket with tight-fitting sleeves, and a bracelet with three cheap turquoises. The only reason she's there is to take her little girl to the dentist! What a life!" Everyone added their bit to the story. "She couldn't marry her cousin even though she cared for him a great deal because he was the youngest son in a big family and had no money. Those feelings of disappointment and resignation still plague her. That's why she looks so glum." "I'll wager that her brother-in-law is a *clergyman*." "Oh, not at all. She has no sisters, I imagine.... She has three brothers, one of whom, the successful one, is "*something on the Stock Exchange*." "And tonight, here, she'll waltz madly with her husband, wearing a frock in black tulle with sequins." They all laughed. "To think this is how we spend our time!"

Maurice protested, "Why not enjoy the fresh air in silence for a moment?" "Aha! That's his new obsession." Maurice's attention was elsewhere, and he stood up abruptly. "Here are the newspapers." Mrs. Atwell's party bought their copies and started leafing through them. Roy read out loud, "The heat in London is intolerable," adding "I'm always glad to hear that." He folded his *Daily Mail*. "I'll read more after lunch." When he was in France, Roy always referred to lunch as "déjeuner." Mrs. Atwell asked, "Are you coming to the concert tonight?" Maurice shrugged, "Of course." "You would never go to something like that in London. We don't even see you at Covent Garden more than five or six times during the season because simply strolling around, looking at the illustrious coats of arms and historic names doesn't interest you, the way it would affect someone less snobbish and more impressionable! In any case, you cannot convince me that we music lovers are breathing a fine and rare concoction of ozone in Dieppe's assembly hall!" Harold said, "I don't care much for serious music, but I must admit that in July the colonnades and open-air passages at Covent Garden are a wonderful spot for a cigarette. You can easily spend an hour between dinner and late supper there." "And the concerts here?" "I go to them the way I go to my club. I settle in my armchair and read the entire program, even the advertisements. That relaxes me for the evening after I've watched the ponies go round and round." Mrs. Atwell smiled. "For me, watching a six-year-old play Chopin brilliantly is terribly painful though I cannot bring myself to look away. It seems immoral somehow, like an act of public indecency. Can you imagine their little minds filled with the passion of Schumann and the romantic revery of Chopin? Do you think they'll fall in love with their tutors or governesses?"

Silence. No one had an answer. For five minutes, everyone savored the bracing sea air. Maurice broke the silence, "Why aren't you doing any work here, Roy?" "Work? Are you mad? I haven't got a minute to myself." Mrs. Atwell chimed in, "It's true. Vacationing at the seaside is so exhausting, the bathing, the newspapers, the lunches, the teas, the dinners, the casino. It will be a relief to go back to London!" She exclaimed all of a sudden, "Stop. Don't budge. Someone is taking our picture. I sympathize with these snapshot photographers. I try not to make a face or a sudden move." "It's the son of the Berkshire lady!" "So, for her, we're no more than extras on a stage or furniture in a room. How disillusioning!" Mrs. Atwell's party moved on, and when they were seated around a table labelled in big letters, *Casino Café*. Roy remarked, "What I like about Dieppe is having my aperitif every evening at the Café des Tribunaux. I feel so deliciously French there, so charmingly small-town provincial." "And you have absinthe or tonic water?" "Tonic water. It's less common." Mrs. Atwell murmured, "Naturally," adding "I'm beginning to feel hungry, no doubt thanks to the fresh air and our vigorous lifestyle...." They began walking back to their hotel. A car passed them, raising a cloud of dust. Harold cried out, "It's them again!" "Who?" He didn't answer directly, but simply muttered, "There are some astonishing, jaw-dropping encounters sometimes. They change once and for all our preconceptions about other people." "Don't speak in riddles." "All right. I'll explain. I have to say I'm never surprised when I see the sinuous grace of Jacques Blanche or Sem's British chic or Count Robert de Montesquiou's[1] white greyhounds, for example. They all look as I imagined they would. But last evening, what a sight! I was in the cafe at the Casino, when a couple turned up, swathed in furs, wearing driving goggles and caps, oozing vigor and health. They sat down near me, and I recognized Madame Georgette Leblanc and Monsieur

---

[1] Jacques-Émile Blanche (1861-1942) was a well-known society painter. Sem (Georges Goursat, 1863-1934) was a popular caricaturist and Robert de Montesquiou (1855-1921) a wealthy doyen of gay Paris, an esthete and poet.

Maurice Maeterlinck![2] Amazing! I couldn't believe my eyes. It was she, the actress who incarnated 'Monna Vanna' and 'Ygraine.' And he, the creator of so many bloodless, dreary characters weighed down by fate, so many hopeless destinies brutally destroyed. They ordered champagne just like everyone else, and they didn't even glance at the shore. They didn't say, 'The sea does not seem happy tonight!'[3] Instead, they talked about flat tires, motors, gears. Oh! What a disturbing contrast. I couldn't stand listening to much more of their conversation, and I left, trying to forget this nightmare. I want to keep in my heart a vision of the lovely pale Mélisande and a poor poet who doesn't hurtle thoughtlessly over Yniold's flock of sheep." Roy said enviously, "Now there's a topic for your next article in *Tragedia*."

AFTER A WHILE, MAURICE LEFT Dieppe and moved on to Biarritz but after spending five weeks there, he had gotten tired of hearing nothing but Spanish and Russian all around him. Neither the waves in the Bay of Biscay, nor the black rocks silhouetted against the orange and purple sunset nor the pleasing sight of battalions of plane trees along the rue Monagran, where the jewelers' shop windows sparkled brightly, nor the lure of three casinos, nor the carriages with jingling harnesses and postilions in short jackets, nor the bustling city's juxtaposition of Second Empire and twentieth century charm, nor the mauve and gray mountains near Hendaye, could excite him any longer. He left for Bordeaux and boarded a ship bound for Southampton. He had decided to spend a few weeks at Bournemouth before returning to London. One October morning he left his luggage at the station and walked around town looking for a room. He passed by one enormous half-empty hotel after another and started feeling hungry when he caught sight of a modest-looking guest house with the pretentious name *Sandringham*. The contrast between this humble two-story building with five windows overlooking the front garden and its royal namesake was so striking that Maurice burst out laughing. *Why not Buckingham Palace?* he thought. He liked it so much that he went inside, asked for a room, and decided on the spot to stay in the modest boarding house with the fancy name. He thought about how surprised his friends would be when they got a letter with the return address: Maurice Verdal, Sandringham. There was no need to dress

---

[2] The actor and singer Georgette Leblanc (1869-1941) and playwright Maurice Maeterlinck (1862-1949) were a couple at that time.

[3] This is a mocking reference to a famous line in Maerterlinck's *Pelléas et Mélisande* (1893).

for dinner here. Maurice had heard about life in this kind of English boarding house in this kind of seaside town and he was looking forward to immersing himself in it. His room, rather large, had a fine view of the cemetery, which was as colorful as an English garden, shaded by pines. He recalled that both Paul Verlaine and Cornelius Herz had walked there, the one dreaming of poetry and the other, of Panama.[4]

Maurice settled into a routine, relaxing in an armchair at the window with a book, a magazine, and a cigarette, not at all drawn to the communal comforts of Sandringham's drawing room or Recreation Room. The drawing room was furnished in stunningly bad taste, in fact, and the hallway walls were inhabited by stuffed birds, fish mounted on wood panels and even a collection of Japanese fans. The dining room had a long rectangular table with chairs upholstered in oilcloth dyed to look like Spanish leather. A pair of ugly still life paintings hung over the mantelpiece. The house had electricity installed on the ground floor, cold running water on all the floors and drafts everywhere. Even though the bathrooms all had a tap labeled *hot water*, in reality, guests had to ring for the maid and ask for a basin of hot water. And the guests in this fine establishment? There were two elderly gentlemen with grey-flecked beards who invariably wore square-toed boots, one rather vulgar young man and ten representatives of the opposite sex. The ladies fell neatly into two categories: ladies of a certain age equipped with false teeth and false hair and others whose age was less certain but were graced with bad teeth, sparse hair and lorgnons. Maurice preferred his own company and didn't have much to do with the other guests, except for exchanging a few words with whoever sat next to him at dinner. The other men boisterously entertained everyone at the table, telling jokes and funny stories, keeping up the chatter in the smoking room afterward. Maurice didn't join in the Thursday whist parties or the Sunday socials either, deciding that he'd rather be shunned as a snob, mocked as a poseur or pitied as a person with limited brainpower and social skills.

One of his neighbors at dinner, an elderly lady who was not too unattractive, would invariably greet him with the same question: "Well, did you go to hear the music last night?" She seemed obsessed with comparing two resort towns, Bournemouth and Southport, and kept this up at every meal. In general, her dinner table conversation was limited to a few banal observations about the weather, local news, the Sunday sermon, and her memories of Southport. At times she shared

---

[4] The poet Paul Verlaine taught English and Latin at St Aloysius School in Bournemouth from 1876-77. Cornelius Herz was a French politician and financier, who fled to England after he was implicated in the Panama Canal corruption scandal.

some observations about literature, especially the novels of Marie Corelli.[5] Once she tried to tell a joke and giggled as she told Maurice, "Miss Barber asked me if you were gravely ill." "Me? Why?" "Because you never come to breakfast!" Maurice replied seriously, "At 8:30 am? How in the world could I bathe, shave, and dress…." She pursed her lips at that as if she was shocked by the intimate turn the conversation had taken. He continued obtusely, "In London…" She cut him off, stiffly, "I know nothing about what one does in London. I've never been there and I'm not ashamed to say so!" He was speechless, and left the table, his rhubarb crumble half-eaten.

Despite Sandringham's dramas and eccentricities, he enjoyed the peace and calm of this seaside town, taking long walks on the shore and on the sandy paths between the dunes where attendants brought convalescents in wheelchairs to take the air. On clear days, he gazed across the water at the rocky coastline of the Isle of Wight, or listened to astounding numbers of church bells, breathed in the resinous scent of pines at dusk, applauded the evening concert on the pier, and watched minstrel shows on the beach. Sometimes he had tea alone at the Bungalow where he was served by a young lady with bouffant Gibson girl curls,[6] a terrifying Cockney accent and the alluring lips of a woman in a Rosetti painting.[7] He savored his quiet daily routine after spending weeks amid the showy elegance of Biarritz. After all, soon he would be swept up in the whirlpool of London. Bournemouth appealed to his *sense of humor*.

ONE DAY, HE WENT FOR a walk despite the gusty wind and threatening weather. A storm broke out as he strolled across the dunes. The wind howled, clouds skidded across the gray sky, and the sun was low on the horizon, flickering like a candle that one more puff would blow out. In an instant, everything around him was pitch dark and he could see lamps lighting up the windows in the villas along the shore one by one. Big fat drops of rain began falling, and he barely had time to take shelter in one of the thatched huts the town fathers had built for bathers. Someone was already inside, and that someone called out in surprise when he entered. "Verdal! you, here? What a shock," Cyril Flint exclaimed. They shook hands heartily. "An unexpected pleasure, one might say. And, Cyril, why are you here?" Maurice asked.

[5] Marie Corelli (1855-1924) wrote about spiritualism, astral projection, and reincarnation, among other topics.
[6] Charles Dana Gibson popularized images of stylish 'new women' in his sketches during the 1890s and early part of the 20th century.
[7] Dante Gabriel Rosetti (1828-1892), was a founder of the pre-Raphaelite school of painting.

"We have a house nearby," Cyril explained, "and I had come to town to buy a few things when I was caught in the rainstorm. Have you been in Bournemouth long?" "Two weeks. I'm staying at Sandringham." "Sandringham?" "It's a boarding house, seven shillings a day, all inclusive! An extraordinary place." "No doubt."

"You won't be surprised if I said it's full of elderly spinsters, only one of whom dresses for dinner. This lady has two outfits that she alternates, one in blue silk and one in black. Once in a while, she puts on a blouse and skirt instead with a jacket that makes a sort of net curtain effect. She only wears jewelry in the evening, a shell necklace." "No!" Cyril guffawed. "Yes, honestly. You know the kind of necklace made of purplish shells that come from Samoa or from Liberty's.[8] I'm terrified of her. Her conversation at the dinner table every night is a quiz that everyone around the table has to answer. The day before yesterday her question was: is rhubarb a fruit or a vegetable? There was a lengthy discussion. She claimed it was a fruit because it's eaten in sweet dishes. Yesterday she stirred up a lot of emotions when she asked after the Irish stew, 'Do you think life is a joke?'" "My dear Maurice," Cyril shuddered, "you mustn't stay there much longer, or you'll lose your mind. Pack your bags tomorrow, call a cab and come stay with me. No, I won't take 'no' for an answer. You'll liven things up since I'm all alone at the moment. I'll expect you for lunch tomorrow."

MAURICE LEFT SANDRINGHAM AND ITS ladies and gentlemen behind for South Lodge, about a mile from Bournemouth. He was glad to join the warm uncomplicated Cyril at the shady rustic cottage. "Honestly," he told his host, "I'm really very grateful. I was yearning, like little Yniold,[9] to have someone to talk to. And staying with you this weekend, I won't be suffocated by the Sunday atmosphere here. In London, it's bearable, but in Bournemouth! Oh, these Protestant Sundays! You don't really need to see for yourself that the shops are closed and the bars are firmly shut. You can feel the Sunday atmosphere in every room, seeping in through the garden walls and the glass in the windows, grabbing you by the throat. But I can forget about that here and not even keep track of the days." Cyril said half-joking, "I take that as a compliment." "A big one! Tell me, why do the guests in the boarding house call Sunday lunch 'dinner' and Sunday dinner 'supper'? This is the only English thing I've never understood." Cyril laughed, "There are things that puzzle me

---

[8] Liberty & Co shop on Regent Street in London opened in 1875 and popularized Art Nouveau syles.
[9] This is a reference to a shepherd in Maeterlinck's *Pelléas et Mélisande*.

about the English too. I'm an Englishman, but I don't know what's comical about a musical comedy. I don't understand the logic of Christian Science nor of Freddy Fisher's fads, for example.... You know I haven't seen him again. His behavior, not that I'm a prude, but still." Maurice nodded, "He is a bit much" and changed the subject. "Do you know I got a letter from Roy? He spent a week in Paris and had a wonderful time. 'I went to the Opera twice. It's so majestic. I always enjoy it. I'm going to spend two weeks at Fontainebleau and then I'm off to Venice, Florence and Rome. I'll be back in March or April.' That's Roy. Now then Cyril, when are you leaving Bournemouth? Will you be coming to London with me?" Cyril shook his head. "No, I'm going to Berlin. Since I left the diplomatic service to study voice, I thought I ought to spend a few months in Germany. But when I come back, I hope that we'll see more of each other than we did last season." Maurice smiled, "I do too." Cyril continued, "You see, I know some rather interesting places in London, not fashionable, but amusing." Maurice interrupted snobbishly, "Bah, there's nothing to match the West End, there's only one Piccadilly in the world, and its crowds...." As he said that, he thought of Reggie. Maurice had received a short, desperate letter recently that began "My dear M.V. I'm going mad in Ireland where I've started drinking every day. This is not the countryside I pictured. Trees, trees, trees, and more trees. But I take a little comfort in thinking that I can tell everyone in London that I've been hunting in Scotland."

CHAPTER XX

london in autumn

MAURICE SPENT HIS FIRST FEW days back in London prowling the city, giving its his undivided attention as he would to a lover. Its sights and sounds amazed him once again and he joyfully sniffed that particular London scent, a combination of blond tobacco and damp asphalt. The news vendors' cries, the sharp whistles of porters calling cabs, the clomp-clomp of horses' hooves, the glaring lights of Piccadilly Circus, the noisy buses and the stolid policemen thrilled him more than ever. Even though he was usually a slug-a-bed, now he felt compelled to get up and walk through the early morning streets, visiting neighborhoods where he was a stranger. He often headed toward the Thames and stood on a bridge over the water, resting his elbows on the railing, enjoying a mesmerizing sight, a stunning Whistlerian symphony in shades of gray. He watched clouds of steam from riverboats and the smoke from factories rising in the sky, mingling with the clouds. Their subtle shades of white and black swirled and melted together. The houses lining the foggy riverbanks were almost invisible and the bridges were only a little darker than the water flowing under them. The imposing bulk of Parliament dissolved into a blurry silhouette in the distance.

Maurice strolled through the vivid green of Regent's Park where sheep still wandered peacefully while the sounds of the city droned monotonously, remotely, in the background. At five o'clock in the morning, he watched the sun paint the sky a milky rose. Although the streets nearby were quiet, occasionally a door would fly open, a maid would appear and whistle twice. Then, the muffled sound of jingling harnesses and clomping horseshoes would come closer and closer until a hansom stopped at the door, rolling almost silently on rubber tires. He heard a Barbary organ begin playing its wheezy tunes off in the distance. The quick marching steps and shrill whistles of the *Boys' Brigade*[1] echoed down a faraway street. A policeman took up his post on a street corner, looking patient and dignified; a postman scurried to each door and knocked on it mechanically like a wind-up toy.

ONE DAY MAURICE WENT ALL the way to Richmond to relive his memories there. The park stretched out before him, green and wide, with that particular intense color one sees in the English countryside. He saw two paths intersecting in the distance. Thick-trunked trees threw their shade on the lawns here and there. A thin mist filled the air tinged with violet and green and merged into the horizon. The countryside seemed to roll on endlessly. A herd of deer ignored him as he passed, but a few rabbits quickly ducked down in their burrows. The silence was broken only by the occasional sharp bark of a dog and once he thought he heard a mail coach trundling past, its rhythmic creaking and squeaking soon fading away. Walking slowly and stopping often to give full reign to his senses, Maurice wandered through this deserted landscape. *How different it was from the flashy and superficial West End*, he thought, though that part of London was vitally, urgently real to him. His nostalgic mood didn't last and one day he lost his taste for wanderlust when after, strolling in Hampstead, he found a bill from his shirtmaker on his desk. He rubbed his eyes and came back down to earth. Maurice had always preferred prose to poetry and that very evening he shivered with delight at the sight of a sunrise in His Majesty's Theater, where the stage set remarkably resembled a Turner painting. The next morning, he ordered a dozen charming shirts that he didn't need at all.

HAROLD AND MAURICE WERE HAVING lunch with Mrs. Atwell. Surveying his friend from head to toe, Harold declared, "You've gotten browner and thinner, Maurice." "How lovely it is to be back in dear old London," Mrs. Atwell sighed. "I hope

---

[1] This was a Christian youth association similar to the Boy Scouts, founded in Scotland in 1883.

you're here for the rest of the year, Maurice?" "Yes," he replied. "I've rented my apartment in Paris to an American who was getting tired of New York." "There are Americans like that?" she exclaimed, "Usually they make a big show of how much they despise Europe." "Especially London, Mrs. Atwell. No matter what they say, I'm convinced they're annoyed at having to speak English with a foreign accent. In France, they speak French with a foreign accent too, but they sound more like Englishmen there. One really can't tell them apart," Maurice laughed. Staring at the ceiling as if looking for inspiration there, Harold said thoughtfully, "I think people are wrong not to think the Englishman, the Scotsman, the Irishman and the American are speaking four very different languages." He sighed, sipped a glass of Bordeaux, and started tapping his fingers on the table. "I do apologize," he continued, "but I'm awfully distracted. My next collection of essays comes out in two weeks, and I just cannot think of the right title. I want something simple, witty and, dare I say it, all-inclusive. Something that excites me. I can't sleep at night anymore because of this and my editor is sending me telegrams twice a day. I'm at my wit's end." "And what's the solution?" "Perhaps I should call it simply, *The Works of Harold Barnes*. When you see something like that in a catalog, you envision a weighty tome, well-researched, but this is a 160-page monograph! Oh well, let's drop the subject. Has anyone heard from Roy?" Harold asked. "Yes" Mrs. Atwell said, "he's traveling somewhere in the south of Italy. He's in Capri, I believe. How odd to leave London at this time. The social season isn't too overwhelming yet, and one still has time for one's friends. But frankly, Roy doesn't like London. I, on the other hand, can't stay away for more than two months before I start feeling very out-of-sorts." "And yet," Maurice said, "London's charm is eroding little by little. Piccadilly is being 'improved'; they're demolishing some exquisite old Georgian mansions and putting up modern apartment blocks. Who knows if soon we'll be unable to find the spot where Mr. Pickwick took his post-chaise or if Dr. Johnson's favorite seat at the 'Old Cheshire Cheese' vanishes because the pub has been knocked down?"

This was a subject dear to Harold's heart. He exclaimed, "Of course, we will always have the historic clubs, the majestic promenade of Pall Mall and ugly, adorable St. James Square. When I cross the square at night, I always hope to see Nell Gwyn[2] on her way home or even the purplish heavy-set silhouette of His Majesty. But you're right. All the little narrow twisty lanes and alleys are going

---

[2] Eleanor Gwyn (1650-1687), an actor, was a mistress of King Charles II.

to be widened and straightened out, alas! London will lose its character and I will lose my entire reason for living. The only thing left for me will be to write letters to the editor protesting some municipal improvement project that's too modern and sterile!" Mrs. Atwell sighed, "That's all well and good. But I won't be around to see it. I'll be dead and buried or so decrepit that I don't dare go out." When the conversation lagged, she sipped her Turkish coffee and idly smoked a thin cigarette. Harold was lost in thought and Maurice leafed through a magazine. He groaned dramatically, "So many new books! And just look at the authors' names! One is starting to think all English novels, except for a handful, are written in boarding houses by middle-class ladies with nothing else to do but see here, there's a new novel by Frank Mattison."

"I've already read it, " Mrs. Atwell commented, coffee cup and cigarette in hand. "*Love at First Sight*. Even though Frank is fanatical about sideburns, he really fell down on the job this time. In the entire book he only mentions them twice and none of the characters talk about waistcoats or Bayswater either. This book really lacks his personal touch. He's quite successful now, but I think he's taking it badly. He has a perpetual stomachache and people say he's going to become a vegetarian and even a socialist!"

C H A P T E R   X X I

bric-a-brac,
the carlton and some
overheard conversation

MAURICE VERDAL WAS SITTING ALONE at a table for six. *What an odd crowd dines at Trocadero these days,* he thought. *Except for a few regulars that I recognize and some others Reggie has told me about, where in the world do these people come from? True, they're not eating their green peas with a knife, but they do applaud the orchestra as if they're in a concert hall. Ridiculous! Would you bring a steak into a theater? Or are they the kind of obnoxious people who munch on oranges, cookies and chocolates in the second balcony and the gallery?*

The enthusiastic crowd at the restaurant called for an encore of 'La Tonkinoise.'[1] It was played by an orchestra led with Germanic ponderousness by a Jewish conductor. Maurice recognized the silhouette of a young man on the other side of the glass panels in the door. It was Fred Fisher, wearing a lovely spray of orchids in his buttonhole and a sneering half-smile of his face. He saw Maurice and came toward him, saying amiably "Hullo, Verdal! I haven't seen you for centuries. May I sit down?" "Please do." He took a seat and the two began chatting. Maurice asked, "And how is your friend Guy Gregory?" "Oh, Guy. We're through. We're

---

[1] "Pretty Little Tonkin Girl" was popularized by the French music hall singers Polin and Fragson at the turn of the century The "colonial love story" written by Vincent Scotto and Georges Villard was later performed by Josephine Baker.

no longer on speaking terms. I absolutely cannot be friends with a chap like that. Impossible, given my position in London." "My word, what a drama!" Maurice laughed. Fred nodded, "Indeed. Drama is the word for it. We weren't getting along very well by the end of our vacation in the Lake District, and now we have absolutely nothing to do with each other. But the funny thing is, we're performing together every night... because I'm at the Haymarket." "Ah, congratulations. Do you have a good part?" Fred smiled, "Oh, I have hardly any dialog but I'm onstage near the footlights all the time." Maurice continued, "And Guy?" "Oh, he only comes on in the last act.... My dear, we had an awful blow-up the other day. He accused me of ruining his reputation, he threw a jar of rouge at my head, and then he waited for me at the stage door... but I didn't dare show my face. That's the situation. I fear for my life. It's jealousy, pure and simple." Maurice prodded him, "Who won this catfight... I mean, this duel?" Fred took him literally, explaining "It didn't come to actual blows. I simply grabbed his wrists and said, 'I think you've lost your head.' That calmed him down right away." Maurice nodded sagely, "I see. Cooler heads prevailed."

Fred sighed, "Guy is such a poor boy, no brains, no ambition. Art doesn't interest him in the least. I know that growing up the son of a pharmacist somewhere in North London affected him, but he ought to put all that behind him!" Maurice interjected cattily, "He's certainly a good-looking boy, isn't he?" "Yes, yes, but a little bland, which is worse. He doesn't stand out. Our dear Oscar said that 'commerce is the last resort for young men who don't stand out.' [2]And the kind of acting he does is precisely that, commercial and nothing more. He has a pretty good part, but I wouldn't take it for all the tea in China." "Oh?" "He plays a groom. Very well, incidentally. Suits him perfectly." Maurice observed philosophically, "Fred, not everyone is meant to be a real artist." Fred agreed, exclaiming, "Thank God!"

Maurice looked at him searchingly, musing, *Oh, what a frail and lovely white lily, buffeted by life's harsh winds. I see the broken stem and withered yellowing petals. He can no longer say gaily 'how marvelous it is to be young' but those words are engraved on his forehead, in his charming features, in his carefree looking choreographed poses. The gestures he makes with his nicely manicured hands, his nimble dancing feet—all sending the same message. Ah, his triumphant attitude. If he only realized.... Where have the rosy cheeks gone? The delicate fresh skin? The golden locks that everyone envied?* Maurice told himself, *I'm sure that every morning when Freddy is shaving and*

---

[2] Oscar Wilde also wrote about attractive but unmoored young men like this. In "The Model Millionaire" (1887). He described Hughie Reskine as "a delightful ineffectual young man with a perfect profile and no profession."

looking in the mirror, he unconsciously avoids noticing his pallid cheeks, his thickening neck and the wrinkles around his eyes.

Maurice thought about beauty, aging, and the indelible influence estheticism in all its forms had had on the young. It was a trend that flared brilliantly and briefly, and then died out like spent fireworks. *What was important in life, after all?* Only vulnerable types like Fred stuck with the esthetic creed. They were pathetic relics keeping the faith and they would never enjoy the 'Glories of Modern Life' that the postcards on Regent Street advertise. In another ten or fifteen years, he estimated, the esthetic movement would no longer be simply old-fashioned but would be considered "amusing," the way Victorian Romanticism is now, featured on magazine covers, in fashion catalogs, and in a few mediocre books. It won't be long before people nod knowingly and nostalgically, remembering the sight of young dandies strolling through Hyde Park with a sunflower in their hands. But they'd be ancient history, like the tales of rambunctious lords who met at Carlton House during the Regency.

History and little glimpses of past lives fascinated him. He and Harold would often stroll down Shaftesbury Avenue and stop at shops to rummage through the display cases of old prints. He liked the odd and out-of-the-way pieces that they turned up by accident instead of the familiar classic scenes for sale. He relished the naive charm of prints that captured real life and treasured finds like "Beau Brummel chatting," "Lord George Hell at Garble's" or a smiling "Nell Gwyn" leaning against a column entwined with roses. He also had a taste for more up-to-date ephemera, caricatures by Spy or editions of the *Topical Times*.[3] He was especially fond of a print of the Newmarket Racecourse that he found. It showed Edward VII, then the Prince of Wales, dressed in riding breeches, beige gaiters and a ridiculous brown hat that was then in style. He was chatting with a very thin Lord Rothschild and the Duke of Hamilton who was wearing a blue necktie. Duchess Montrose stood nearby, smiling, dressed in a light-colored gown with three rows of fur-trimmed ruffles and a silly green Tyrolian hat decorated with a short violet veil and a single peacock feather. Her bustle was a big as a well-padded footstool and she held a parasol nonchalantly in one hand. Newmarket 1885! Maurice adored these snippets of the past for the same reason he loved modern-day London. He

---

[3] Caricatures by Spy (Sir Leslie Matthew Ward) were published in *Vanity Fair* from 1873 to 1911. *Topical Times* was a weekly humor magazine founded in 1887.

kept busy storing up memories and cultivating his sense of humor. He enjoyed life and would rather be an onlooker than anything else.

ONE NOVEMBER AFTERNOON AT THE Carlton Maurice caught sight of his unpredictable friend Reggie, dressed in a gray suit and a remarkable waistcoat. He was having tea with two rather elegant ladies. Maurice watched his friend eating, drinking, smoking, laughing, and restlessly swiveling his head from side to side, surveying the room, radiating an aura of frivolity. As soon as he spotted Maurice, he stood up and rushed to his table. Maurice noticed he had gained weight and had a little trouble walking. "Hullo Reggie!" "My dear Maurice," Reggie drawled, emphasizing every syllable. "I'm thrilled to have found you. You're exactly the person I've been longing to see." Maurice protested, "But, I should think number 7 St. James Place …." Reggie blinked. "True! It hadn't occurred to me… and then I haven't got a minute to myself…. Gosh! So much to tell…I'm moving into a superb apartment near Park Lane but…" he hesitated a moment.

Maurice prompted him, "And? What is the 'but,' Reggie?" "Well, not by myself!" Maurice probed, "Not alone? Kemball? Or you've worked out something with Mrs. Henderson?" Reggie exclaimed, "You're mad! Kemball is in Liverpool where he belongs and as for Mrs. Henderson, my dear, it seems someone introduced her to… .guess who? Fred Fisher! That's so unlike her. She's mad about chicness and youth! He would do well to get some keepsakes while he can, before… before… because I know once she takes a look under his trousers and sees his pink garters, she'll have a hard time to keep from laughing. And when Mrs. Henderson laughs at him, he'll have no choice but to leave. Also, he is way too artistic. Poor Freddy!" He gloated over the prospect of his friend's downfall.

Maurice chided him, "You are cruel, Reggie!" "No, not at all. Don't assume that I have anything against him. He's an idiot and dresses badly. I can also be an idiot, but I dress well. I can convince people I'm witty and I'm also a terrible gossip. Maurice, you're the only person who really understands me; that's why I don't keep anything from you." He leaned toward Maurice as if he was about to tell a secret, but he didn't lower his voice at all. "You see, I'm having tea with Miss Houston…. We aren't engaged yet. I always wonder if she takes my proposals seriously. Do you like her hat? I don't! And she is too dressed up for the season. As for Freddy, the day I see him wearing a tie pin from Cartier, I'll say: That's done! Mrs. Henderson always gives a tie pin from Cartier… after the first time. People say she has a special design on order, and all the jeweler has to do in put in a different gemstone for each one. Nothing funny about that! When you see a young actor with a sketchy reputation who didn't own any jewelry to speak of show up with a tie pin from Cartier, you know he's been paid off. That's the price of his honor!" Maurice murmured, "You haven't changed at all, Reggie. But have you grown or…?" The young man was little disconcerted and put on a surprised look. Maurice continued, "And you don't walk as quickly as you used to. An old injury, perhaps?"

Reggie exclaimed, "No, no. I'll tell you the truth, but don't let it out. I'm wearing heels now. I've been feeling too short lately, but I'm not used to them yet, and these heels are wearing holes in all my socks. It's costing me a fortune. But let me tell you… about my apartment. I'm living with someone quite proper, not a person known to frequent certain undesirable circles, and who has excellent contacts. I also took singing lessons in Ireland so, we are going to host a salon, invite chic ladies, have gypsy musicians and flowers everywhere. I'm going to hobnob with an entirely different class of people because all those young men and those ladies with no standing in society, they're a lot of fun but somewhat hazardous to one's reputation. Ah well! If Kemball neglects me, if Mama doesn't pay my allowance, what will become of me? I often think about it and it's going to give me wrinkles. I know there's always the theater or the cabarets in Paris, but I'd rather have a position in society." Reggie sounded determined.

Maurice thought he ought to nod solemnly and approvingly, but he couldn't help grinning. Reggie burst out in his usual shrieking laugh. He continued, "And this do will annoy a whole lot of people. The apartment is really superb. You'll see. I'll order the finest things to eat and drink…. Norman will pay for it and that's that!" Maurice asked, "And you're going to invite three hundred people?" "Of course." "Are you inviting Lady Ward? She's the type society columnists always write about, reporting she was dressed 'in black' and putting her name next to last on the list of notables." Reggie smiled, "About Lady Ward…. Do you know she's still friendly with Freddy? I wouldn't have been surprised if she had cut him after the charity matinee or when he was at Haymarket…. And…." He was getting agitated, and made a quick decision, saying "Wait here for five minutes, will you? I must say good-bye to Miss Houston and her aunt. I know it will be all right if I let them go because I absolutely must tell you something…." Maurice waited until Reggie returned and said, "I think I already know the story. A quarrel in the theater?" "Yes, Guy really got his goat and Freddy was absolutely furious. Apparently at the end of it, poor Freddy had one cheek completely bare; their tussling swiped off all the makeup. People backstage were rolling on the floor with laughter." Maurice observed mildly, "Fred tells it differently." "Naturally, his side of the story! I prefer Guy's." Maurice said patiently, "No doubt about that. But everyone here is getting ready to leave. It's closer to dinner than to teatime."

Reggie shook himself, "And I'm invited to the Berkeley." He rushed to the door but stopped short, letting loose a sincere and disgusted "Dammit." A thick fog blanketed the streets. The lantern lights on the cabs were scarcely visible from where the men stood on the pavement. "It's impossible to get to Green Street by cab," Maurice said, "so let's try walking up Haymarket on foot, using the housefronts to guide us and then take the Tube from Piccadilly Circus." They took a few steps in the swirling fog that seeped everywhere, yellowish and penetrating. It was the worst kind, suffocating, filling your throat and eyes. The two men could almost believe they were breathing out this pestilential fog from their own lungs. Street sounds were much louder in the murky atmosphere, frighteningly so. They could hear hansoms crashing somewhere, stretchers creaking, shouts, arguments, policemen's whistles, and the monotonous roaring of a broken-down bus. It was all too close by, too terrifying, but invisible. Maurice said, "I've had enough. I'll go back to the Carlton for dinner and then perhaps later the fog will dissipate or at least clear up a bit." "All right," Reggie replied. "Good evening, then. See you soon. I'm going to keep trying. How awful! At least, if I reach the Tube, I'll be safe. But to get to the Berkeley after that, I'd give anything to have a guide with a light…. So long." When he said that, he was only a few steps away from Maurice and his voice sounded close, but his body had already vanished into the fog.

CHAPTER XXII

springtime and unexpected respectability

ONE DAY EVERY LONDONER KNEW spring had arrived. This was not because they saw tender green leaves on the trees or daffodils popping up in the lawns in Hyde Park. It was the society calendar that officially heralded this change of seasons. All at once, you saw tall ladders leaning against the housefronts in every street in Mayfair, Saint James, and Belgravia. A regiment of workers in white overalls rushed along the sidewalks to their destinations and busily got to work, paintbrushes in hand, to redo those house facades in the latest fashionable shade. Soon the houses would rebloom, painted white, yellow, or green. Window boxes would overflow with colorful miniature gardens and footmen would wait in the doorways for their mistresses. The season had begun once again. Just as lilacs bent in the gentle breezes and the hedgerows lining the country roads burst into bloom with little white five-pointed stars, Hyde Park was suddenly vibrant and alive. It got livelier around noon every day as the globe-trotting English gradually returned from Monte Carlo, Rome, and Cairo to a London that, refreshed and refurbished, was ready to welcome them.

Everywhere things were coming back to life. New fashions caught the eye in tailors' shop windows, Bond Street was superb, and passers-by slowed down to take it all in. If you stayed in town on Sunday, you went in all your glory like a good Protestant to the mass at the Catholic cathedral on Brompton Road or you motored to Brighton in an open car to dine at the Metropole Hotel and meet the same people you saw all week long in Piccadilly. We Londoners have to follow fashion, don't we? And follow it slavishly, unashamed to admit it, taking care not to lag behind the speeding chariot. It's an English sport for a certain class, actually, like golf, salmon fishing or dining in town. We have to follow rigorous social protocols, know what to say and how to say it. Gentlemen, do you realize there's a correct way to take a seat in a cab, to lean at the proper angle when chatting with a lady, or to enter a restaurant with the right kind of step? Learning all these rules is a rite of passage although your instincts and natural tact should help you along. The English aren't snobs in the French sense of the word, but instead they are students, sincere students of Fashion. Not everyone earns a bachelor's degree but at the very least, to the credit of British universities, if our pursuit of Latin, history or science faltered at Oxford or Cambridge, we still graduated with an aptitude for fine manners that ought to last a lifetime.

In London, fine manners make up for many other deficiencies. That's why the young and elegant men strolling through Piccadilly, Berkeley Square and Dover Street all look alike: the same hat, the same jacket, the same silhouette. They are slaves to fashion. They carry a walking stick even on rainy days. The City men in central London have their umbrellas, no matter the weather. But as we French understand, England is a different country, and every country has its customs. Perhaps the start of the social season affects other parts of London too, but who's to know? We can avoid going there and spend an entire lifetime knowing nothing about them even though the people living in those benighted neighborhoods do have to visit us from time to time. The West End can brag about its attractions and has the prices to prove it. Turnabout is fair play. For instance, if Reverend Father Vaughan excoriates his parishioners for their sins during the Lenten sermon, he is also secretly grateful. This gives him a pretext to inveigh against Mayfair in the pulpit of the most fashionable church in the heart of Mayfair. What a feeling! Mayfair shivers a little in the Reverend Father's blast and then goes merrily to lunch after mass, just as one goes to dinner after the theater. Such is life in London.

ONE NIGHT AFTER CYRIL FLINT returned from Germany, he burst into Maurice Verdal's study. "Hello, I'm back. Are you free tonight?" Maurice had no plans, so they decided to dine out casually, not in their dinner jackets, and go out on the town. "Go out on the town in London?" Maurice smirked. "Certainly! I'm going to bring you to places you've never heard of, places you didn't even know existed, and even ones you won't much like," Cyril bragged. "Everyone goes on about Whitechapel and its sleazy dives, but Soho, the French-Italian part, is just as bizarre. Be prepared for a bad meal, though. For once, it won't hurt you!" They ate in a little restaurant on Lisle Street that was popular with a motley clientele: foreign actors, musicians down on their luck, women whose station in life was unclear. The bread was French, the waiters were Belgian, the proprietor was Swiss, the dishes were unrecognizably international and the prices more than reasonable. The place wasn't as sparkling clean as Lyons or Slaters and the cuisine wasn't as impeccably English, but a customer might appreciate the comforting Mediterranean grime of the interior and chuckle at the odd locutions on the menu.

Cyril and Maurice shared a table with two German singers from Covent Garden and enjoyed 'risotto á l'anglaise,' 'rosbif á l'inglese,' and *french beans* á la française.' After they put in their order with a man who was supposed to be the wine steward and even vaguely resembled one, that gentleman left the restaurant in search of an 'Australian Burgundy.' The 'Turkish coffee' on the menu seemed to be a muddy chicory blend. Maurice started to fidget nervously when their tablemates, the singers from Berlin, left and were replaced by businessmen from Paris. "One feels quite far from London there," Maurice observed, once they were out in the street. "It was interesting, but I have no desire to go back." Cyril nodded, "Wasn't it awfully European and surprising?" "European, yes, but surprising, no. Not behind Leicester Square!" Cyril laughed, "And to top it off, for an after-dinner liqueur they served cherries in aquavit. What a menu! Let's move on," he continued. "Lisle Street is filthy, the thoroughfares crowded with children playing and fighting, the shops selling second-hand clothes and the prostitutes in rented rooms.... Soho Square used to be chic years ago and it has some fabulous houses from the time of Queen Anne."

Maurice joked, "You sound like a Baedeker guidebook tonight."[1] Cyril smiled, "I have a guide's temperament. Would you like me to use Dantesque metaphors and talk about circles of hell?" "Bah," Maurice scoffed. "So far, your tour has been a flop. I'll take my West End, more elegant, more typically English, and actually more louche. The people around here seem terribly decent." "Just

---

[1] There's a long history of journalists and novelists trawling in London slums as in James Greenwood's *In Strange Company: Being the Experiences of a Roving Correspondent* (1883).

wait," Cyril cautioned. They stopped at a tiny Turkish cafe, ordered shots of mocha for two pence, and sat on straw-bottomed chairs at an iron table. Prints of Constantinople hung on the walls, and they were surrounded by dirty bearded men with heavy-lidded eyes and olive complexions. Cyril claimed they were dangerous anarchists, but Maurice assumed they were local merchants. The coffee, however, was marvelous, fragrant and boiling hot.

Then, they killed time until midnight in a working-class music hall, the Middlesex, where for six pence they watched clumsy comedians, tuneless balladeers, pretentious jugglers, and an extraordinary melodrama in which several people were murdered in the space of six short scenes. The audience joined in vociferously, booing the villain and singing along to the choruses of the popular songs. Young women sitting next to young men in caps munched on unidentifiable treats. Babies snoozed in their mothers' arms. Maurice groaned, "Not so unusual. All these working-class types look alike! We could be in Paris at the Gobelins or the Gaîté Montparnasse." Cyril chided, "You've been out of sorts all evening, Maurice." "Not at all," he protested. I enjoyed the melodrama when the audience called out 'Princess, Princess, I love you' and the princess replied 'You forget that I am a great lady' with that abysmal accent.'"

THE TWO LEFT THE SMOKE-FILLED theater and returned to Lisle Street. "Let's try something else!" They stopped in front of small dark door and Cyril knocked softly. A peephole slid open, and light filtered out. Then the door opened silently, and the two men entered. A man asked abruptly, "What name?" Cyril replied, "Smith and this is Mr. Brown." He signed a grimy page in a register, and was handed two tickets. "Mr. Brown," Cyril said, "here's your membership card to the club." They walked down some stone steps and entered a small room with brown-painted walls that had a piano and an 'American bar.' "My word," Cyril muttered. "What a disappointment. They've redone everything! Where are the peeling walls covered with graffiti, the stale basement smell, the usual crowd? I can hardly recognize the place." A waiter wearing a classic white apron and alpaca vest brought them a printed program that read, to Cyril's dismay, *'Grand Concert for the Inauguration of the New Saloon annexed to Artisten Heim.'* He explained that after the last police raid, the club had been cleaned and renovated. A great many members were struck from the rolls. Times have certainly changed. The waiter, a conservative fellow, dismissed the improvements with a wave of the hand. After listening to a rendition of 'La Berceuse' by 'Goudard' and a melody from 'Marthe' attributed to 'Mr. Floutan,' the two friends fled.[2] Only one thing in the club tickled them, a poster hanging on the wall near the entrance that had evidently survived the renovation: 'Inebriated gentlemen are asked to leave the premises as quietly as possible.' Cyril said mournfully, "We wasted an evening, I know. It's my fault." Maurice protested, "No, not at all. I saw a part of London that wasn't very memorable, but it's one I didn't know. Believe me, Cyril, maybe I could show you some odd corners of the West End. Did you realize that certain bars, some orchestra seats in theaters, la Rivière on Sundays and the Savoy at night have plenty of astonishing sights for people who know where to look? At least, I've always thought that. That's the real London. Something is going on behind those elegant facades."

"Don't overwhelm me, Maurice. Let's make one last try. Let's go to Mrs. Sachs'." "Who is Mrs. Sachs?" Cyril chuckled. His friend didn't know Mrs. Sachs! "She's a nice woman who lived an upstanding but impoverished life for forty-five years, then inherited a small fortune and started making up for lost time. She's enjoying her mite with a simplicity worthy of the ladies of Antiquity." Maurice smiled, "She had better hurry, then!" "Don't worry. It's quite amusing there sometimes. Let's go." At 1:00 a cab left them in front of Mrs. Sachs' house. Light streamed from the windows. People were still there. The lady of the house, chubby and wearing a pink peignoir, welcomed them with a distracted air. The empty bottles of whiskey and champagne strewn about were proof that her guests had not wasted their evening. Three chic young men were romancing the old lady and another woman that one of them had picked up on the street. Maurice and Cyril had to drink a lot to catch up with the other guests who seemed to be teetering on the edge of eagerly joining in an orgy or rapidly falling into a deep alcoholic slumber. Mrs. Sachs sat on each man's lap in succession, with remarkable impartiality. The other woman, Molly, seemed more attached to one of the young men. At first, she was tough as nails, announcing "An hour, two pounds, all night, five pounds," but quickly softened, murmuring about tenderness and other high-minded feelings. Mrs. Sachs seemed determined to experience as many different sensations as possible, letting herself be embraced and then insulted in turn. Cyril, the faithful guide, had fallen asleep in an armchair. Around 3:00 after a little more whiskey, an argument broke out. Molly and her young man leaped apart. She was

---

[2] The program notes are misspelled, as historian Jacques Dupont observed. The actual composers' names are Godard and Flotow.

in tears; he was indignant. "It was going so well," she confided to a sympathetic Mrs. Sachs. The young man exclaimed to Maurice, "What nerve! She kissed me right on the lips. Can you imagine? So forward. She can go to the devil. I wasn't in the mood for kisses. I'm going to bed. This dump disgusts me." Meanwhile, Mrs. Sachs, stretched out on the sofa, looked fascinated by the two other young men's chatter even though they tried to be discreet, given their inebriated state. Molly fell asleep on the floor, drunk as a lord. Maurice nervously smoked cigarette after cigarette. Gradually, Cyril woke up and he wanted to leave. "Wait," Maurice said, "I must say good-bye to the lady of the house. Let's remember our manners." He took the lead and spoke for both of them, "Farewell, Mrs. Sachs. No, please, don't bother getting up. We'll see ourselves out. Good night, everyone!" And Mrs. Sachs, summoning up her dignity as a fine lady for a few seconds, replied from the depths of the divan, "Farewell, Mr …?" "Verdal." "I do hope, Mr. Verdal, that you haven't been too shocked by the informality. It's an odd way to get acquainted. Please don't put too much stock in appearances," she sighed. "I am at home every Wednesday at teatime." Outdoors again, finally! Cyril and Maurice breathed in the fresh early morning air.

childhood memories and madame lenore

SINCE REGGIE DE VERE SEEMED to have disappeared from Maurice Verdal's orbit, he decided to stop at 24 Green Street one afternoon after tea to satisfy his curiosity. A very proper-looking maid wearing a lace-bordered apron showed him into a comfortable drawing room, exuberantly decorated in pink, generously upholstered and accented with flowers and silk ribbons tied in bows. Maurice waited there until the maid returned, having been instructed to bring Mr. Verdal to Mr. de Vere's bedroom. Reggie was stretched out in his bathtub, stark naked, while a woman who was about sixty years old, with the face of a wily peasant, soaped and massaged him from head to toe. The odors of iodine and cologne wafted in the air. Reggie exclaimed from his bath in the midst of vigorous slapping sounds, "I didn't want to make you wait, Maurice, and I want you to meet Madame Lenore." Madame Lenore nodded politely in his direction without interrupting the tempo of her work. Reggie cried, "It's the latest in scientific massage. A marvelous woman! Mr. Verdal will be a good and loyal client, Madame Lenore, especially when he puts on some weight!" "I don't need any new clients," the masseuse replied in a heavy German accent. Reggie continued proudly, "She took me on as a favor, my dear, because I am not nobody and was very highly recommended." He leaped out of the tub, and Madame Lenore enfolded him in her arms adroitly, and began toweling him off meticulously. "I can't get enough of it, Maurice! And it's frustrating, she's hardly ever free. Just think about it… to be massaged by such famous hands…. All the European celebrities who have gotten undressed for her." She beamed and her chilly attitude thawed a degree or two. "It's true," she admitted. "I've had some extraordinary clients." She cocked her head to one side as if to say *I could tell some tales if I wanted to….and reveal some secrets….*

Reggie wheedled, "Go on, tell us something." He bragged, "My dear man, she's massaged Wagner!" Maurice was taken aback. "Really?" "Yes, sir," Madame Lenore nodded, "He's the one who first brought me fame and fortune. Since then, without counting all the Royal Highnesses, I've had the Duchess of Harland, Mrs. Mikey, the famous American millionaire, Madame de Jordalès, the well-known Second Empire beauty, Otero[1], and Lord George Cannon." Maurice asked hesitantly, "Cannon… the one involved in the scandal?" "Yes, sir, "she replied calmly. "He's a piece of filth, that one." Reggie interrupted, his jaw dropping and his eyes wide with surprise "Gosh! Filthy? Dirty? Not even a sponge bath?"[2] "No," she answered crisply. "I said he's a filthy one. I mean he's only attracted to his own sex." The two men could hardly keep from laughing. Madame Lenore's funny accent and odd choice of words made her gossipy tidbits hard to understand. She went on, "I was supposed to massage Sarah Bernhardt but at the first appointment, she made me wait twenty minutes, so I left. I don't have time to wait." Maurice changed the subject. "Do you like London, Madame Lenore?" No, she didn't like London. She only came to work. She didn't even bring any formal clothes with her since she never went out here. She confided, "It's my only weakness. I love fine clothes and I adore the opera."

Reggie couldn't bear imagining her in a low-cut gown at Covent Garden, and he burst out laughing over the head of the woman who knelt in front of him. "Oh, oh, I'm so silly, " he cried, out of breath. "When will you come back, Madame Lenore?" She leafed through her appointment book. "Not earlier than next week. Thursday, if you wish, at 7:30." Reggie asked, "At 7:30? What about dinner?" "Mr. de Vere, I mean 7:30 in the morning." Shocked, he echoed, "In the morning!" "That's the only time I have open for the next ten days. Let me see… at 8:30 I have

---

[1] Jordalès probably refers to Countess Louise de Pourtalès (1836-1914), a celebrated beauty and French socialite. Otero is Caroline Otero, (1868-1965) who performed in France as a "Spanish dancer," and was also a high-priced courtesan.

[2] Though "the filth" is a popular British slang term for police, the German woman is alluding to a sex scandal.

the prince of… anyway, the name doesn't matter. Yes, that's it. The only time." He gave in, "All right. To think I'm agreeing to such conditions. I'll have to get up at 7:00 on Thursday!" Maurice smiled, "Wonderful. You can take a ride around the park at eleven, then. You never go any more, Reggie." "No, I'll go back to bed instead. So there!" Having pocketed her fee, Madame Lenore left after giving her client some tips on the correct way to wash and dry off his stomach. Reggie listened attentively, with a serious look on his face. "I'll never remember it all," he cried in frustration. "Of course, I was rubbing in the wrong direction. She said it was quite risky. Do you think I'll bring on an attack of appendicitis?" He sank into an armchair after pouring out a generous slug of brandy and lighting a cigarette. Reggie commented, "I'm on brandy now. After drinking Irish whiskey, I can no longer tolerate Scottish ones. And you know the old saying: 'Whiskey and women, brandy and—'" Maurice interrupted, "Yes, I know. Have you gone to the dogs, Reggie? Don't forget your country's unwritten rule: 'Do it but don't talk about it.' That's what makes Great Britain morally superior to all the other civilized nations. It's not hypocrisy; it's modesty. In fact, I admire it."

Reggie wasn't listening. He began, "My dear, I'm awfully miserable here…." He jumped up, having been struck by a thought. Plucking up his dressing gown, which was too long and trailed on the floor, he said, "You've never seen the apartment. I'll show you around. Rayner is out. You'll see. It was very ordinary-looking, but I rearranged and redecorated as well as I could. It might be a little too slutty now." Actually, the words 'ordinary' and 'slutty' filled the bill. Reggie's familiar portrait photos, plus a few new ones, had pride of place on the walls. Maurice asked, "Well, who is this Rayner chap?" "That's the friend I live with." "Ah!" Maurice's 'ah' was restrained, polite and only a little inquisitive, but it persuaded Reggie to go on. "I've known him for years… since Jersey. He drives me crazy anyway. Can you believe he keeps all the cigarettes under lock and key? But he's the one who introduced me to society…." Maurice murmured, "I didn't know any of this, Reggie." "Well, let's sit down, shall we? Another whiskey? A cigarette? I'll tell you all." "Go ahead." "Well, I should say first of all that I grew up partly in London and partly in Jersey with my mother. You know her, I think. Poor Mama! She saw I had some talent for drawing, and she wanted to send me to Kensington to study art. I was fifteen then and knew nothing or almost nothing about the world. Mama always had lots of friends, dinners, parties, the whole shebang. I enjoyed it because I was already very social. My dear, would you believe that I would chew on rose and geranium petals before going to dinner to make my lips look redder? Ha, this is in my nature, I suppose. And I would dip into Mama's rice powder..."

Maurice interrupted, "Don't go off on a tangent, Reggie. What about Norman Rayner?" "Well," Reggie continued, "Norman had been invited to stay for a week and he paid very special attention to me.... without going too far, however. One night, after dinner, in the moonlight... the roses in bloom scenting the air, etc. I went to sit in the garden with a friend of my mother, a woman older than she is, whom I was flirting with, naturally. And for the first time, I dared to kiss her. Well, who should appear but Mama herself! She had seen everything! I ran to my room, under a hail of angry words and dramatic threats. When I think about that... cursed by my mother for a simple kiss!" Maurice smiled, "How times have changed." Reggie said thoughtfully, "The next day, Mama walked into my room. She acted just like a character in a melodrama at the St. James Theater! She had a serious look on her face and was wearing an outfit that meant business. I said, 'Mama, you always know how to dress for the occasion!' but she didn't appreciate the compliment, apparently. 'My dear Reggie,' she said, after your scandalous behavior last night I cannot keep you here under my roof. You're leaving for London tomorrow to finish your education.' I didn't know whether to laugh or cry. And then I learned... I know it's hard to believe... that Mama had put me in Norman's care. He would supervise my studies... and... a mother's love is blind... and, and what? Do you think she wanted to get rid of me without too much fuss? Anyway, the next day I left for London with Norman. He set me up in an apartment, but kept the key.... What do you think? I've never shirked from the task... Of course, I had never worked before. Norman kept my mother up-to-date from time to time and always reported good news....Then, after two years I left him for someone else.... I had become very chic and spendthrift. One must live, after all...."

Reggie continued, "Then, the other day or actually last summer, Norman invited me to go to Ireland with him. I had actually lost touch with him, and I didn't know what to do.... I accepted the invitation and when I came back... naturally I asked Kemball what he thought about my taking this apartment with Norman. He approved; he thought Rayner was a solid fellow, one who could advise me, he thought I'd do fewer stupid things under his eye.... Yes, but I'm already frustrated. I always used to have friends over after midnight to drink and chat.... So now I'm trying to be respectable. Kemball's support and this apartment depend on it. I have to watch my step, you know! To tell the truth, I really miss Mrs. Henderson!"

MAURICE INTERRUPTED THE TORRENT OF words and said gently, "You ought to think a little about the future, Reggie." "Say no more about it. It's driving me mad. Honestly, I'm not showing my age too much…. Do you think I could write my memoirs and make some money that way? Everyone in London would buy a copy. You could have your journalist friends write about it, eh? That would be chic." Reggie stopped and stared off in the distance dreamily, past the graceless furniture, the bottles of liqueurs and his photographs. He sighed. "I would like to do theater again, Maurice. I really can sing a little." Maurice nodded, "Reggie, you're full of ideas. But you never stick with one…. It's either theater in London or cabaret in Paris or marrying a wealthy woman or publishing a book." Reggie groaned "Don't make fun of me. I barely have enough strength to stick with the life I'm living now and the days go by so quickly. Ah, well…. Ha ha!" He seemed to forget his troubles instantly. He laughed loudly, showing his teeth as he always did. "Maurice!" he exclaimed. "I forgot the most amusing part. When I said good-bye to Mama in Jersey after our big blow-up, she said very solemnly, 'Reggie, my child, when I'm in London, come and invite me to lunch from time to time, as often as you like.' Believe me, she's no ordinary mother. She is still quite lovely, you see. Here's a photo. Do you think I look like her?"

number 24 green street, park lane

THE INVITATION CAME. IT WAS engraved on the best quality card stock. It read:

MR NORMAN RAYNER (printed) and
MR REGINALD DE VERE (added in handwriting)
at home
Sunday, June 3 from 4:00 to 7:00
24 Green Street Park Lane W. (Music)

When Maurice Verdal arrived, the guests had already filled the drawing room and overflowed onto the stairs. And what a crowd! Some of the women were dressed in typical English style, in fussy gowns trimmed with flounces, draped in shawls and strings of false pearls. Some of the younger ones looked demure, in uncomplicated virginal white frocks, but many of their elders, oh so many, had festooned their silk muslin and satin gowns with eye-catching brooches. A few less respectable-looking Frenchwomen joined the party, sporting lustrous blond hair and enormous hats. Some unknown actresses mingled in the crowd. And the men?

There were a few actors and chorus boys from Reggie's stage days; other young men in fashionable frock coats lounged around the doorways. Reggie's friends, dressed in form-fitting jackets with gardenias or orchids in their buttonholes, had taken refuge in the smoking room where they were chatting, smoking and making catty remarks about their host, who stood at the top of the stairs greeting his guests.

Garlands of flowers and greenery twined around the doorways, along the curtains and over every piece of furniture in the apartment. The doors between the dining room and the salon were open, making one big space. Reggie had emptied out his bedroom, turning it into a temporary buffet stocked with the most alluring dishes. Many of the women were busy filling their plates and kept going back for more, as if they expected this meal to tide them over until Sunday dinner. Snatches of conversation drifted through the air. Some guests were singing or doing impersonations of well-known actors. Maurice knew almost no one there and was starting to feel bored when Reggie rushed to his side. "Come into Norman's room, will you? I need to talk," Reggie said. When they were alone, he exclaimed, "Well, isn't this a wonderful party? What a crowd! The decorations are gorgeous, and the buffet is fantastic, you know. It's going to cost him a fortune. Look at this." He showed Maurice something he had written in the style of a society column: *The floral decorations consist entirely of Malmaison carnations… the most costly, etc. Invitations have been sent to the duchess of Harland, to Princess Tatanoff, to….* His friend scoffed, "Invitations have been sent! What an odd way to put it, Reggie." "It's better to put it that way," he explained, "since they certainly won't come!" He sighed, discouraged, as if he suddenly realized that his social climbing was futile, a sham. Reggie was undoubtedly part of a "Fashionable London" crowd, but even he was astute enough to realize that his crowd was a poor imitation of the genuine, elite and selective club of lords, ladies and millionaires. He could only hope to mingle with that High Society at restaurants, theaters or charity galas and they were, in fact, the sort of people who kept their distance and smirked as he walked by. He wondered, was this really worth sacrificing his happiness and his freedom? A frown creased his forehead; he wasn't sure.

"Listen, Maurice," he exclaimed in despair, "who would come here after all? I was crazy to think I'd be accepted into High Society and could invite them into my home. Just look at the people Norman invited. Awful women and men who are nobodies! *The Evening Post* will print a paragraph about this party, but what a joke that is! Oh, my dear, what a disappointment! I even sent an invitation to Mrs.

Henderson, and she hasn't shown up! The one thing that makes me happy is that this reception will cost Norman a pretty penny and all my sweet little friends in the smoking room can't help but notice that. At least no one will say I'm broke. I'm not going to introduce you to Rayner, all right?" Without waiting for an answer Reggie continued, "It really isn't worth it. Now, have a glass of champagne and eat something… or would you prefer iced coffee? It's very good."

Back in the buffet room, Reggie was all smiles, chatting gaily with everyone and accepting their compliments with a charming false modesty. Maurice enjoyed watching him play the role of host. Today Reggie looked even more elegant than any of his guests. His mind wandering, Maurice asked himself *Who in the world was the boy's father?* He had inherited all his mother's frivolity. His rackety upbringing had shaped him in a certain direction and nurtured his worst instincts. He was egoistic, superficial, and manipulative, if truth be told. Without a doubt, a flower like Reggie could only sprout in British soil and thrive in a hothouse like London's West End. Maurice wondered what would become of him. At the moment Reggie wasn't worried about his future. Like a well-bred society lady, he was working hard at charming his guests even if they bored him. A few minutes later he left the buffet and decided to go to his temporary boudoir, Rayner's bedroom, to check on his complexion. He was worried that the heat had made him too flushed. He walked quickly up the stairs but stopped outside the closed door, surprised to hear the muffled sound of voices inside. He pushed the door open brusquely and saw two of his friends, red-faced, standing together at the foot of the bed. The bedspread was slightly rumpled.

A furious Norman Rayner barked at him, "Ah, what fine friends you have, Reggie! I just found these two asleep on the bed, my bed! This is too much…. And my brand-new bedspread is all wrinkled. Such manners!" "My dear Norman," Reggie's voice was cold as ice; he stood his ground. "My friends are at home here, in my home. I suppose they were tired and wanted to take a little break from the crowd. That's absolutely understandable. Nothing is as exhausting as an 'at home,' especially one as uncomfortable as this. It's so hot. Anyway…." Norman was not appeased. "To behave like that! It's unacceptable, intolerable. In my bedroom!" The flush vanished from Reggie's face. He was furious. His two friends gave him a comradely wink as they tiptoed out of the room, leaving the men alone. "Enough! I'm done. No more lectures. I'm leaving this dump tonight," Reggie blustered. He stormed out of the room, leaving a flummoxed Norman behind, and walked demurely down the stairs, a hospitable smile on his lips.

Just as Maurice was about to leave, he ran into Guy Gregory. He seemed to be trapped between an oily obese woman and a girl with a yellowish, consumptive-looking complexion. "Hello, Guy. How are you? Your name came up just the other day when I was speaking with…." Maurice hesitated, "Fisher." "Oh, did he say something nice?" Guy asked snarkily. "Of course not. What are you up to these days?" He shrugged his shoulders, a hangdog look on his face. "Nothing! I'm bored to tears, stuck in a rut." Maurice exclaimed, "My word, that's too bad. Is it because you quarreled with Freddy?" They both burst out laughing. "Precisely! And then Sundays in London are always depressing. One never knows what to do on Sunday nights…." Guy said in a defeated tone of voice. At that moment, a young, very elegantly dressed man with a weary-looking face popped into the conversation. "Guy! I've been looking for you." Maurice politely turned away from the two of them, making such a show of his discretion that the second man bristled. He couldn't help but overhear their conversation. Guy asked, "Why?" and the man replied "We're having dinner together. I'm not letting you go. We'll dine wherever you like, formally, casually. So, are you coming?" Guy, blushing and with a regretful look in his eyes, said good-bye to Maurice, who teased him, "Now, now. You were just complaining about having nothing to do on Sunday night!" The man pushed through the crowd to the door, making a show of waiting for Guy to join him, and the two walked down the stairs together. Maurice watched them go, a quizzical expression on his face. He noticed Guy's shoulders sagging eloquently. Reggie, always well-informed about his guests, whispered in Maurice's ear "A very fine fellow!" Then his shrill laugh cascaded down the stairs with the two men, all the way to the street.

old acquaintances

REGGIE DE VERE SAID TO Maurice Verdal "I just ran into Guy Gregory. He was leaving your apartment." Reggie settled into an armchair. "So, he's coming to see you now?" Maurice shrugged indifferently, "Occasionally. He enjoys my company. He tells me his troubles." "Ah ha!" Reggie laughed. "Well, my dear, I'm becoming a paragon of virtue." "I don't see the connection." "So much the better!" Reggie got up and wandered around Maurice's study, looking at his books and magazines. He even opened a package that had just been delivered and gushed over the new shirts made of very light silk, with initials embroidered on the left sleeve at the shoulder. The insignia, a circle with intertwined initials, was his own idea, Maurice explained. "Gorgeous!" Reggie exclaimed. "The next time I order shirts...." He perched on the arm of a chair and put his feet on the seat, assuming a pose favored by English actresses when they want to look casual and natural. (Otherwise, they sit on the floor in front of their beloved and lean back, their head resting on the man's knee.) With his arms dangling, a cigarette between his fingers and his face eagerly turned toward Maurice, Reggie very much resembled the young men in Charles Dana Gibson's sketches. But this was the English version.

"I must tell you, Maurice. I've moved out of Green Street, and I'm back in my old flat on Clarges Street." Reggie said. "My word, I have no idea how I'm going to pay the rent." Maurice asked gently, "Wasn't that a bit rash, Reggie?" "No doubt. But after that argument the other night, you know, when Norman found Esmé and Algie in his bedroom… and the way he yelled about it! It was nothing at all, really. They were fed up with sitting at the children's table." Maurice protested, "But they went upstairs!" "Yes, they wanted to rest for a little while. I think they might have drunk too much." Undeterred, Maurice continued, "Really? You leave Norman just because he scolded two of your friends for behavior that was—" Reggie interrupted, "He's too, too annoying. I've had it with him. You have no idea! How could I stand spending all that time with him in Ireland? It's true, I'm sick of all the gossip about us. And in fact, the situation, Maurice, to tell you the truth…." Reggie got up, stood face-to-face with Maurice, and grasping his friend's shoulders, asked dramatically, "Can I tell you a secret?" Maurice laughed, "My Lord, where did you hide the body, Reggie? I would never have imagined…." "Oh, don't make fun of me. It's too painful, for me at least. My dear chap…" Reggie paused, just as he would on stage, and then burst out, "Norman isn't my protector." Maurice exclaimed, "Reggie, that's awful." "Indeed. I was a boarder at his apartment, paying my way! I had to pay for my room, my meals, my laundry, my electricity. I gave him the entire allowance my mother has been sending… or almost all of it. He made sure she paid him directly… to prevent any mistakes. And then, he used all his connections in London to bring me into his social circle. What do you think about that, eh?" Maurice shook his head. "I can't get over it. But why be so cagey about it?" Reggie smiled, "You're mad! I'd rather people think I've been taken under the wing of someone wealthy. That's good publicity. Mama insisted that I could economize living there with Norman. I could eat well and live at a chic address. I'm willing to put up with a lot, you know, but that scene with him was the last straw. I'm so much happier now in my old rooms even though I haven't got a penny to my name. I'm going to have to ask Liverpool for a little extra help. And I have a big tailor's bill. But you know, Kemball is going to complain now that I'm living alone, left to my own devices, as he says." Maurice murmured, "My goodness, what a shock this is." "Wait," Reggie added. "That's not all. Another thing… Mama says she's coming to London. That's fine, but she's going to stay with one of her friends and that is a bad sign. Not a word to anyone about any of this, all right?"

Just as Maurice was promising not to mention it to anyone, his valet ushered Fred into the room. Maurice settled back in his armchair, eager to see how the two young men would react. Fred stepped back into the hall as if he was going to leave immediately. Reggie stared at him brazenly, silently. Then, he burst out laughing and said in a rush, "Freddy! This is ridiculous. There's no reason for us to be angry at each other. You say terrible things about me, and I do the same about you. My word, what a chic outfit you're wearing. Honestly…. I see you've got a different tailor now, and so…." Reggie started taking inventory, looking him over from head to toe and he shrieked with laughter when he caught sight of Fred's tie pin: a discreet circlet of rubies and diamonds. "Freddy dear! My compliments. Yours is much nicer than the one she gave me. This new design is a vast improvement, seriously. And how are you handling the situation?" Fred's dignified facade started to crumble. He said with a half-smile said, "You are absurd, Mr. de Vere." At this, Reggie almost choked with laughter and had to take a moment to catch his breath. "That's too, too hilarious! 'Mr. de Vere.' My dear Freddy, that is the funniest thing you've ever said. 'Mr. de Vere.' Wait until I tell Mama!" "Now see here, Reggie…." After that, the two started exchanging compliments, flattering each other knowingly. Reggie started, "Really, I mean it, Freddy. You are so well-dressed now." "Mrs. Henderson insisted. I wasn't so sure…." "I'm not at all surprised. You weren't conventional enough for her taste. She prefers a look that everybody recognizes. It's 'today's chic young man.'" Fred didn't quite know how to respond. Was that a compliment? Maurice intervened to say "Reggie means that your artistic personality, being an actor and a dandy, was too unique. Mrs. Henderson is happier with something more ordinary, a more middle of the road style."

"Exactly, " Reggie chimed in. "Can we take a closer look at your tie pin? It's very chic…. Do you think an all-diamond one would be more valuable? You can't get much, you know, for colored gemstones…." "I'm going to have buttons and cufflinks too, made with caliber-cut diamonds," Fred explained.[1] "We ordered them the other day." Reggie demurred with an expert air, "I don't really like special orders. I'd rather find something I like at the jeweler's and walk out of the shop with it in my pocket. That way you're sure you've got it." Fred explained, "You know, Reggie… it's not what you think, between me and Mrs. Henderson, not at all. Nothing has happened yet. I prefer it that way!" Reggie tut-tutted, "My dear Freddy." He spoke slowly and deliberately to emphasize the significance of his

---

[1] Caliber-cut gemstones are faceted and cut into squares, rectangles, or oblongs, popular in Art Deco jewelry.

words, "That's very odd, indeed. Even concerning. In your shoes…. She doesn't like to be kept waiting. You'll never get those buttons and cufflinks, I'm afraid…. And your suit?" "She put it on her husband's account. This one and another, a tuxedo." Reggie nodded, "Very good. But just remember what I'm telling you. She doesn't do business on credit." Their conversation was distressingly professional. What would Lady Ward, Mrs. Hallet, or even Cyril have thought if they had overheard these two young men discussing the costs and benefits of their relationships? Maurice wondered. He changed the topic. "Fred, have you heard from Lady Ward at all? How is she?" But Reggie answered instead, "She's enjoying the warm weather in Cannes with Mrs. Hallet and her false fringe. You didn't know that, Maurice? Oh, Freddy, you put a foot wrong with her too, you know. You ought to know… a platonic affair costs almost nothing and is worth its weight in gold."

Fred blushed slightly. He suspected that Reggie had heard something about him and Lady Ward but what exactly? "We're still friends," he stammered. Reggie continued, "Of course. But when she comes back from Cannes and finds out you've been seen with Mrs. Henderson, things will get a little messy. Too bad! She'll go to the theater for the umpteenth time and see Sidney Martin in *Monsieur Beaucaire* and that'll calm her down." Fred said brightly, eager to change the subject, "Speaking of the theater, the King and Queen came to our performance the other night." Maurice exclaimed, just for the sake of saying something "Really?' "Yes indeed. And can you imagine, I was walking past Buckingham Palace when the royal couple arrived in their carriage. I was standing right at the curb. I was stunned, I can tell you, when everyone in the crowd looked at me and I noticed that the Queen was greeting me with a friendly gesture. There's no question it was meant for me. That's why everybody was staring. They wanted to know who I was. I'm sure she must have recognized me from the theater." Reggie agreed heartily, "Of course." Fred continued, "I took a look at the royal carriage. Not bad at all." That offhand remark was his parting gesture, and he left, convinced he had greatly impressed the two men.

Reggie could barely restrain himself. He cried, "What an idiot! If he talks to Mrs. Henderson like that, he won't last very long, and to be honest, Maurice, his relations with her sound awfully odd to me. They're not at all going according to the program. She doesn't want anything more to do with me. Even so! Oh, I know her too well. He'll never get his buttons. As I've always said, he's not the right type. Ibsen and the esthetes are not at all in style. You see how she had to order a new wardrobe for him from a different tailor. Not in terribly good taste, eh? His clothes.... But people are used to seeing him so badly dressed that now he doesn't stand out from the crowd, that's all. Bah! No matter what he does, no matter what he wears, he will never be chic! And then, I don't know if you noticed, but he's looking a little worn. He was never very fresh looking, but now he seems so old and tired. These last few months have taken their toll.... Oh, he didn't even ask us to come to his cottage this Sunday and pay him a visit. What does that mean? Is he broke? Poor Freddy! He looks like he's 100 years old.... It's a fact that he's no longer really young!"

the big scandal
at the savoy hotel

PEOPLE SAY THAT THE CLASSIFIED ads on the first and last pages of London's biggest newspapers are genuine and even the ones from moneylenders are trustworthy. That's why one day Reggie de Vere went to an office on the second floor of a lovely building on Regent Street, persuaded by one such ad. The sight of an office with ten typewriters, two telephones and an array of comfortable armchairs was meant to give visitors a certain degree of confidence. Surely, the ad hadn't been placed by an unsavory and unreliable outfit. A very proper-looking gentleman greeted him with the respect due to a well-dressed, self-assured young man. This business, he explained, was a brand-new concept. It specialized in supplying sophisticated and well-mannered male guides to wealthy Americans. These escorts had to be able to navigate London society and introduce their millionaire guests to its wonders. The agency's well-heeled clients happened to have no friends or connections in London, and arrived without letters of introduction to open the right doors.

Reggie was thrilled by the idea. He was, he thought, the ideal candidate. He needed to earn money and would rather use his connections to introduce wealthy clients to London society. That was much better than toiling in an undistinguished office job or leaving for Jamaica to manage a banana plantation. This position, he supposed, would revolve around carriages, cars, dinners, travel, chic people and, as he learned, a regular salary of three guineas a week, with the expectation of generous tips in the form of jewelry. The proprietor of the gentleman-guide business apologized for not being able to offer a higher salary, but as he explained persuasively the cost of starting this business was prohibitive. Still, only the Good Lord knew how generous a satisfied customer, undoubtedly an American millionaire, could be. In the past clients like these had always complained about the poor quality of ordinary London guides who were generally lower-class and badly educated. They lacked the manners, savoir-faire and proper wardrobe to be seen with these gentlemen, accompanying them to theaters and restaurants. Someone like Mr. de Vere, though, met all the requirements; he was well-dressed, clever, and knew London like the back of his hand.

"And never a bad word said against me," Reggie laughed. Then, a little worried, he asked, "I won't have to get up too early, will I?" "Certainly not," the man replied, "but first there a few formalities to take care of: a contract for you to sign and a small deposit to make. Thirty guineas for security, you understand." "Why, of course. That's to be expected." Reggie left the office, thrilled by his prospects. He sent a telegram to Mr. Kemball, then telephoned him, dispatched a letter and finally got hold of the money he needed. He promised that this was the last time he would ask for help or listen to his endless stream of advice. 'Had he done his due diligence? Wasn't the escort service a scheme operated by crooks to defraud trusting souls like Reggie? etc. etc.' He ignored the advice and the warnings, eager to earn his three guineas a week and proud of himself for finding a real job without anyone else's help. This was an unusual job, surely, but it didn't sound too demanding. For the next two weeks he kept checking his appointment calendar, but sadly, he had no clients to escort around town yet. He wasn't too worried, however, and spent his days and nights as he always had. He did devote a little time to reading a *London Guide* since he knew almost nothing about monuments and historical sites and thought that information might be useful.

MAURICE HOSTED A SMALL DINNER party one Sunday evening to celebrate Roy's return from Florence. He invited Harold and Mrs. Atwell to the Savoy where the four of them sat at a little table decorated with red roses. Everyone who's anyone in London goes to a restaurant for a late dinner on Sunday evenings. There's not much else to do when theaters and concert halls are closed, so instead people meet in hotel dining rooms to chat and listen to the orchestra until closing time. Of course, you have to make reservations a week in advance even for the most crowded rooms where tables are crammed together. Though the menus are not the best on Sunday evenings, customers have neither the time nor the inclination to complain. You absolutely must dine at the Savoy or someplace like it on Sundays.

"What awful weather!" Mrs. Atwell exclaimed. "These cold temperatures! This rain in June is so extraordinary that one can talk about it without feeling ridiculous." For the first time in a very long time, the temperature was an important topic in London salons. Roy sighed, "I miss Florence. If only I had known—" Mrs. Atwell immediately protested "Look here, Roy. You should be glad to see us again, us and London! How brilliant and bustling the Savoy is tonight." Maurice and Harold agreed. London, for them, had everything they needed, close by and convenient, but Roy wasn't satisfied with living in the present. He was always thinking about the future. "Mrs. Atwell, are you going to Dieppe?" "To Dieppe? If I go anywhere, it will be to Cannes or Monte Carlo. I'm dying to see the sun again. Don't you think it would be nice to spend the winter season in the sun on the shores of the Mediterranean? I had to light a gas fire this afternoon. I was freezing to death while I was correcting my proofs." "Your proofs? Did you finish your book? Is it going to be published?" "My word, no." Mrs. Atwell said. "The first two chapters have been typed up. That's what I mean by 'my proofs.' I can assure you that for someone like me, who's not used to publishing, seeing the typed pages and making corrections was really gratifying. One imagines one's work is actually in print! Perhaps in Monte Carlo, in the sunshine, I could start on my third chapter."

Maurice added, "Speaking of Monte Carlo, it seems Lady Ward is still wintering in Cannes." Mrs. Atwell said, "That doesn't surprise me. She's probably taking long convalescent walks along the shore, leaning on Mrs. Hallet's willing arm." "Why do you say convalescent?" "Because she's not at all ill, Harold. She's one of those women who think they should seem peevish and languid after a disappointment, suffering from either heart trouble or nerves, and with her neuralgia flaring up, she needs fresh air and lots of rest. You look as if you don't know what heartbreak I'm referring to? It's ancient history, by now. Do you remember the charity matinee where Fred Fisher played Herod? Lady Ward lent a certain sum of money to the organizers, expecting to be reimbursed by the money earned in ticket sales. But the box office collected almost nothing because Fred told most of the ticket-buyers to write checks directly to him." "How in the world did that happen?" "It was quite straightforward. The publicity posters said 'Get tickets at the theater or from Mr. Fisher....' It's not unusual. Except he kept almost all the money. And someone, I think one of his friends, found out about it. And that's why the very sensitive Lady Ward, who didn't know what to do, politely decided to leave the country. And also, the winter has been so awful..." "This Fisher chap...." Maurice wanted to say something about Mrs. Henderson, but he hesitated. Maybe his friends would wonder why he was so well-informed about this sketchy young man's affairs. He stammered, "I mean, this chap Fisher, what is he up to now?" Mrs. Atwell scoffed, "Bah. Nothing. He will never be anything.... He's vegetating, with no personality and no talent. His mother was such a weak-willed woman, a chinless wonder. Poor Freddy! I feel sorry for him sometimes—" Roy interrupted her, "I don't! No reason to waste time thinking about him." "He's living a happy life, don't worry. He's the 'little cottager.' He makes me think of an old print called 'The Little Cottager' with a sentimental picture of rural life, sheep and simple pleasures." "Simple pleasures? Not so simple!" "Poor Freddy. We once nicknamed him 'Better than Nothing' but now I don't remember why. I don't know what it was supposed to mean or why we did it. I still see his father sometimes. He never talks about his son. He's like a father in a melodrama. Freddy is dead to him!"

Mrs. Atwell didn't want to stay up late since she had gotten up so early that morning. The sky was so dark that it woke her up, she explained, as she left the restaurant with Harold. Then, Roy pushed back his chair, saying he was meeting someone at the Automobile Club. Maurice sat alone at the table, smoking and sipping a glass of 'Forbidden Fruit,' a delicious pineapple liqueur. He idly glanced around the room, watching the other late-night diners. There was Reggie!

Reggie smiled, waved and bustled over to his table. "Maurice! What good luck! I've had my eye on you tonight. You and your party looked awfully respectable!" "I always am, Reggie!" "That's true," Reggie chortled. "But I want to introduce you to my mother. I do so want you to meet her." Mrs. de Vere, very charming and terribly sophisticated, told Maurice that she knew how kind he had been to her dear Reggie. "The poor boy is so flighty, so unsuited for anything serious." "Oh, Mama," Reggie protested, "you are so wrong. I've been earning a salary for almost three weeks now, getting paid for doing practically nothing." Mrs. de Vere said severely, "I don't like that job, Reggie, either for you... or for me. A gentleman-guide! How ridiculous. Will you have to wear a cap with gold lettering when you're on duty?" He smiled, "That is just so like you, Mama!" "I'd rather see you working as somebody's secretary, my dear child. In any case, I think you were wrong to have words with Mr. Rayner and move out of his flat. He's always been so good for you.… But children are always ungrateful, aren't they, Mr. Verdal?" Maurice felt a bit uncomfortable. The obliviousness of this mother, with her dyed hair and brittle worldly manner. Was it all a facade? What was underneath it: raging egoism and an unscrupulous, manipulative nature? He remembered Reggie explaining how his mother had arranged for him to leave Jersey when he was younger, but neither seemed bothered by that now.

"You know" Reggie cried triumphantly "I am treating Mama to dinner. The world is topsy-turvy, eh? But she claims she has some frightful bills to pay and no more money to give me. That's what she always says to keep me from asking for a loan. Ha!" With that exclamation, he grabbed his mother's arm. "Look! There's Mrs. Henderson. Five or six tables away…I hadn't noticed her in this crowd. People are staring.… Really chic, really! Who in the world is that with her?"

Mrs. Henderson, distracted by the sight of a handsome Italian waiter, hadn't noticed Reggie yet. Other women in the room, however, were looking at her, admiring the fabulous pearls and gorgeous gown, taking note of the somewhat ordinary, not terribly youthful man dining with her. Even though she was used to being the center of attention, Mrs. Henderson soon realized that something was amiss. She couldn't quite put her finger on it. A few well-informed guests began whispering a name in their tablemates' ears, something to do with Mrs. Henderson's escort. The whispers and glances swelled into a torrent. It was rude. People grinned, they smirked, they muttered about her unspeakable audacity, but in the midst of all this tumult, Mrs. Henderson was calm and collected. After all, her dinner companion was neither too young nor too showy, so she was somewhat puzzled by the atmosphere in the room. Reggie, never subtle, stood up to get a better view. He was stupefied. "Oh, this is too much. Impossible! But actually… I recognize him quite well. I've seen his photograph. Mama! Maurice! Do you know who is dining with Mrs. Henderson? Take a guess. It's her husband! No one has ever seen them together! Everyone here is astonished, you know. Her husband! Dammit! This is the biggest scandal of the season!"

CHAPTER XXVII

rain and dark skies

THE SUN SEEMED DETERMINED NOT to come out in the skies over London. Not a single day in the frigid month of July passed without a violent rainstorm or even more annoying, a thick blanket of fog to ruin everyone's plans. It was turning into a pathetic season on the river. The Henley regatta took place under drenching showers and even the match between Eton and Harrow fell victim to a vindictive Deity. And that, the last great event of the season before everyone was allowed to leave town was not even granted a single ray of sunshine. Everybody's summer outfits, the straw hats, light cotton dresses and eye-catching flannels, stayed in the closet and the newspapers were filled with meteorologists' predictions and astronomers' explanations about why the English summer had gone missing. The planet Mars got much of the blame for having come too close to the Earth and the *Weekly Mail*, always on the hunt for the latest news, launched a survey asking, 'Will we ever see the sun again?' It was a follow-up to the burning question of women's suffrage in the *Weekly Mail*'s already stale query: 'Should women get the vote?' Harold got into the act and published an "open letter to Apollo" in the *Evening Post* that was widely praised.

Because Londoners didn't want to leave for Maidenhead and Henley in this weather, more spectators than usual showed up for the ever-popular Sunday morning "Church parades" in the park.[1] They came to watch the marching men and chat about the temperature, the flower in the King's buttonhole, his visit to Kiel, Yvette Guilbert's hit show at the Palace, the third marriage of a well-known actress and other very important topics. One Sunday morning Maurice was strolling in the park with Cyril, who was spending half his time in voice lessons and the rest of the time worrying about his voice or mulling over any sins he had committed in the past. These days he thought he was in love with an actress of unblemished moral character. Maurice asked, "But will you marry her?" "Oh no," Cyril replied. "She's engaged to one of my friends who's out of the country. I'm simply keeping her company. We chat about ourselves and about him. We flirt a little, that's all." "That word can mean anything!" "No, in fact, it does not. I make a few charming observations of the most cloying sentimentality and also tell some home truths. I thought you were English enough now to understand these kinds of situations." Maurice said "I have to admit the way English actresses behave always surprises me a little. For example, with very few exceptions, they're constantly assuring the public that they're proper, upstanding women. They pose for publicity postcards with their children and if they're not already married, they claim their burning ambition is to make the right match and land a good husband. Parisian actresses, on the other hand...." Cyril laughed. "Let's not overgeneralize. The kind of actresses you're describing, the ones with no real talent, are like the Parisiennes you call 'actueuses.'" "Agreed." "They're no more than a pretty face, a stage decoration. They don't care at all about morality or decency; they'd rather show off their shapely legs than pose for photos with their children. In fact, they take great care not to have any!" "That's why we enjoy Paris, Maurice. 'The gay city' as operettas call it. I think most Englishmen appreciate Paris, but don't love it. Your city doesn't have enough bourgeois cuisine or respectability. I mean, the typical Englishman visits Maxim's or the Rat Mort when they go to Paris. Here at least we keep up appearances. In Scotland the bars close at 10:00 pm but you can buy drinks to take home. I tend to think that's better." "I agree completely," Maurice nodded, "I've always said so. Modesty isn't the same as hypocrisy, but it's a principle that certain societies uphold and treasure. It's not at all like Tartuffe's famous cry 'Cover up that breast.'"[2] "Or you can add 'the one I cannot gaze upon in public!' That's

---

[1] The longstanding tradition of British Army soldiers marching to church services on Sunday was abolished in 1946.

[2] In Act 3 scene 2 of Molière's play '*Tartuffe*', *the hypocritical main character says to Dorine*:
"*Cover* this *breast* which I cannot behold: Such a sight can offend one's soul. And it brings forth guilty thoughts."

the difference in a nutshell and it explains the vast disparity between London as it actually is and London as it appears, which I find especially fascinating. But Roy, who is a more continental Englishman..."

At this point, with a glance at his watch, Cyril abruptly ended the conversation, explaining that he had an appointment on Stanhope Street. "But you'll have lunch with us, won't you?" Maurice asked. "I'm going to stop at the Bath Club for ten minutes and then I'll meet you back at my flat in two hours. We can take a drive to Richmond if the weather is good." Maurice kept on walking, just strolling idly, and eventually came upon Mrs. Henderson and Mrs. Morell. He walked alongside them. The two ladies exclaimed, "It's been years since we've seen you," after the usual chorus of "How d'ye do?" Mrs. Morell had just come back from Paris with her friend Mrs. Adams. They frequently traveled together. They had, she explained, visited such an artistic and charming salon hosted by an American woman in Neuilly who organized Greek-inspired receptions in her garden. "A lovely woman, she could have stepped out of a portrait by Burne-Jones."[3] Mrs. Henderson announced "I'm leaving for Marienbad, Mr. Verdal. Otherwise, I would have invited you to come and see me. I'll go as soon as my husband leaves for Canada. I'll be traveling alone" she added. No one mentioned Reggie's name. That poor chap was at his wits' end after the director of the Gentlemen-Guides Company had disappeared, having collected a tidy sum from a number of hopeful applicants. The office, the telephones, the typewriters, all the business-like decor of that luxurious setting had reeled in dupes who never recouped a penny of their investment. Naturally, the director left no forwarding address.

Nevertheless, Reggie would never consider lodging an official complaint with the authorities. His unflappable confidence evaporated when he had to speak with police officers or lawyers who used unfamiliar complicated words. Once he had tried to decipher a document sent by his tailor and it frazzled his brain. Stamped with imposing seals, it began 'H.M. Edward VII by the grace of God.' Now he asked himself, *what should I do now?* He stretched out on the bed, revisiting all the brilliant plans he had concocted in more optimistic times. They all seemed a bit fantastical to him in the bright light of day. And the timing of this latest catastrophe, coming at the end of the season, made everything more difficult. It was either too early or too late to be hired by a theater company, Miss Houston was leaving for the Alps, and his mother was no longer in London. For the umpteenth time he

---

[3] This is another reference to lesbian author Natalie Clifford Barney (1876-1932) who hosted salons in her garden in Neuilly and in Paris on the rue Jacob.

muttered, "I've got to tell everything to Mr. Kemball," but just the thought of it upset him terribly. The gentleman from Liverpool had in fact paid a great deal for brief and infrequent encounters.

REGGIE TOYED WITH AN IDEA. Couldn't he use his secret weapon and threaten to reveal everything to Kemball's wife? But he shied away from such drastic measures. He didn't like them and didn't even feel he had the courage or the cleverness to break English laws and get away with it. Or, he could ask his mother to let him stay in Jersey during the summer when she was at Trouville or Aix-les-Bains. But would she say yes? No doubt, she would claim she was broke and couldn't pay his fare. Also, she would stop his allowance for the months he was there. No, it wasn't worth it for him. Should he make up with Rayner and go with him to Ireland? He shivered at the thought. Actually, telling his troubles to Mr. Kemball was the only possible solution, perhaps in a well-crafted, remorse-filled letter. He could always expect Kemball to bail him out, and give him the thirty pounds he had lost. With that, he'd be able to keep his head above water until the fall and not count on the irregular and unpredictable allowance from his mother. Kemball would have to come through. Reggie was sure of it. He sighed with relief. He had found a temporary solution and had no need to worry about it any longer. He thought as philosophically as Ascyltos in Petronius' *Satyricon*, "If a thing doesn't happen today, it will tomorrow." Of course, Reggie had no way of recognizing his idea's literary pedigree.[4]

He stopped worrying about his fate, stopped making calculations and instead sat in front of his big well-lighted dressing table mirror. He looked searchingly at his face, ran his finger along his cheekbones, his forehead, and the corners of his eyes. He wrinkled his forehead, relaxed it, poked the flesh under his chin and checked the gleam of his teeth, sighing deeply. Then, he got dressed. That evening, dining at Trocadero with Fred, he said forthrightly, "My dear chap! I have a fabulous beautician, an extraordinary masseuse, the chicest tailor in London, and I don't know what else. In short, exactly what everyone wished they had. But I honestly don't know what in the world people see in me." After Fred protested politely, he started on another topic, "By the way, how is Mrs. Henderson?"

---

[4] The *Satyricon*, or *Book of Satyr-like Adventures* is attributed to Gaius Petronius, 1st century AD.

departures

THE REGISTERED LETTER ARRIVED AT exactly the same time as a package wrapped in brown paper. The package was from Reggie de Vere's tailor in Hanover Square and the registered letter was from Liverpool. Even though the sight of the letter surprised him, he decided to open the package first. He was overcome with joy at the tailor's work, which was utterly perfect, but as he read Mr. Kemball's letter, he felt a chill penetrating deep into his bones. "Damn!" he muttered when he finished reading it. Then a check fell out of the envelope he was impulsively ripping up. The check for 150 pounds, however, came with a letter that stiffly but firmly put an end to their relationship. Yes, the 'Liverpool uncle,' had been apprised of certain facts and was undoubtedly tired of the extravagant costs of his trips to London. Therefore, he had no desire to continue such a taxing endeavor. He was, with the most profound regret, *'yours sincerely,'* but would remain no more than that. Reggie was livid. He didn't even say "oh my bad luck!" as he usually did under such circumstances. Instead, he cursed poor Mr. Kemball loudly, in the harshest terms. Then, he sat down and dipped his pen into the little purple Morocco leather box he used as an inkwell.

THAT SAME EVENING A SMILING, radiant Reggie, dressed in a gorgeous white piqué jacket, strolled into the orchestra section of Covent Garden. Patiently waiting in the aisle behind the usher, he paid little attention to Madame Melba who looked like a tiny doll on the vast stage as she sang her signature aria with characteristic artistry and cool sang-froid.[1] Reggie only went to Covent Garden on "Melba nights" because her performances were deemed more chic than the other concerts he might attend there. His companion was a young, tall, square-jawed man with broad shoulders and an American-style tailored suit, obviously a New Yorker. Maurice was smoking a cigarette in the lobby during the intermission, leaning against a column. Reggie left his American, looking thrilled to see his old friend. "My dear chap, I so wanted to see you!" he exclaimed. "Some new piece of gossip, Reggie?" "Rather! Kemball decided to dump me. It's all over!" Reggie was so excited that he blurted out, "But then I wrote him a letter, one that will make him think and… will help me with money from time to time." Maurice said ironically, "Congratulations! Well done!" Reggie continued, feigning more courage than he actually felt, "He'd better not forget who he's dealing with! Anyway, Mama will back me up…. And I'll have 150 pounds more the day after tomorrow. So there!" Maurice smiled, "You are truly astonishing, Reggie. An American, if I'm not mistaken?" he asked, glancing at Reggie's companion. "Yes, an American, why not? And he is awfully American, don't you think? The clothes, my Lord! And what an accent! I met him through a friend, and we're getting on very well." Maurice nodded, "I see he's wearing some lovely jewelry, a bit flashy…." "But expensive! Come on, I'll introduce you."

Mr. J. Parker H. Drayton assured Maurice in an unbelievably nasal voice and with a great deal of enthusiasm that he really liked the French. Besides, he wouldn't have taken Maurice for a Frenchman. "And me," he continued, "it's very funny. Even when I'm with a crowd of people all speaking English, everyone knows immediately that I'm an American. I can't see why." Reggie couldn't manage to stifle his laughter. Mr. J. Parker H. Drayton had a habit of starting his sentences with 'why' or 'say' and he seemed to find any number of things 'grand' or 'bully.' Maurice asked politely, "What do you think of the performance tonight?" The Yankee said seriously, "Of course, it's Melba, but you know at the Metropolitan Opera in New York—" Reggie, interrupting, burst out with "Oh, I adore Melba and *La Bohème*" as if he couldn't hold back his passion for music. Maurice said thoughtfully, "Just so. Melba is magical, an unforgettable summer pleasure. I think this very special artiste's voice is so refreshing. Like a cold drink at the perfect

---

[1] Nellie Melba (1861-1931) was a celebrated Australian soprano, well-known for her role as Mimi in the opera *La Bohème.*

temperature, it calms everyone's jitters at the end of the season. And why should she give a melancholy tone to the words in the aria? We're all content just to immerse ourselves in her crystal-clear voice singing 'Ah! Ah!' or even just 'a-a-a-a.' She knows quite well that she doesn't have to overdo the tragic aspects here. She's chosen her path wisely." Mr. J.P.H.D. honked nasally, "Isn't he bright?" Taking matters in hand, Reggie said firmly, "We three will dine at the Savoy. Drayton, have someone call the hotel right away and reserve a good table for us." Drayton obeyed promptly.

MAURICE WAS BUSY GOING OVER his wardrobe, sorting piles of clothing and underwear, when Reggie stopped in without waiting to be announced. He wasn't his usual smiling self and instead seemed to have put on a dignified sorrowful look. Maurice explained his packing system, "I'm trying to combine winter undergarments with summer clothes. I absolutely must wear my new outfits even if I'm freezing to death!" Reggie sighed deeply, "Oh, I have no time for clothes now. If you only knew the jam I'm in…." Maurice said dismissively, "You can't be in such bad shape, Reggie." "You think so?" Maurice continued, "You've always managed quite well. Just imagine Fred, Paul, and their rotten luck…." This prompted Reggie to forget his troubles for a moment. "You know, Maurice, Freddy never got his cufflinks and buttons! Mrs. Henderson took off for Marienbad and left him flat. I knew it! He's gone into exile, joined a theater company touring South Africa or is it Australia? I can't remember which, for the next eighteen months. How awful! Being away from London for eighteen months, among the savages, at his age! No one will be able to recognize him when he gets back. My God! It makes me laugh. And he's in *Floradora*. After his two lines in *Hamlet* and *Herod*, he's performing in a musical comedy. It's hilarious." Reggie twirled around in a pirouette, gaily. All of a sudden, he seemed more optimistic. He continued, "Listen, Maurice, I think you're right after all. I shouldn't feel sorry for myself…. It's just that I haven't been able to profit from certain situations. I ought to have saved some money…. Now, I'm going to have to be very, very thrifty." His friend scoffed, "I'd like to see that!" Now that Reggie was back to his old carefree self, he simply shrugged. Maurice continued, "And your business as a… guide, Reggie? Anything new there?" "No, I'm done with that…. Bah! I lost twenty pounds, that's all. And I learned a lesson…. If I ever take on another job, I will have to succeed at it." He frowned, convinced by his own words.

Maurice probed, "And Kemball? Is it really over?" "Over and done," Reggie said indifferently. Maurice shook his head skeptically. "Reggie, if you are taking these setbacks, these personal catastrophes, so lightly, you must be cooking up some scheme." "Yes," Reggie admitted. "I've got plans, fantastic ones. If I'm successful…." Maurice continued, "And, my dear boy, your marriage to Miss Houston?" "No, absolutely not. She mangles the English language intolerably." "And what about performing in music halls in Paris?" Reggie said nonchalantly, "That may happen later, my dear chap. For now, I have something up my sleeve. You'll see. I'd rather not talk about it today. It'll bring me bad luck. Touch wood…." Maurice nodded, "All right. What are you doing this summer, Reggie?" Leaning back in an armchair, he said mysteriously "Dunno yet," and puffed on his cigarette, staring vacantly at the ceiling. Then, he asked brightly, "What do you think of my new cigarette holder? It's the latest thing. I had someone buy it for me the other day on Bond Street. And, do you think I ought to get one of those new walking sticks at Percy Edwards?[2] They're so *smart*! I'd really like to get out of London for a while. Everyone is leaving. It's the end of the season. It's depressing." Maurice agreed glumly, "And it's so cold, I'm freezing to death. I'm leaving next week." "Oh yes, too bad. I'm going to miss you. You're the person I'll miss the most, Maurice." He looked terribly sincere, sighed several times and then glanced at the watch on his wrist, one with an expensive-looking leather band. "Hell, I'm going to be late! I'm supposed to dine at Jules at 7:00 on the dot with Drayton. Come and see me one morning soon, sometime before noon and we'll chat. Really, I've been so out of sorts today that I forgot to gossip about anybody. Good-bye!" He left, trailing a cloud of cologne. Maurice would not see him again for a long time.

Harold, Roy, and Maurice were having lunch together at the Carlton for the last time this season. Harold was leaving for his beloved Dieppe the next day and Maurice and Roy were leaving two days later for Boulogne. They intended to meet Mrs. Atwell at Le Touquet. "We'll make witty remarks and sit at the seaside. The sand will blow into our eyes and our feet will be tormented by the pebbles on the beach that came all the way from Dieppe. We've got to make the most of it!" "Oh Harold," Roy signaled the waiter and joked, "This is why I love London. What could be better than this fine restaurant where no one understands you when you

---

[2] Percy Edwards and Company was a luxury jeweler in Piccadilly.

order in English?" Harold said, "Perhaps they're Italian?" "Maybe, but they're speaking French here," Maurice commented. "Also, Roy, think of all the different brands of cigarettes you can buy in London, the neckties, the amazing socks. And let's not forget the unforgettable sight of Hyde Park on a Sunday evening when musicians are playing selections from operas, preachers are preaching at every corner, and the Salvation Army are booming out hymns. Imagine the sight of couples stretching out on the lawn, twosomes of different sexes and some of the same sex, and then you see a Horse Guard's red vest adding a touch of color.[3] It's a jollier spectacle than the Bois de Boulogne in the evening, isn't it?" he asked.

"AND WHAT ABOUT THAT SPECIAL tradition, 'closing time?'" Maurice continued. "Restaurants and bars abruptly switching off their electric lights, the streets suddenly bustling, the whores streaming out of the Continental as policemen bark 'Move on,' the silhouettes of the hustlers lurking in Piccadilly Circus, giving the eye to the men in evening clothes heading for their clubs. And so much more!" Roy protested, "My dear man, you'll find all of that in Paris with a French twist." And he began explaining in such crude terms that the others quickly cut him off. "Good Lord," Maurice exclaimed. "I forgot the best part… I was treated to quite a spectacle the other day. You know that I prefer taking an omnibus over a hansom cab. The other day, I took a bus and as it was moving slowly along in Piccadilly, the driver turned and said a few words to me. I was quite proud. He told me, in a volley of slang and an almost impenetrable Cockney accent, that the weather was getting better and more like summer every day. And when I replied, he noticed my French accent and very tactfully predicted a long life for the Franco-British alliance. I agreed. We were going down Wardour Street in Soho and a noisy crowd attracted my attention. I saw a woman dressed in red, who looked like Sarah Bernhardt's twin sister, speaking and making sweeping esthetic gestures. She was waving a tiny trowel that seemed to be made of silver, but her voice was pure gold. A short, bearded man standing near her looked a lot like Mr. Clarkson.[4] I saw a chap I thought was Mr. George Alexander and a lady I supposed was Countess B. at his side. All of them made different gestures and spoke different languages as the crowd whistled and applauded. It seemed like quite an extraordinary show to

---

[3] Guardsmen were popularly associated with prostitution. Public gardens like Hyde Park and the Bois de Boulogne were well known cruising spots.
[4] William Berry "Willy" Clarkson (1861-1934) was a theatrical wigmaker and costumer with a shop on Wardour Street. He was rumored to be gay. A public lavatory in Soho on Dansey Place was nicknamed "Clarkson's Cottage."

me and the driver soon put me right, in his inimitable Cockney pronunciation, no 'h's' anywhere. They were indeed Madame Bernhardt, Mr. Clarkson, Mr. George Alexander and Countess B. They were giving speeches and acting out parts from their stage roles in honor of Clarkson's new shop. Sarah Bernhardt was setting the first brick. That's why she was holding a trowel. I thought the driver was absolutely right about the Franco-British alliance. Here it was in action. I felt quite moved."

Harold smiled broadly and then said in a serious tone, "My dear Maurice, I must tell you your reputation is getting worse by the day. You were seen more than once with Reggie and Mrs. Henderson. They're notorious. Everyone knows about them and their tendencies. You, my dear sir, are charming enough to be saddled with two bad reputations at the same time. That's one too many and quite serious, as we say! I'm awfully attached to my own good reputation, and I intend to keep it." "Oh, Harold, bad reputations! How unfair! Perhaps I was wrong to go about with Reggie in public, but I don't regret it.... If you saw him as I did, a lazy, frivolous boy struggling to make his way in life with occasional bursts of energy and cowardly tricks, he would have intrigued you too. At least, as much as George Moore's *The Memoirs of My Dead Life*.[5] Listen, ten days ago, he came to my flat, broke, depressed, at his wits' end but also superbly confident. Just now I got a letter from him saying, 'Dear M.V. Please forgive this quick note. I'm leaving for New York. Life is beautiful! I'll write you once I'm on board.' What do you think of that? Reggie the young acrobat is so entertaining. If associating with him harmed my reputation, I'm not responsible for that. It's really the fault of society's cruelty and small-mindedness. Why are we always taken in by appearances? The only thing we know about other peoples' lives is what we can see on the outside and we draw our conclusions from that evidence. Why should that matter to me, Harold? Roy, all is well. This is the very definition of poetic justice. I'm innocent of the sins one accuses me of. I'm not guilty but perhaps I harbor other, more terrible and unspeakable thoughts that you know nothing about. Maybe I've committed horrendous crimes. I am expiating unnamed sins that people have attributed to me. I find it all perfectly natural."

Roy nodded and muttered, "Just so," and ordered another carafe of Claret Cup.[6] Harold changed the subject. "The *Weekly Mail* has asked me to write a series of articles about Italian cities. I think I'll start working on it in Dieppe." Roy

---

[5] The Irish poet and novelist George Moore (1852-1933) published several scandalous novels, including 'Confessions of a Young Man" and 'A Modern Lover."

[6] This is a cocktail made with brandy, red wine, sparkling water, lemon juice, and other liqueurs.

smiled fondly. "I can just picture Harold describing the sky reflected in the lagoons of Venice while he's sitting comfortably in his hotel room in Dieppe on the rue de l'Hôtel de Ville. No doubt the room Whistler stayed in." Maurice smiled and chimed in, "And why not?"

nancy erber

NANCY ERBER is professor emerita of Modern Languages at the City University of New York. She has translated French 19th century LGBTQ books and memoirs and 20th century gay liberation flyers.